MANY DEADLY RETURNS

MANY DEADLY RETURNS

21 stories celebrating 21 years of Murder Squad

Edited by Martin Edwards
Foreword by Margaret Murphy
Introduction by Martin Edwards

With stories by

Ann Cleeves, Martin Edwards, Kate Ellis, Margaret Murphy, Chris Simms and Cath Staincliffe, as well as John Baker, Chaz Brenchley and Stuart Pawson

SEVERN
HOUSE

First world edition published in Great Britain and the USA in 2021
by Severn House, an imprint of Canongate Books Ltd,
14 High Street, Edinburgh EH1 1TE.

Trade paperback edition first published in Great Britain and the USA in 2022
by Severn House, an imprint of Canongate Books Ltd.

severnhouse.com

British Library Cataloguing-in-Publication Data
A CIP catalogue record for this title is available from the British Library.

ISBN-13: 978-0-7278-9093-1 (cased)
ISBN-13: 978-1-78029-819-1 (trade paper)
ISBN-13: 978-1-4483-0557-5 (e-book)

All Severn House titles are printed on acid-free paper.

MIX
Paper from
responsible sources
FSC® C013056

Typeset by Palimpsest Book Production Ltd.,
Falkirk, Stirlingshire, Scotland.
Printed and bound in Great Britain by
TJ Books, Padstow, Cornwall.

ACKNOWLEDGEMENTS

The members of Murder Squad would like to thank all those who have supported us during the last twenty-one years. A special shout-out to Roger Cornwell and Jean Rogers of Cornwell Internet, who have maintained our website and newsletter for many years. We are very grateful to Kate Lyall Grant and all those at Severn House who have worked on this book, and also to Doreen Pawson for graciously permitting the reprinting of one of Stuart's stories, as well as to our friends and former Squad colleagues John Baker and Chaz Brenchley.

CONTENTS

FOREWORD

I n 1999 I was getting great reviews, but sales didn't match the reviewers' enthusiasm, and with no marketing or publicity budget, that wasn't likely to change. When my then editor bemoaned the sales problem, I ventured (perhaps naively), that I'd done my bit by writing books worthy of glowing reviews, surely selling them was her job? 'Oh, but it doesn't work like that,' she sighed. I fumed and contemplated homicide. I calmed down and considered self-promotion. But with a meagre writing income and a pathological aversion to hyping my own books, I was stuck. Many sleepless nights and aborted plans later, I decided that a collective approach was the way to go, and I invited six other crime writers whose work I admired to join forces. They were Cath Staincliffe, Chaz Brenchley, John Baker, Martin Edwards, Stuart Pawson, and Ann Cleeves.

Some of those on my list of brilliant-but-unknown writers might surprise you, as Cath Staincliffe has since become well-known for her popular *Blue Murder* TV series, Martin Edwards has won multiple awards for his non-fiction work *The Golden Age of Murder*, and Ann Cleeves is now an international best-selling author with three major TV series to her name. But back then, Ann had only just completed her first Vera novel, Cath's *Blue Murder* was still three years away, and Martin was yet to embark on his Detection Club opus. In year 2000, none of us sold spectacularly well, which made each and every one of us, by definition, 'midlist' authors, which put us on an equal footing from the outset.

Our very first glossy brochure, published in year 2000, described Murder Squad as 'a group of northern writers keen to gain a wider audience for their work, which has been extremely well received by reviewers'. We set up a website, worked our local contacts, approaching festivals, journalists and TV with surprisingly positive results, including a slot on the BBC's *Inside Out* programme. We also took the innovative step of sending out a regular e-newsletter. Our newsletter continues today, covering a wide range of topics, from book news, competitions, events and award nominations to our perspectives on surviving the COVID-19 lockdown. You are cordially invited to join us at www.murdersquad.co.uk

In the years since our inaugural event at a Borders Bookshop in March 2000, the squad line-up has changed a little – John and Chaz stepped down, and sadly, Stuart Pawson died a few years ago, but Kate Ellis and Chris Simms have since joined us, and we continue to bring our wide-ranging fiction to new audiences. Between us, we've won over twenty national and international awards and published three anthologies – one of which won *two* awards. I have chaired the Crime Writers' Association, as has Martin Edwards, and both Martin and Ann Cleeves have been awarded the CWA's highest honour, the Diamond Dagger.

This anthology, appropriately named *Many Deadly Returns*, celebrates our twenty-first anniversary, with three stories each from the existing squad, as well as contributions from the squaddies who have since retired. Twenty-one years on, we continue to sustain and encourage each other, sharing not only the highs and lows, but also writing opportunities with others in the squad. One notable example was an email Ann forwarded to the squad from an ITV producer looking for a strong female detective for a new series. This was eight years before *Vera* first aired on TV, and that generously shared email resulted in Cath's long-running *Blue Murder* series.

Frankly, I never imagined Murder Squad would last so long. I feel blessed that it has not only survived but has evolved and in particular that its individual members (and they are highly individual!) have grown in stature and achieved international recognition – giving the lie to the popular notion that having acquired the dubious and often pejorative label 'midlist author', a writer is pigeonholed for life. Finally, I am grateful that alongside the day-to-day benefits of shared experiences and opportunities is the joy of having made friendships that have not only gone the distance but have been enriched and deepened with time.

Margaret Murphy

INTRODUCTION

Many Deadly Returns celebrates the twenty-first birthday of Murder Squad and showcases the range of our fiction. This is our fourth anthology and the most ambitious so far. We thought it would be truly appropriate to put together no fewer than twenty-one contributions – three stories from each of the current members together with one from each of our former colleagues.

The members of Murder Squad trade in fictional murder and mayhem, but at the heart of our joint activities is friendship, closely linked to a shared aim of mutual support. Over the past twenty-one years, we've enjoyed plenty of wonderful times together, as well as one or two sobering occasions. Among the latter, one that stands out in my memory is of us all gathering together in Formby, Merseyside, for a joint event – to which nobody came. People did turn up in droves to the venue where we were booked to appear, but they were all taking part in a line-dancing class in an adjoining room. It didn't matter; we went off to the pub and had such a convivial evening that the occasion wasn't really sobering after all. I also recall being booked through Murder Squad in our early days to give a talk at Pudsey Library. I was impressed, as I approached the venue, to see crowds of animated individuals swarming around both sides of the pavement outside the entrance. Unfortunately they turned out to be more concerned with a political demo and counter-demonstration than with listening to a discussion about crime writing.

We've taken part in fascinating joint events such as a specially scripted live performance in an old courtroom during Cheltenham Literature Festival. Over the years we've also participated in festivals held in places such as Carlisle and the Word in South Shields, as well as at countless bookshops and libraries up and down the country. We've given talks and readings, taken part in panels, and offered workshops for aspiring writers. One memorable afternoon at Knutsford Literature Festival, Stuart Pawson entertained the refined Cheshire ladies with a reading from a bawdy and very funny scene in one of his Charlie Priest novels – and they loved it. Often we've collaborated in smaller numbers. I have fond memories of a 'murder dinner' in Derby, when Cath Staincliffe and I gave readings in between courses of a rather splendid meal, while hoping not to spoil their digestion; there was also a fun event at Harrogate's Majestic Hotel when Stuart, Ann, and I spent the evening with a group of visiting Americans.

When we took part in a BBC TV show, *Inside Out*, we were filmed having a delightful dinner at the home of Ann and Tim Cleeves. Ann was also interviewed while roaming around her old stamping ground, Hilbre Island in the River Dee, while I was asked to wander along the bank of the River Mersey at Runcorn, a setting which I adapted for a scene in *Waterloo Sunset*: for a writer, any experience may one day find its way into a story. In the days before streaming, we produced a CD of readings from our books, and we've sent out a regular free newsletter for many years (details of how to subscribe can be found elsewhere in this book) as well as running our own website.

Our first book of short stories, *Murder Squad*, appeared in 2001, and was followed a decade later by *Best Eaten Cold and Other Stories*. The latter book yielded two nominations for the CWA Short Story Dagger: 'Laptop' by Cath Staincliffe and 'The Message' by Margaret Murphy. To our collective delight, the CWA judges demonstrated the wisdom of Solomon by awarding the Dagger – uniquely – to two stories, rather than one, choosing those written by Cath and Margaret.

Our third book, *The Starlings and Other Stories*, appeared in 2015, and was a particularly unusual project. We took black-and-white photographs of Pembrokeshire scenes by the accomplished photographer David Wilson and wrote stories inspired by the images he'd captured. Each of the six Squad members wrote a story, and we invited half a dozen friends to contribute as well, so the book as a whole became the work of Murder Squad *and accomplices*.

We had plenty of celebrations planned for our 20th anniversary. Alas, the pandemic put paid to those events; undaunted, we decided to produce this book. The majority of the stories are either freshly written or have not been previously published in the UK. We hope that they will entertain our fans and interest readers who may not be familiar with our work. At the time of writing, society is still battling the pandemic, but we look forward to meeting readers in person again just as soon as circumstances allow. In the meantime, please do sit back and enjoy *Many Deadly Returns*.

Martin Edwards

ANN CLEEVES – WILD SWIMMING

Four of us swim every day in the sea at Cullercoats. We have formed, I suppose, an informal bubble, though we still keep to social distancing and we bring our own flasks of coffee, and hot-water bottles to stem the chill afterwards. There's no nipping up to the Boatyard Café to stay warm while we wait for takeaway drinks, no sharing of bags of chips or homemade cake, though some other wild swimmers seem to be less careful. I'm a teacher and breaking rules goes against my instincts. Besides, my mother died of COVID in the first wave of the virus, so this is personal for me. Grief gets me in the gut when I'm least expecting it. We were very close. I'm being sponsored in my swims, raising money for the NHS, for the staff who cared for my mother, who held her hand when I wasn't allowed to visit.

We didn't know each other before we started out on this crazy adventure of the daily dip throughout January. On New Year's Day, there were lots of swimmers, celebrating the start of 2021. A new year and new hope. A vaccine at last, a new US president in prospect. A glimmer of light on the horizon, just like the glimmer of white light to the east as the sun started to rise.

The four of us began talking afterwards as we climbed awkwardly out of our costumes, shivering so the words came out in stutters. We'd each decided that the lifeboat station provided shelter, a degree of privacy to get dressed. The sun came up, blasting the bay with its rays, and it felt, to me at least, that something important had happened. I had been in at the beginning, a new dawn, metaphorically and literally.

All four of us found the swim exhilarating. More than that. It felt like a life-changing experience. It's hard to explain how that shock of freezing water acts on the body: the skin, the flesh and the nervous system. I have never taken drugs, but Liv, one of our number has, and she says that winter wild-water swimming gives her the best high of her life.

Liv runs her own business – something to do with financial services – and she spends all day crouched over a computer screen, trying to juggle home-schooling her kids with earning a living. I sense that her husband isn't a lot of help. She seldom talks about him and I don't know what *he* does for a living. There are days though when she seems desperate. She says she could murder her teenage son, who slides his attention away from his streamed lessons to YouTube, his Xbox or Fortnite, if he's not under constant supervision. There's something impulsive about her. On some days she's very excitable, almost manic, and on others she seems a bit low and barely speaks as we prepare to swim. The cold water is almost miraculous on those days. It seems to reset her energy level. She steps back on to the shore a new woman.

Holly has never told us what she does for a living. Something demanding, I think. She seems driven. When she hits the sea, she powers off, with a crawl that takes her easily between both piers, much further out than I'd ever go. She's the youngest of the four of us, and at first, she seemed separate, not a real member of our group. Very much apart as if, every day, it was chance that brought us all together. She mellowed as the month went on, though, and joins in now when we decide on a time to meet for the swim. Often, we fit in with her plans, because the rest of us are more flexible about timing. I think she must work shifts. She could be a doctor. She's very bright and she dresses very smartly. I imagine her coming to the Bay straight from ICU, needing to wash away the stress and the blood. I could ask her, of course, but something about her manner prevents me. She is a very private woman and I wouldn't want to intrude.

Holly never talks about a family and I can't picture her with a husband and a couple of kids. It occurred to me that she might be gay. I build stories in my head about the people I meet. I see her in a beautiful house, uncluttered and ordered, completely in control of her life.

Then there's Maria, who's on her own too. She's not a spinster like me, and she has grown-up kids to look out for her, but she's a widow. Her husband died in a car crash four years ago, and she's still bitter. She still blames the woman who came out of the junction too fast without looking.

If Holly is silent, Maria talks a lot. She's fixated on the driver of the other car.

'The cow had been drinking. They breathalysed her and she was just under the limit, but all the same . . .'

We hear the same story a lot. About how the woman was charged with dangerous driving, but was only given a suspended sentence, because she had an otherwise clear record. We listen sympathetically as we undress for the water and drink coffee afterwards through icy lips. I don't think Maria talks to anyone else about her husband's death any more. I've seen her occasionally bumping into other people she knows. She lives in Cullercoats and many of the dog-walkers are her friends. With them, she seems sunny, easy-going. The wild swimming allows her to express her true feelings to people she will probably never meet again once this month is over.

Maria has a style that I suppose might be called hippy chic. She wears loose trousers, that make her look a little like a clown, big hand-knitted jumpers, and chunky jewellery. She's not a small woman so I suppose the clothes hide her bulges. I recognized her when we first met on the beach. She's furloughed now, but she worked in the new bookshop in Whitley before the last lockdown. It's called The Bound. She's passionate about reading and recently our post-swim meetings have turned into a book group. We've all decided to read the same title, and buy copies through Maria. We thought we would continue to get together when the restrictions are eased, in the sunlit room above the shop, sharing our reading passions. Now, at the beginning of 2021, that idea seems like an unachievable fantasy.

It was Maria who almost tripped over the dead body. It was 31 January, the last day of my challenge, and my birthday. We'd decided on a dawn swim to see the month out. It was a weekday and we were the only people there. Liv had brought a balloon filled with helium, with the number fifty in gold painted on it. It was still dark when we ran into the water. I'd tied the string of the balloon around my waist and, as the sun came up, it glinted on the gold paint. I'm usually rather sensitive about my age, but today I didn't mind celebrating it with my new friends.

I was very moved by the fact that Liv had remembered my birthday and had gone to the effort of bringing the balloon. She wanted to take a selfie of all four of us, but that would have been impossible if we were to abide by the social distancing rules, and there was nobody else on the beach to take the photo for us. The others were prepared to take the risk, but I put my foot down. Now, I wish I'd allowed it as a record of the day, the last time all four of us would be together. Later, I discovered that Liv had brought a bottle of prosecco too, and plastic glasses still wrapped in polythene so they'd be entirely safe, but we never got to drink the wine because of the body.

It had been wild and stormy the day before, with rain and a gusty wind. Although the weather had cleared, the sea was still mountainous. It was just past high tide and the waves were crashing over the jetties. Liv loved these conditions and swam close to the north pier, so she could experience the breakers as they hit the outside of the jetty at full strength and were forced into the air before landing on the other side. It was as if she was under a waterfall, and she waved at us through the curtain of spray. I found the power of the waves intimidating and just watching her made me breathless, a little anxious. I don't have her courage, or I'm not as reckless, so I bobbed in the calmer water, with the balloon floating above me. Holly was doing her usual solitary crawl way out in the mouth of the bay.

Maria is always the first one out of the sea. She seems to feel the cold more than the rest of us. I watched her run across the sand toward the bench by the lifeboat station where we'd all left our clothes. Then she stopped suddenly. I thought at first that she'd trodden on a piece of glass. It couldn't have been a jellyfish sting, not at this time of the year, though there'd been an invasion of them earlier in the autumn. She started waving and shouting. Holly responded first. I thought again she could be a doctor, used to dealing with emergencies. But when Maria didn't stop screaming, we all followed Holly out on to the shore, shivering, our skin that strange pink it always turns after exposure to icy water.

I recognized the dead woman immediately. We all knew her as the 'lone swimmer'. She was a middle-aged, rather frumpy person, with flabby arms and a belly only held in by her floral bathing costume. She wasn't as big as Maria, certainly, but Maria had a certain style and carried her weight well. She was fit, easy in her own body. If anything, she flaunted it, not caring at all if her towel dropped and her breasts were exposed to the world. The lone swimmer was timid, nondescript, grey-haired and sallow-skinned. Occasionally, I'd wondered about approaching her, inviting her to join our group, but in the end, I could see that it wouldn't have worked. Not that the others were snobbish exactly. I don't want you to think that. But I sensed that they wouldn't have welcomed her.

It was a matter of pride that none of our team wore wetsuits, but we four had some of the kit, the special gloves and hats and long-sleeved Lycra bathers, the orange floats. The lone swimmer had none of these things, nor a dry-robe to warm her immediately she came out. All she had was a rather threadbare towel. It can't have been much fun, but we often saw her, and, like us, she must have gone into the water every day.

It's dangerous to swim alone in cold water. Regular wild swimmers who can't find anyone to go in with them will ask a 'spotter', a friend, to stand on the shore and watch out for them. This woman had appeared entirely isolated. There seemed to be no pleasure for her in the activity. It was almost as if it was a penance. I'm not religious myself, so I find it hard to understand such a thing, but I did wonder if that was the case. I'd become quite fascinated by the woman, and intrigued by her motivation. I noticed when she wasn't there.

When Holly reached the body, she took charge. She told the rest of us to get dressed, and asked me to bring her clothes to where she was standing, on the most exposed stretch of beach, almost guarding the site.

'I'll need my phone,' she said. But she didn't look at me.

All her attention was on the body, lying on the high-tide mark. She didn't touch the lone swimmer, which seemed odd for a doctor, but we all realized that nothing we could do would bring the woman back to life. After all, she hadn't died in the last hour. It was pure chance that we hadn't stumbled over her as we'd entered the water. It had still been dark then, that grey dawn at least, when everything's shadowy. By chance, we'd all taken a path into the sea which would have avoided her.

I didn't want to look at the woman's lifeless body – I've always been squeamish and I worried that I might be sick – but I carried Holly's clothes to her, passing them a garment at a time, so she could get dressed without having to put them on the wet sand. As soon as she had her dry-robe on and the shivering had stopped, she got out her phone and I heard her talk to someone on the other end of the line.

It was the words 'unexplained death' that caught my attention. Because what was unexplained about the lone swimmer having drowned? She must have been in the water the evening before, when the weather was still wild and the sea was at its coldest. Without a spotter, she'd always have been taking a risk swimming alone, and clearly a current had pulled her out of her depth and then the tide had spewed her back on the shore. But I suppose doctors always have to be cautious.

Sometimes, I teach from home in lockdown and I didn't have live lessons that day, so I was in no hurry to get back, but the others were dressed now and eager to get away.

'You OK to deal with this then Hol?' That was Maria. She seemed to have got over her shock, wrapped up in her long, red coat.

'I'll need you to hang on, I'm afraid,' Holly said. It was getting quite light now and there were more dog-walkers on the beach, curious, standing a bit apart, but staring. 'We'll need to take statements.' She looked at the gathering crowd. 'Stand away please. I'm a police officer. I've got this.' She spoke with an authority that shocked me. Not a doctor then, but a police officer. I would never have had her down as that.

'Do you mind waiting here?' she said to me. 'I want to go and see if I can find her clothes, see if there's some ID, and someone has to stop the gawpers messing up the locus. Don't let anyone get close. My boss will be here soon.'

That surprised me too. I'd supposed Holly would be in charge of a team. I did have a moment of satisfaction that she'd chosen me rather than one of the others to be her second in command, and I stood with my back to the body, giving the rubberneckers the glare that I'd perfected for silencing a class of fidgety Year Eights. In the end, they got bored and wandered off, though some were taking photos of the scene on their phones. No doubt they'd soon be posted all over social media.

Holly walked up the beach and I saw her chatting to Maria and Liv. They both seemed reluctant to hang on for Holly's colleagues to arrive, and I could hear snatches of the conversation. Liv said she had a Zoom meeting booked for nine o'clock and if she wasn't there to get her son logged in for his first streamed lesson, he'd still be in bed. Maria claimed she needed to be home for childcare duty, but we all knew that she only looked after the grandchildren in her support bubble in the afternoons. They both sounded like excuses to me.

Holly had moved round the lifeboat station to the place where we'd seen the lone swimmer always prepare for the water. From where I was standing, I couldn't tell whether she'd found what she was looking for, and she was still there when a battered Land Rover made its way down the slipway towards the ice-cream kiosk. Parking is not allowed there, and I was wondering whether I should say anything, but Holly came back into view to approach the driver. I assumed she was about to send the woman on her way, but instead they had a conversation. The Land Rover door opened and a large, rather scruffy woman climbed out. This was obviously the boss for whom Holly had been waiting.

She and Holly made their way to Maria and Liv. They seemed unimpressed with the new woman and started to argue with her, but I suspected that they'd end up doing what they were told. I've known head teachers with the same sort of presence, professionals who carry great authority and who are highly competent. It's easy to underestimate women of a certain age, especially when they don't bother much with their appearance. And Maria and Liv did seem resigned to staying where they were because they both took out their phones. I assume they must have been explaining to their families that they'd be delayed.

The detective – she *must* have been a detective because she wasn't in uniform – had walked round the corner of the lifeboat station to where the lone swimmer had left her belongings. I was tempted to move a little way from the body to see what she was doing, but Holly had asked me to stay on guard, and besides, I didn't want to appear too curious. There was the sound of a siren and I watched a police car drive down the slipway and park behind the Land Rover. It all seemed unreal, rather theatrical, as if somehow the scene had been set up just for my entertainment.

Holly walked across the sand towards me. By now there was a pale sun and the wind had dropped completely. It was one of those mild days that makes us feel that spring isn't so far away. The uniformed officers from the police car were clearing the beach, sending everyone who still remained on their way.

'I found her clothes and her bag,' Holly said. 'She's named Rosemary Parr. Lives in Wallsend. Does that mean anything to you?'

I shook my head. 'I don't know anyone who lives there.' Wallsend is a somewhat poorer area of North Tyneside. Most of my friends live on the coast.

'I'm not sure that this was an accident.' Holly was talking almost to herself. 'There are marks around her neck and her shoulders. Bruises.' A pause. 'I'd say someone drowned her.'

I didn't know what to say. I was shocked, of course, but I supposed that was why the older detective had been called in. Again, I was pleased that Holly was taking me into her confidence. It gave me a certain status. My mother and I had always enjoyed watching crime dramas together on television, and here I was observing a crime scene in real time. I looked over to Maria and Liv, who were sitting on the bench at the top of the beach, all thoughts of social distancing forgotten. They were whispering together in a rather conspiratorial way, and I had a moment of feeling left out, the rather prim child at the front of the class, liked by the teacher but not by the other pupils.

Holly looked every inch the professional now, in her leather boots and smart black coat, and her next words confirmed my suspicions about the woman from the Land Rover. 'That's why I called in Inspector Stanhope,' she continued. 'She's doing some background checks but she'll want to talk to you all in a while.' One of the uniformed officers was standing by the slipway turning people away. The other joined us. He hardly looked more than a boy and was vaguely familiar. I wondered if I might have taught him. I'd forgotten my balloon in all the excitement. I'd untied it as soon as I came out of the water and must have let it go. Now it was floating low over the beach and towards the sea. I almost chased after it, but I'd never have reached it in time.

'Sam will look after things here now,' Holly said. 'You can go back to your friends.' As though until an hour before, they hadn't been *her* friends too, that we hadn't laughed together, jumping into a moonlit sea during an evening swim, or shared tips on the best gloves and hat to wear when there was ice on the shore.

Liv and Maria were fed up at having to wait. I suppose they'd assumed this was an accidental drowning, as I had, and they couldn't understand the fuss.

'I imagine they have to go through certain procedures, as it's an unexplained death.' I lowered my voice, although now there was nobody to hear. 'There are bruises on her neck and shoulders. I believe that Holly thinks it might be murder.'

Maria went very pale at this. Perhaps she was thinking about her husband. She'd always claimed that his accident had been almost as bad as murder, and she'd been in the car with him when he'd died. Finding the lone swimmer's body must have brought back a lot of memories.

'Her name's Rosemary Parr,' I said. 'She's from Wallsend. The police are running background checks.'

It occurred to me that they might be running background checks on all of us too. I wondered what they'd find out. I'd done a quick Google of my swimming buddies not long after we'd met. As I say, I've always been curious and I like to

know who I'm mixing with. I hadn't been able to find anything
about Holly, though. She hadn't even given us her second
name.

Liv had appeared in an article in *The Journal* when she was
named north-east businesswoman of the year. The reporter had
done some digging too, and it seems that she was a very wild
child when she was younger. She'd hung out with footballers
and pop stars, and had a spell in rehab in her early thirties
before reinventing herself. Still, I couldn't see that anything
there could make her a suspect in the murder of a middle-aged
woman from Wallsend. She and Rosemary Parr would scarcely
mix in the same circles.

Maria was all over the local press immediately after her
husband died. I'd read about her at the time, and I had seen
her on *Look North*. She'd started a campaign against the woman
driver who'd crashed into them. All her grief had turned into
anger and there were some very intemperate posts on social
media. I could understand that, of course, but she'd ended up
making herself seem vengeful and unbalanced. I wondered if
there was guilt in there too. If maybe she'd distracted her
husband just before the crash occurred, or they'd had an argument and he'd lost concentration. It's a very easy thing to do.
It seemed impossible to believe that the dead woman had been
the driver who'd killed Maria's husband, though. That would
have been too much of a coincidence, and besides, these days
Maria only expressed her anger to us.

I was about to ask Maria for the driver's name, because
after all coincidences do happen, when Holly's boss came up.
She'd come well prepared for the beach and was wearing
wellington boots and a big coat. She introduced herself.

'DI Vera Stanhope.'

The sun was well up behind her now, and that made her
look bigger than she really was. Intimidating, somehow.

'Sorry to have kept you,' she said. 'You can all get off now.
I don't expect we'll be bothering you again. Hol can give a
statement about finding the body. She said that none of you
had any contact with the woman while she was swimming.'

I don't know what I was expecting, but certainly not just
to be dismissed like that. It occurred to me that I'd never

hear the full story of the investigation. I'd enjoyed the sense of being an insider for once, of knowing a little more than everyone else. But in reality, of course, there was nothing I could do. This was the last day of January and there'd be no more sponsored daily dips. We gathered up our bags filled with damp, sandy towels, and told each other that we'd keep in touch, and perhaps meet up again for that reading group.

I was following the others up the slipway when Inspector Stanhope called me back.

'Margaret, could you give me a minute?'

I thought then that she might be able to use my advice after all, that all the digging I'd done might be useful.

'Rosemary Parr,' she said, when the others were out of earshot. 'You knew her, didn't you?'

'Only here. On the beach.'

'We've checked with her employer. She was one of the agency staff going into your mother's care home. You told Hol where your mam spent her last days. You didn't see Rosemary there?'

'No! How could I? We were allowed nowhere near, even when the old folk were dying. Not even in all the protective gear, just to hold their hands.'

There was a silence, apart from the gulls and the waves breaking on the beach.

'That must have been hard.' Her voice was gentle. 'My father and me, we never really got on, but still I was glad I was there at the end for him.' Another pause. 'I think you and your mother must have been really close.'

'There was never anyone else. My mother and my work.'

'Ah well, maybe I just have the work!' She gave a sad little smile. 'It was Rosemary who gave your mother the infection, wasn't it? She'd suspected she might have COVID, but still she went into the home. She was on one of those zero-hours contracts, so she'd not get paid if she didn't work. And it was before care home staff got the proper PPE.'

'My mother was only there because she'd had a hip operation and she wasn't ready to go home. They booted her out of hospital to free up beds for the COVID patients.'

'You couldn't have had her at yours?' That sad little smile again.

'I was at work all day!' And I love my work. The kids bring me to life every morning when I go in. The head said I could have compassionate leave, but I work with the vulnerable ones and they've been in school all the way through lockdown. I thought I was indispensable, and, besides, I didn't want them building the same special relationship with another teacher. I've been feeling guilty ever since. Blaming myself and wanting to hit out. Like Maria after her husband's accident.

'Tell me how it happened,' the inspector said.

And so I told her. What else could I do? I've never been a liar and there was something about Vera Stanhope which would have made lying impossible anyway. I knew Rosemary Parr had brought the infection into the nursing home. She worked for an agency, and the owner of the home was glad it hadn't been one of her permanent staff.

'Our girls wouldn't have been so irresponsible,' she'd said when she'd phoned to tell me of my mother's death, to offer insincere condolences.

She let slip the care assistant's name and that gave me a starting point. I followed Rosemary from the agency where she went each week to check for work. She never noticed me. Once I followed her on to the metro, scared of catching COVID myself, because nobody was wearing a mask at that point. She got out at Cullercoats and I watched her swim. I bided my time, and throughout the summer I watched the beach from a distance and I made my plans.

Then it was January. A new year and a new start. Time to act, I thought; otherwise I'd never be rid of the obsession. So I started swimming too. I knew that Rosemary mostly swam after dark. She swam every day, as if she thought the water would wash the infection and the guilt from her body. I suppose I should have felt sorry for her, have had some sympathy for her situation, but I was haunted by thoughts of my mother, dying alone, scared and helpless. And by my own guilt.

The night before my birthday I went to the Bay and I waited. Rosemary came just as it was getting dusk. It was perfect weather for my plans. Huge waves crashed on to the beach.

Her death would be seen as a tragic accident. She might even be blamed for being foolhardy, going in without a spotter. I shouted to her:

'Hi! We must be mad, don't you think, going in today? It'll just be a quick dip for me.'

She seemed grateful that another swimmer was befriending her at last. 'I need it,' she said. 'It's all that's keeping me sane.'

We went into the water together, gasping at the cold and the ferocity of the tide. There was some traffic on the road behind me, but lockdown meant that the bars and cafés were closed and there was nobody else about. We jumped the waves, laughing, until we were nearly out of our depth. I felt almost a kindred spirit with the woman, but when she started to swim away towards the shore, I put my hands round her neck and with all my strength I pushed her under the water. She hardly struggled. Perhaps it was the shock or the cold, or perhaps she didn't really want to go on living. Not enough to fight back. In a strange way I could have been doing her a favour. At last, she went limp, and the outgoing tide took her away.

Vera Stanhope and I were sitting at opposite ends of the bench now, looking out to the sea. A couple of tankers were moored, waiting for high water to enter the Tyne. The light reminded me of daffodils in suburban gardens, the end of a long, dark winter. Vera had round brown eyes, the colour of conkers, young eyes, and they were looking at me all the time.

I told my story.

'It must have been a shock, finding her here this morning. Did you think she'd just float away and never come back to haunt you?'

I couldn't answer. I hadn't thought beyond the drowning.

'But maybe you thought this would be for the best,' she said. 'That she'd be haunting you anyway, which would be very much worse.'

I took a last look at the Bay, nodded, and followed her up the slipway to where the young policeman was waiting for me.

MARTIN EDWARDS –
LUCKY LIAM

*B*etter to be born lucky than rich. The phrase had stuck
in Liam North's mind ever since he'd first heard it as a
child, during a family get-together at a pub on the front
in Seaton Carew. His mother's brother had been talking about
a distant cousin, who had announced her engagement to a
banker she'd met at university. Uncle Graeme wasn't lucky
himself – a tree surgeon, he'd been killed six months later in
an unfortunate accident while felling a Lombardy poplar a
mile outside Hartlepool – but it seemed to Liam that his
philosophy was spot on. Money comes and goes, but if you're
born lucky, in the long run you'll get pretty much everything
you could possibly wish for.

Liam's family was far from rich, but he believed he'd been
born lucky. An affable manner and a love of words that
endowed him with the gift of the gab eased him through child-
hood and the teenage years without suffering the consequences
of his incurable indolence. He loved reading, and the way he
surrounded himself with books gave everyone the impression
of a likeable but studious young chap who was destined to go
far. In examinations at school and university, his fluent way
with words did not compensate fully for his lethargic attitude
to revision, but ensured that his grades were borderline respectable. Good enough, as far as Liam was concerned, and when
he blamed his failure to do better on recurrent migraines,
everyone sympathized. People liked Liam, and were willing
to give him the benefit of any doubt.

After a few inconsequential schoolboy romances, he met a
fellow English student at the University of Sunderland during
his first week on the campus. Sally was blonde and stunningly
attractive, and she loved books just as much as Liam. She
confided on their first date that she dreamed of becoming a

writer and, during their student years, a stream of poems, plays, short stories and fragments of novels flooded from her laptop. None achieved paid-for publication, but Liam kept encouraging her. He wasn't convinced that Sally possessed literary talent, but never mind. One day, she might drop lucky.

They married three months after taking their degrees. Sally took an Upper Second, but Liam had to make do with a Third, even though she'd helped him with his course work, to the extent of writing most of it. She felt guilty about her own success because he'd suffered migraines during the whole of finals, and dismayed because the job market in the north-east didn't offer much for inadequately qualified English graduates. The tricky question of how to make a living demanded an answer. Sally, keen, energetic, and a self-proclaimed 'people person', soon started climbing the greasy pole in human resources, but Liam drifted from job to job, working in bars and restaurants while he tried to write the Great North-East England Novel. He seldom made it past chapter one.

Reading other people's books was less like hard work than writing his own. He was taken on by an elderly fellow called Gidman who owned a second-hand bookshop on the Headland at Hartlepool. The building reeked of musty old tomes, and its out-of-the-way location on a road meandering between the Spion Kop Cemetery and the lighthouse meant that customers were few and far between. The peace and quiet suited Liam perfectly. More opportunities for reading, less scope for anyone to stop him pleasing himself. Gidman suffered from emphysema, and had recruited Liam simply because he wanted to keep the business afloat. Earning only the minimum wage didn't worry Liam. Sally was picking up good money, and at least they didn't have any extra mouths to feed.

Sally proved unable to have children, the result of a rare genetic condition. When the medical advice was finally confirmed, she wept throughout one long, long night. Nobody could have comforted her more assiduously than Liam. He kept repeating that it didn't matter, it really didn't matter. Sally, inconsolable, feared that he was simply being kind, but he was speaking nothing less than the truth. Kids would take a lot of looking after, and he preferred being the centre of Sally's universe. Thanks to her salary, they'd been able to put down a deposit on a tiny house in Seaton Carew, a stone's throw from where Liam had grown up. From the upstairs bedrooms, you could glimpse the sea. Life was good, who could want more? *If it ain't broke, why fix it?* That was another of Uncle Graeme's maxims, although it may have contributed to his inadequate maintenance of the circular saw responsible for his premature demise.

His idea for cheering Sally up was brilliant in its simplicity. She loved books too, so she could help out in the bookshop at weekends, and assist with cataloguing and stuff on the evenings when they had nothing better to do. It wasn't reasonable to expect Gidman to cough up any more money, given the paltry takings, but it was a way of taking her mind off babies.

Sally proved agreeable and, for a while, things went well. She'd developed an entrepreneurial streak, and soon she came up with several ideas to boost footfall, including occasional author visits. Inviting real-life authors to sign their latest books in a second-hand shop – where dog-eared copies of their earlier work were on sale for a pittance – seemed counter-intuitive to Liam, but Sally was extremely persuasive, and before long she'd lined up a series of events featuring the north-east's more prominent literary figures.

Liam congratulated himself. Sally was kept fully occupied, and he was free to devote more of his own time during business hours to reading and daydreaming. One or two of his fantasies were inspired by what Sally told him about her oldest friend, a talkative, seriously overweight woman called Maxine. She'd been deserted by her husband, who waited until twelve months after their wedding to discover that he was gay. Maxine was generous and good-natured, always doing good deeds for others, but she never had much luck. The poor woman was as plain as the back end of a bus, and she didn't care for books. Nevertheless, she was legendary for her sex drive and, according to Sally, her maxim was *try anything once.* Physically, she repelled him, but he couldn't help wishing that Sally was equally adventurous. Some of the spark had gone out of their love-making, he couldn't deny it. If only she were less consumed with ambition – especially ambition for him. She wanted him to take over the shop once old Gidman died, and 'make a proper go of it'. All Liam wanted was for her to leave him to his own devices – except in bed, of course. Once or twice, he noticed Maxine giving him a longing glance, but he pretended not to notice. He only had eyes for his wife. Life with Sally might not be perfect, but he couldn't deny that he'd dropped lucky with her. The very idea of sleeping with Maxine made him break out in a cold sweat, and even if it hadn't, he certainly couldn't contemplate the fuss and acrimony associated with divorce. *If it ain't broke . . .*

He didn't suspect that their marriage might be in the process of breaking until Sally invited Heath Morrison back to Headland Books for the second time in six months to conduct a workshop for aspiring writers. Morrison came from South Shields, and eighteen months earlier, his third novel, an introspective character study of a priapic coal miner, had been long-listed for the Man Booker Prize. Liam found Morrison's bleak worldview depressing on the page, and his cocksure manner – over-compensation, people reckoned, for a depressive streak – irritating when encountered in person. But Sally was smitten with his work, and eventually it crossed Liam's mind that she might also be smitten with the man himself. Morrison had a formidable reputation as a philanderer. He'd once spent six months in jail after beating up a lover's boyfriend following a violent row in a Gateshead bar.

At first, Liam tried to shrug off the jealousy that Sally provoked whenever she rhapsodised about Morrison's poetic prose. But she kept harping on about it, and when she mentioned that the great man had offered her advice on how to sharpen up her own writing, he made the mistake of blurting out that Morrison was an arrogant shit who ought to mind his own business.

'Liam!' Her cheeks were pink with outrage. 'That's a disgusting thing to say. I thought you liked Heath.'

He hadn't meant to let the mask slip. 'I only meant that you've as much talent as he has,' he improvised. 'You can't deny that Heath Morrison is a nasty piece of work.'

'Rubbish!' He took a step back, as if she'd slapped his

cheek. Surely he hadn't lost his knack of mollifying her with a few well-chosen compliments? 'Heath is a true artist. You may not realize it, but he's tormented by self-doubt. People who say he's violent and arrogant don't have a clue what he's really like.'

She stomped off so angrily that he couldn't be confident that she would set about making their evening meal. In the end, he had to ring for pizzas to be delivered to their door.

Liam began to fret. He suspected that the only doubt tormenting Heath Morrison was whether he could add Sally's name to his list of conquests. How fortunate he was to be able to depend on her loyalty. All the same, it was a mistake to be complacent. Better keep an eye on things. Check her mobile phone account, that sort of thing.

He was shocked to discover that his luck was about to run out. Sally and Morrison exchanged calls and texts with startling regularity, far more often than was justified by making arrangements for readings at the Headland Bookshop. On a Saturday morning at the end of May, he eavesdropped on one of their conversations, and confirmed his worst fears.

'I'm in the shop on Bank Holiday Monday,' Sally murmured. 'Liam asked me to help out while he visits this old bloke who wants to sell his book collection . . . yes, we can lock the door as soon as you arrive. We're opening up, on the off-chance a few visitors to the gun battery get caught in a downpour. I've promised to get stuck into some overdue tidying, and that's enough for Liam to make himself scarce. He's such an idle bastard. Whatever the weather, there's no way I'll be rushed off my feet by customers . . . no, I don't want anyone to watch us, thanks very much – I'm a highly respectable woman, I'll have you know . . . honestly, Heath, you are the limit. Just as well you're so gorgeous, huh?'

The conversation subsided into a long, helpless giggle. Crouched in his hiding place, behind a bookcase full of battered self-help books, Liam barely managed to suppress a howl of pain. At lunchtime, when Sally went out to buy ingredients for their evening meal, he checked out the loft space at the top of the building. She'd starting using it for storage – but why would she want to store half a dozen luxurious velvet cushions? He had no difficulty in guessing their intended purpose.

Later that evening, as they ate together, he noticed that Sally was distracted, and realized that she'd not had much to say to him for quite a while. He'd simply not noticed her increasingly perfunctory replies to his remarks, or that so often nowadays – in the shop, in the kitchen, and most of all in bed – her mind seemed to be elsewhere. Now he understood where her thoughts were roaming. A rage consumed him that felt unlike anything he'd ever experienced before.

Would Sally pack her bags, and leave him high and dry? The financial and practical consequences hardly bore thinking about. What if Morrison dumped her? She was evidently far from content with the marriage, and in time some other literary Casanova would seduce her. She was no longer the innocent girl he'd married. Things could never be the same again.

While brushing his teeth, he remembered that her firm had recently bestowed upon her a new perk, to supplement a measly rise in pay. Life insurance for employees. What a pity Sally couldn't have an accident. Frankly, it would serve her right.

It occurred to him as he shaved the next morning that, of course, accidents did happen. All the time. Why couldn't one happen to Sally? And to Morrison too, come to that? Killing two birds with a single stone was always attractive; economy of effort combined with maximum achievement.

Thinking furiously, he made an excuse to pop out to the shop, even though it was closed, and set about putting his plan into practice. He was acutely conscious that it wasn't a perfect plan. A good deal could go wrong. But then, you constantly read about supposedly perfect crimes that unravelled because of one piece of bad luck. Might as well trust to fortune, same as always.

'When will you be back?' she asked, as he dropped her off at the shop the next morning.

'Not quite sure. You know what Ernie's like. He'll insist on a good long natter, and it will take me ages to price up all the titles. We'll probably just grab some fish and chips for lunch.'

'Fine, there's no rush.'

'I might be able to get back by mid-afternoon to give you a hand.'

'Really?' The flash of alarm in her eyes gave him intense pleasure, and it confirmed his belief that he was doing the right thing. The only thing. 'There's no need. The weather's so nice, I don't expect we'll get many people in. Everyone will have better things to do than bother about books.'

Everyone, including you and Heath Morrison, Liam thought savagely. 'Yeah, I suppose you're right. I may as well go straight home.'

She smiled, her relief as visible as face paint. 'Good idea. Would you mind picking up some salmon from Sainsbury's on the way back? I'll bake it in white wine for you.'

His favourite meal. She was trying, in her crude way, to atone for her betrayal. He patted her hand. 'Marvellous. I'll see you later.'

She waved happily as he drove off. Ernie Cobb lived just outside Hart, in a quiet cottage with a vast garden which had defied the occasional tidying efforts of Maxine, his god-daughter, and become an overgrown wilderness. He had no close family, but somehow he still managed to live on his own. He was in his eighties, and his memory was failing. Liam was sure he was in the early stages of dementia. Carers came in twice a day to look after him. Except on bank holidays, that is, when – as Liam gathered – they only turned up at tea-time. It took Liam five minutes to reach the cottage, and five more to greet Ernie and ask how he was, before making a vague excuse and nipping out of the house. Less than twenty minutes after dropping Sally at the shop, he parked behind a small auto centre that had gone bankrupt the previous winter. He satisfied himself that the spot wasn't overlooked before striding along the alley that ran behind the bookshop, past a disused pub and a semi-derelict warehouse. A gate gave on to a small yard. He undid the padlock, and scrambled up the rickety iron fire escape, right to the top. Nobody could see him. Stepping on to a railed walkway, he pushed open the skylight that he had left unlocked. The loft was dusty and cramped, the only means of exit a small trapdoor. He opened the trapdoor, and contemplated the long, narrow wooden ladder which led to the floor below. Bending double under the sloping roof, he steeled himself to wait in silence until the time came to do the necessary.

And it *was* necessary. Whichever way you looked at things, he really had no choice. True, he was taking a huge risk. Would his luck hold?

Distant noises came from downstairs, as Sally moved around at street level, three floors below. There were rooms crammed with books on the ground, first and second floors. On the second floor was a small office, and, immediately below the loft, an open space accommodating stacked chairs. Sally had come up with the idea of turning this into a compact venue for author events. Liam remembered her saying that it was perfect for an intimate occasion. He'd never guessed what sort of intimate occasion she had in mind.

Ten minutes crept by before he heard the light clatter of her footsteps on the stairs. Coming to retrieve the cushions, at last. He'd wondered if she might have done so as soon as she'd arrived at the shop, so that by the time of his return, she'd already have had her accident, but he'd guessed that her first priority would be to glam up for her lover. Putting on her make-up was a job she never rushed. On balance, he was glad nothing had happened yet. What if she'd had a slice of luck in his absence, and escaped with a few cuts and bruises? He slid the trapdoor shut and waited.

He'd sawn through the ladder in three places, before putting it back together so that, at first sight, you'd never guess he'd tampered with it. Certainly, Sally didn't have a clue. Her crash and scream were simultaneous. When he peeked out through the trapdoor, it looked as though she were unconscious, but still breathing. There was no carpet on the floor, and she'd had a hard landing.

He'd fixed a length of rope to a rusty old hook in the roof cavity. It would be a bitter irony if, in the absence of the ladder, the hook gave way and he broke his own neck, but he made it down safely. In his imagination, he'd pictured Sally opening her eyes as he crouched over her, and experiencing a terrible moment of realization about what was to happen. He'd brought a short length of wood in order to club her into silence if the need arose. Thankfully, she didn't stir. As he'd expected, she'd heaped on mascara and her favourite purple eye-shadow, although the blood oozing from her cracked skull ruined the impression of loveliness.

The bell that rang when someone opened the shop door tinkled from downstairs. Liam was sure it was Heath Morrison, even before the bastard called Sally's name. When there was no reply, he could be heard springing up the stairs, taking the steps to the first floor two at a time.

'Sally! Where are you?' Morrison chortled. 'Playing hard to get? A bit late for that, sweetie.'

Liam decided to risk mimicking Sally's high-pitched giggle. He'd practised endlessly, but in the excitement of the moment, his impression left a good deal to be desired.

'Sally?' Morrison sounded suddenly wary. 'Is that you?'

The stairs to the second floor turned at a right angle near the top. Liam stationed himself out of sight, behind a tall stack of books. He was sure that Morrison would only have eyes for Sally's body. People were so predictable.

'Sally, are you playing hide and seek?' The wheedling note in Morrison's voice was truly odious. He deserved his fate, no question. 'OK. Coming, ready or not!'

Once again, he raced up the staircase, but his first glimpse of Sally, stretched out on the floor, halted him in his tracks. He had a book in his hand, but Liam had his club. No contest. Liam swung wildly, miscalculating the angle of his strike, and caught Morrison a glancing blow on the forehead. To his infinite relief, it was enough, coupled with the shock of seeing Sally's body, to send the novelist tumbling backwards down the steps with a strangled cry of pain and horror. Liam leapt after him, kicking Morrison down as he fell, before hitting him a second time as they landed on the floor below. The other man groaned, but did not stir. Like Sally, he wasn't dead, but he wouldn't be getting up any time soon. So far, so good.

Liam picked up the book Morrison had dropped, before checking to make sure that the writer was, as usual, carrying a packet of Player's and a box of Swan Vestas in the pockets of his jeans. The man smoked eighty a day; filthy habit, he'd have died young anyway. Liam eased both boxes on to the floor with a handkerchief, because you couldn't be sure what might survive in a fire, and he worried vaguely about finger-prints. He'd never smoked in his life, but he'd nicked an identical box of matches from Ernie's sideboard when the old man wasn't looking, and he lit a couple. The first set alight a stack of *Book Collector* magazines he'd left on the floor close to Morrison, creating a merry little blaze. Going back upstairs, he put the second match to a heap of old newspapers. The results were quicker and more impressive than he'd expected. Both fires took hold, and started to spread. Within seconds, the smoke was bringing tears to his eyes, even as he hauled himself back up to the loft, and detached the rope from the hook. He didn't venture a last look at Sally, as the flames danced around her. It was a shame, but he couldn't afford to be sentimental. Destroying the books was equally dreadful, come to that.

By the time he wriggled out through the skylight, still clutching the book that Morrison had brought, the building was ablaze. There was so much tinder in a second-hand book-shop. He stumbled down the fire escape, desperate to make good his escape before anyone saw him, and almost fell down the last flight of steps. Would it have served him right to break his neck after committing two murders and destroying Gidman's business? Liam didn't believe so for a minute.

Nobody saw him running down the alleyway, or jumping into his car. He heard the fire engine's siren when he was a mile away from the bookshop, and for a moment he wondered if, against all the odds, Sally and Morrison might be rescued. But no, it was unthinkable, so he didn't devote any more thought to such a nightmarish possibility.

'Shall I go to the chippy and get us each a cod and chips with mushy peas?' he asked Ernie a few minutes later. The old man nodded absently, and Liam wasn't sure that he under-stood the question. Going downhill rapidly, sad to say, but he was supplying a near-unbreakable alibi. Later, Liam would leave him a cheque for a box of books, and load them into his car. Ernie would swear blind that he'd been there all the time, but even if he got confused, that was Liam's story, and he meant to stick to it.

The police rang when he was on his way back from the chip shop. He hadn't expected them to track down his number so quickly. They'd got hold of poor Gidman within minutes of arriving at Headland Books, but it didn't make any difference. He expressed just the right amount of horror and disbelief at the news of the fire.

'But my wife . . .'

'What's that?' A sharp intake of breath from the young woman officer. 'You're not saying there's anyone inside the shop? On a bank holiday?'

'But yes – she was doing some tidying up. And a friend of ours was supposed to be coming over to lend a hand . . .'

'A friend?'

'Yes, Heath's a writer.' Liam clutched the phone tightly in a hand greased by the chip wrappings. 'Nice chap, always willing to help a chum. But my God, you're not telling me – you did get the two of them out of there, didn't you?'

By the time he arrived back at the shop, it was a smouldering ruin, but still too dangerous for a serious rescue mission to be mounted. Liam did his best to be brave, but he couldn't help crying. To think of all those lovely books, burnt to a cinder.

In the days and weeks that followed, there was universal agreement that the place was a deathtrap. The wretched Gidman was only saved from serious trouble with the Health and Safety people by a fatal heart attack. Liam was fairly sure that the superficially sympathetic police officers had their doubts about the cause of the fire, but its intensity had, as he hoped, disposed of the evidence of the sawn-off ladder and the rope, and there was no forensic evidence to prove that Sally and Morrison had been attacked, or that anyone else had been in the shop when the fire broke out. Morrison was notorious for his heavy smoking, and he proved the ideal scapegoat. One rumour had it that Sally had resisted his advances, and he'd set fire to the shop in a fit of blind fury.

The police questioned him closely about Morrison, but he insisted (while taking care not to protest too much) that the author was a really good sort, devoid of airs and graces despite his fame. He'd known that Morrison was visiting the shop on the day in question, and had meant to return there himself as soon as he left Ernie's. The more suspicious detectives seemed to conclude that, even if Liam had been cuckolded, he was to be pitied rather than suspected. Crucially, the investigation was led by someone on the verge of retirement who only wanted a quiet life. Liam played the part of bereaved loser to perfection. All in all, he was asked fewer tough questions than he'd expected.

Everyone was very kind. His crime might not have been perfect, but what mattered was to be lucky, and he'd made his own luck. Naturally, he took care not to make a claim on the life insurance until the inquest was out of the way, and he waited for Sally's firm to raise the matter with him. He explained that she'd never mentioned the perk.

At Sally's funeral, Maxine made a great fuss of him. Warm-hearted as ever, she'd insisted on popping round on a daily basis after the fire, to make sure he was all right and to do the housework. Although he much preferred to be alone with his books, he could hardly object. One day, when he was reminiscing sadly about Sally, she took him by surprise.

'Yes, she was gorgeous. Pity she was such a slut.'

'What?' Liam gaped at her.

'I mean, the way she carried on with that bastard Morrison, for instance. And he wasn't the first, not by a long chalk, I'm sure you know. She loved telling me about her flings, you know; she gloated over them. And over me, since there was no way I'd ever pick up handsome men the way she did. I never said anything, but I really loathed her for it. She was always the successful one, I was poor old Maxine. As for the way she treated you, it turned my stomach.' She stretched out her hand, and brushed his. 'I'm so glad you did it.'

'Did . . . what?'

'Got away with murder, of course.' She squeezed his arm, making him wince. 'Let's not beat about the bush. I'm impressed, to be honest. Never thought you'd have it in you.'

He swallowed. 'I haven't the faintest idea what you're talking about.'

Maxine sighed. 'Liam, please. I was in Ernie's back garden

that morning. I always felt guilty about not doing enough for him. I popped over to do a bit of weeding and such-like, it was like hacking through a jungle. I'd not been there for months, but to be honest, he'd mentioned that you were coming over. I thought we might have a nice chat, just the two of us, while Ernie had a good zizz after lunch. A chance for us to get to know each other better, eh?'

She gave him a meaningful wink. Liam couldn't bring himself to utter a word.

'Anyhow, imagine my surprise when you dashed off in your car again, five minutes after you came, without buying a single book. It baffled me, never mind Ernie. I was so fed up, I abandoned the garden and went home. It was only afterwards that the penny dropped, when I heard that you'd claimed to have been at Ernie's all along, except when you went out to the chippy. But that was later, wasn't it?'

'You're making a terrible mistake,' Liam said.

'Believe me, I know what I'm doing.' Maxine beamed. 'I did wonder about the fire, remembering what Sally told me about her insurance. Kind of me not to mention that to the police, wasn't it? I did my best, insisting on how happy you and Sally were together. The perfect couple, that was my phrase. To be honest, I can't find it in my heart to blame you for what you did. I reckon she and that pig Morrison drove you to it. You're a gentle soul, you just need the right woman. As for what happened, I wasn't absolutely sure until yesterday, when I took a look around your study. Guess what I found?'

She flourished in front of his eyes a fat paperbound book marked *Advance Proof Copy*. Heath Morrison's new novel, a pretentious finale to an over-hyped career. Even before she turned to the title page, Liam knew what she'd spotted. The graphically phrased inscription to Sally, bearing the date of Bank Holiday Monday, the last day of the lovers' lives.

'I've taken a photocopy,' she said. 'Another sort of insurance policy, you see, against the risk that I might suffer an accident, like Sally. It's in safe hands with my solicitor.'

Liam glared. *It's a bluff*, he was thinking. *You don't have a solicitor*.

'Tristram acted for me in my divorce.' For God's sake, the

woman was a mind-reader. 'We had something going for a few weeks, but . . . I suppose he couldn't stand the pace. I can't deny it, I've got a huge . . . well, appetite.'

Liam's throat was dry. 'What . . .?' he began.

'Don't worry,' she said. 'You can cope with my demands, I'm positive. I'm looking forward to showing you how. We'll have a quiet wedding, obviously. Something flashy wouldn't be right, when we're still coming to terms with the grief. Our shared loss. That insurance money will be really handy, while you're looking round for another job. In a library, perhaps? I know you love books, though personally, I've never seen the point of fiction. What's so good about something made up? Real life is what matters, if you ask me. Anyway, I'm not expecting you to kill yourself. Or me either, come to that, though you can do your best at bedtime. We can both work part-time and spend the rest of the week together.'

Her face shone with happiness as she took his hand. He shut his eyes, trying not to show his revulsion at being touched by her damp, flabby flesh. To his horror, she mistook this as an invitation to force her slithery tongue between his lips.

'It will be lovely, promise,' she said as he gasped for breath. 'Sally wasn't right for you; under-sexed and indiscreet. Very different from me in every way. At long last, after all these years, I've finally dropped lucky. Just like you.'

CATH STAINCLIFFE – SCORPION

'Smoky bacon or roast chicken?' Cody says. He's sitting on the floor of the cell, back against the wall, knees bent. I'm opposite, lying on my bunk.

'Nathan?'

'I'm trying to decide.' Cheese and onion are my favourite crisps but that's not an option. 'Smoky bacon.'

'Rank.' Cody screws up his face.

We've had lunch and the day stretches ahead. Just like all the others. Hours until association. And the next meal.

'Jet ski or quad bike?' I say. I know Cody will pick quad bike. I know him like a brother. We grew up together. Lived across the street. Same primary, secondary. Spent half my life around his. Safer there.

'Ended up with twins.' His mum would joke. We aren't anything like each other. I'm dark, he's blond. He's skinny, I'm solid.

'Quad bike.' Cody flexes his wrists, tilts his shoulders, leans like he's taking a corner. Grins. Default expression, that wonky grin. One of those people who go through life smiling even when there's bad shit going down.

'Remember that quad bike the Leesons had?' Cody's eyes light up.

'And they got it stuck up the clough.' We'd all gone to look.

'Twats,' he says. 'Wasted on them.'

'Life's wasted on them,' I say. Ben and Reece Leeson. Thieving, fighting, lording it over the estate. Clones of their dad, Pete Leeson. Hard man. Robber.

They used to rob my dinner money. Cody was OK, he was on free school meals, but my folks were both in work. Least until my dad got promoted and my mum gave up her part-time admin job. He liked her to stay at home. Keep her close.

Now I'm stuck in here and she's—

'Mountain climber, deep-sea diver?' Cody says.

'Can't swim,' I say.

'Not much swimming involved, is there? More like sinking. Flippers and wetsuits and that.'

'You'd have to swim back up,' I say. 'Into the boat.' Then again, freezing my nuts off halfway up a glacier doesn't exactly appeal.

'I can't drive but I still picked a quad bike,' Cody says.

'You don't need to drive to ride one of them,' I say. 'Your Jaden could do it.'

Jaden's five. 'Our little surprise,' Cody's mum says. We were thirteen when he showed up.

'He couldn't reach the controls,' Cody says. He shakes his head, fringe flopping around. He keeps it long. His mum trims it. I used to tell him he should come round the barber with me, get a proper cut.

'Deep-sea diver,' I say. Because you'd get to see fish and wrecks and maybe whales and that.

I roll on to my back and stretch. Yawn. 'Batman or Spider-Man?'

Cody likes Spidey best. I used to think Batman was cool, though, the Dark Knight. They all wear masks, don't they, superheroes? A disguise. That probably started with the highwaymen. Stand and deliver and all that.

The Leesons were our highwaymen. Didn't need masks. Find yourself in the wrong place at the wrong time and they'd help themselves. Phones, cigs, weed, cash. Say no and they'd cut you.

Cody would turn his pockets out. Show them he had nothing worth the bother. His phone was always some out-of-date model from Cash Converters that took a million years to load anything.

One of Cody's cousins had an iPhone and he wouldn't give it up and the Leesons put him in hospital. Life-changing injuries. Everyone reckoned the police would get involved then but no one was willing to snitch.

Just think if they'd been sent down for that. In here, having to shit in the bog in the corner and stare at breezeblock day in day out. Going slowly insane. No peace, not even after lights out, always shouts and cries and sudden thumps. Misery.

'Spider-Man.' Cody picks just like I knew he would.

'Did Robin Hood wear a mask?' I say.

'Who?'

'Robin Hood. Rich and poor. Sheriff of Nottingham.'

'He wore green,' Cody says.

'Yeah, but did he wear a mask?'

'A green mask?' He's being thick now. Winding me up. 'Lone Ranger had a mask,' he says. 'And a beaver hat.'

That was Davy Crockett. Was it beaver? Racoon? I look at him. 'A beaver hat?'

'Like beavers wear.' Then he's cracking up, laughing, and I am too. I couldn't tell you why. Cody can't stop. He's banging one hand on the floor, the other across his stomach. Gasping.

When I can breathe again, I wipe my eyes. I swing round and sit up on the edge of my bunk.

Cody leans his head back against the wall. 'Man,' he sighs.

It was Cody bought the knives. One for me, one for him.

'Protection,' he says, showing me.

We're in his bedroom.

'How much?' I say.

'My treat.' He smiles. He's got pointy teeth at the corners, like a vampire. Makes him look a bit crazy sometimes.

'How come? Where d'you get the money?'

'One of my mum's sisters died. She hadn't any kids. We all got a bit.'

It's heavy in my hands, heavy and cold. A flick knife. A button on the side. I snap it open. Gleams silver. Sharp. I feel a bit sick. Think how easy it would slide in, how quickly it could slice open. The blood that would follow.

'Stormzy or Skepta?' Cody says.

Neck and neck. The beats, the words, telling it like it is. It's like tossing a coin.

'Stormzy,' I say. 'Today, anyway. Adidas or Nike?'

'Nike – got to be,' Cody says.

He nudges my foot with his. 'Steak and chips or chicken and roasties?'

We always come round to food again. The food in here is crap. Reheated till it's lost the will to live. Mush or shoe leather. Not fit for a dog.

That's what my dad says that tea-time. He's just got in from work, well – from the boozer after work. And I can tell, by the way he sits, by the way he breathes, he's going to go off on one.

Mum's opened wine and there's one of those little vases with a yellow rose from the garden.

She's cooked ham and leek pie, homemade, with peas and broccoli and new potatoes.

He takes a mouthful and spits it out. 'It's cold,' he says.

She jumps up. 'I can microwave—' Before she can finish, he throws his plate across the room. 'Not fit for a dog.'

'Dad, don't,' I say.

'Don't?' He looks at me, eyes sparking. Gets to his feet.

'Nathan.' Mum warns me.

'We can heat it up,' I say, standing too. The food isn't cold. We all know. It's a code, a dance, a starting pistol.

'Don't what?' he says.

Any of it.

He shoves me in the chest and I stagger back.

'It's not cold,' I say, losing control. 'There's nothing wrong with it. It's fine.'

'For a dog, maybe. For a bitch like her.'

'Nathan. John.' Mum is trembling.

'You eat it then, bitch,' he says to her. And he points to the mess on the floor. The broken plate and the muddle of pastry and sauce and veg.

'Please Dad?' My eyes burn.

'Down,' he says.

She gets on her knees.

I think of the knife upstairs in my drawer.

I stare at the flower on the table and try not to hear the little noises my mum makes as she picks the chunks of food from the carpet with her fingers. Chews, swallows.

I won't cry. Crying makes it worse. And I don't want to give him the satisfaction. So I sniff hard and he says it anyway. 'Oh, for God's sake. You're like a little kid. Pathetic. When are you going to grow a pair?'

I tried stopping him once, physically grabbing him. And he punished her extra for it.

He sits down. Drinks wine. Then he nods at Mum's plate – she's not had a mouthful – and tells me to go microwave it.

I have to go past her to get into the kitchen. There are lumps of food splashed on to the skirting board and greasy stains on the wallpaper.

It's dark outside already and I see my reflection in the kitchen window. *Coward.*

I've asked her to leave him. Three times. Begged her.

'I love him,' she says. 'He can't help it,' she says. 'He doesn't mean it,' she says.

The plate is hot as I carry it back to him, but the burn helps wipe out everything else for a few seconds.

I picture creeping up behind him while he stuffs his face. Slipping the knife between his ribs. Or leaning round and cutting his throat, the blood gushing over his meal.

He tells me to eat up. I force my food down, trying not to gag. Lumps of clay in my throat.

'You can go,' he says when my plate is clean.

I don't need telling twice. It's worse when I argue.

'Steak or chicken? Final answer.' Cody claps his hands.

'Steak and chips. With onion rings and loads of ketchup. A pint of cider.'

'Mate.' Cody groans. 'Lager. Pint of lager. Ice cold. On a hot day. A nice big spliff.' He smiles that crooked smile at me. 'Next.' He reaches forward, pats his hands on his ankles. A drum roll.

'I'm thinking.' It's too easy. We know each other too well. I want some category that he won't be able to answer straight off. I flick through possibilities.

'OK,' I say. 'Venus or Neptune?'

'What?'

'Planets,' I say.

'What's the difference?'

'Venus is boiling hot. Loads of volcanoes, thick clouds. It spins the other way from all the rest of them.'

'What colour is it?' he says.

'Colour?'

'I'm trying to see it, aren't I?'

'Yellow,' I say.

'And Neptune?'

'An ice giant. Dark, freezing cold. Supersonic winds. It's got fourteen moons. It's bright blue.'

'Yeah, that one – Neptune.'

'Cos it's blue?'

He gives a smile. 'Scorpion or jellyfish?'

'Scorpion.'

I take the knife with me over to Cody's.

'Here he is,' Cody's mum says. 'Our ray of sunshine.'

I laugh but my eyes sting.

They've had pizza from Tonio's up the road.

Jaden shows me his Lego *Star Wars* set.

Most times we stay in Cody's room. Play games on his Xbox. We can't smoke at his. Nothing. Not even vape. His dad's on oxygen and they've Jaden too. His mum can sniff anything a mile away. We've got some weed so we head off down to the square.

I don't tell Cody what's happened. No point. He knows stuff goes on, times I've gone to his to get out of the way. His mum does too. She took me aside one summer, said if my mum ever needed help with anything, a fresh start, she could help. There were places could help. I felt like dying when she said that, my face on fire.

Everyone else? Well, they all know John's a gent, isn't he? This charming man, do anything for you, fundraises for children's cancer. Always says hello. First to buy a round at the pub.

Everything my dad says is true. I'm weak, spineless. Waste of space. I can't even talk her into leaving.

When we get to the square, Cody rolls a big one. It makes me mellow at first. Then we see Ben Leeson come down the alley by the Chinese.

'We should go,' Cody says, sucking a last drag.

'No,' I say. 'We'll stay.'

'Nathan!' He's worried. Still grinning though.

I pull my hand out of my pocket, show him the knife.

'You're off your head,' he says.

Reece Leeson pitches up next to his brother. He's on his phone. Turning in half-circles, scoping the square. A bunch of girls come out of the Chinese and they scurry away. They're joshing each other, voices high and bright, swooping on the night air, but it's like an alarm call. Like birds make when there's a predator near the nest.

'Was your idea,' I say to Cody.

'Protection,' he says. 'A last resort. Not to start a fucking war. Come on.'

Reece has clocked us from over the way. He puts his phone away, nudges Ben.

Cody stands up. 'Don't be a dick,' he says to me.

I don't move. 'You go,' I say.

'Like I'm gonna leave you here for them two.'

The Leesons are coming across the square. I've got my thumb on the switch.

A gust of wind lifts the litter by the War Memorial and swirls it about. Cody swipes his fringe. He's standing at the edge of the bench. His feet straining like he wants to run.

Ben and Reece reach us. I look at each of them, slowly. Cold deep inside me and my heart thudding in my ears, a fast, deep bass.

Come on, I think. Come on, try it. My blood's racing. That wild feeling, like when you let go. Like a rollercoaster. Heading down. No way back.

'Got any green?' Ben Leeson says. Cody moves his hand but before he can pull out what's left, I say, 'All gone.'

My hands are sweating, mouth dry. I keep staring.

I push my toes down getting ready to spring at them. Reece first, he's nearest.

Then Ben's phone rings. A blast of drum 'n' bass. He turns

away, answers. Nods to Reece and they walk. They walk away. Backs to me.

Oy! I want to shout. Get back here!

I stand up. Shaking.

'Man!' Cody crows. 'That was totally mental.' He pushes me in the chest.

'Leave it!' I say.

But he won't. Jabbering on and on. 'Suicide mission, man.' He pushes me again. 'You must be bricking it.'

'Get off me.'

'Aw, Nathan, you're shaking. Look at you man, you're shaking.'

'Shut the fuck up.'

He won't stop pushing me. 'Like a little kid,' he says. 'You'd never use it, can't even hold it straight. Shaking like a leaf.' Chattering at me, grinning, off his bonce on the weed.

I flick the knife. 'Don't laugh at me.'

'Burial or cremation?' Cody says.

My heart stops. I wasn't expecting that.

I swallow. 'It's not your go,' I say, knocking his foot with mine.

'What if I want an extra go? You owe me that.'

Someone is banging on a door, again and again. Howling. I try to shake the noise away.

In court I told them how I slipped. Messing about and slipped.

The knife in his leg and Cody folding, falling. I grab him, to break his fall. Hold him. So much blood. A great black pool of it, shiny under the streetlights.

I pull the knife out and that's worse. I call his name over and over, freaking out. Holding him.

His eyes flutter open and he looks at me. 'Oh, mate,' he says. The smile dies on his lips. The light goes out in his eyes.

'You didn't slip,' he says. He's not smiling now. He lifts his head. Eyes beneath his fringe are steady and cold on mine.

'I never meant— I'm sorry,' I say. 'I'm so sorry.' I'm crying.

For Cody. For his mum and Jaden. For me. Smacking my head on the wall. Harder and harder. Blocking it all out.

Next door screams, 'Keep it down, you fucking psycho.'

I lie on my bunk, shivering. Curl up small.

I just want him back.

CHRIS SIMMS – SKELETON CREW

The tip is quiet. Always is last thing on a Friday. Guy in a Volvo estate dragging sheets of cardboard out of the boot. An old lady – sixty-five, seventy? She's at the railings, dropping all of three jars down into the container for glass. Why drive all the way out to the edge of town for that? Daft old bat, should have used the collection point at the local supermarket.

I look at the items which have been used to decorate the little cabin. The bloody things shouldn't be here. Mutilated teddies. Heads of decapitated dolls. Action figures with missing limbs. I recognize that one – it was on the telly the other day. Stupid advert: garish and shouty and too fast. Military drums, camera swooping jerkily down from the sky to a close-up of the manikin. Transfigurer, was it? Something like that.

Next to it on the windowsill is a grotesquely muscled wrestler, face contorted in a snarl. He only has one arm – and that's been placed round the slender shoulders of a naked female figurine. Her legs make up two thirds of her height, pinched waist and high, jutting breasts. But she has no hair and her eyes are missing. Is it any wonder the country's going down the pan? Kids playing with this kind of rubbish.

Need to put a message out to the site staff: no collecting items deposited in the containers. This is a council tip, not an opportunity to amass unwanted toys.

The Volvo bloke's carrying the cardboard towards the wrong container. Imbecile. I fold the copy of the local newspaper on the article about another young adult going missing. 'Excuse me, sir. That's for non-recyclable waste.'

He turns to the half-open door of the cabin with a lost look. I step fully out, and zip up my fluorescent tabard. 'Cardboard goes in number four. The one to your left.'

He's staring at me like I'm speaking a foreign language.

'Number four,' I repeat. 'To your left – that's the one for cardboard, sir.'

In the restricted-access area below us, the JCB revs its engine. The vehicle's cabin has been raised up to its maximum height. The front of it is fitted with a long pair of hydraulic arms that clutch a cast-iron scoop. This allows the driver to reach over into the various containers and rake smooth the piles of debris within. But more often, he simply uses the heavy bucket like a pile-driver, smashing it down to compress everything inside.

The member of the public nods at number four. 'This one, you say?'

A safe guess, I want to reply, judging by the three-foot-high sign marked with the word 'cardboard' attached to the front of it. I incline my head in agreement and he slings his armful of squashed boxes over the railing. They drop down into the container where, in due course, they'll be battered lower by Rick, the JCB driver.

The vehicle approaches the waste-to-energy container and the scoop hits the mound of bin liners that have built up in one corner. Plastic bursts and the shrivelled remains of carrots and potatoes tumble out. The bucket lifts and drops again, sending a chicken carcass scurrying down the slope. It comes to rest behind a fading bunch of carnations, as if it's hiding there. The cloying smell of rotting fruit wafts up. Lorry will be here soon to ferry that lot to the incinerator at the borough's main site.

I watch as Rick backs the JCB away. There shouldn't be that silly registration plate propped up behind the vehicle's windscreen. CD R1C. Not CD now, though. Not since I banned him from listening to music while working. Ear protectors? A valid item, perfectly permissible for a site such as this. Not earphones, though. That's a safety hazard, plain and simple.

The JCB's engine growls as he heads off to the container reserved for timber. The one for small household appliances looks a bit full, too. Get that collected first thing tomorrow morning.

The old Cortina passing under the height barrier at the

entrance catches my eye. Hey up, it's them again. Tweedledum and Tweedledee. A right pair, these two. Quick glance at my watch: six fifty-five. Always the same. Seconds ahead of when the lorry arrives to take the waste-to-energy container away.

As I walk down the ramp to unlock the main gates in readiness for the lorry turning up, their battered old Cortina stops alongside the container for unwanted clothing. One bag goes in, but the flap isn't able to close completely. Thing must need emptying, too.

Here comes the lorry, as I knew it would. 'Evening Harry,' I say to the driver as he slows to a halt. 'How's things back at base?'

He gives me an awkward glance as I swing the gates open. 'Same old, same old.'

As he steers the lorry towards the waste-to-energy container, I can see Tweedledum and Tweedledee standing at the railings above it. Even though one's lost most of his black curls, they must be twins. The same jowly cheeks and squashed-out bottom lip. Sad, droopy eyes that are devoid of life. Open-mouth-breathers – that's what Trevor, my ex-policeman friend, calls their type. Both are wearing hideous, cheap-looking leather jackets that end in thick elasticated waistbands. Shapeless jeans tucked into black wellington boots that are caked in manure, or something similar.

Every time they reach over to drop a shoebox-sized package into the container, the waistbands of their leather jackets ride up over their fat stomachs. Tugging them back down in unison, they turn to the boot of their car and repeat the process, avoiding eye contact with me all the while. Something's not right about them, I just know it.

The fruit machine lets out a burst of flashing light. Coins chunter into the tray. I look at the young man playing it and sigh. 'Bloody thing. Why did Dave let them put it in?'

'Brewery said so,' Trevor replied. 'Dave's hands were tied.'

'Well, even so. He could have insisted.' I turn to my friend of over forty years. Trevor and I schooled together. Two young lads in baggy shorts, our barm cakes in snap boxes over our shoulders.

I got a job with the council – or 'corporation', as it was once known. Trevor went into the police. Rose to sergeant before retiring last year. Every Friday we meet for a pint, come rain or shine. You need routine in life. Everyone does.

I take a sip of mild and adjust a beer mat before setting my glass down. 'Another went missing this week, I see from the local paper.'

'Another what?' He sits back, a hand resting on each knee.

'A lad. Or vulnerable young adult, as they like to call them. Which means one from that council care home in the town. It's up near the old mill, apparently.'

Trevor is watching my hands. He has an uncomfortable expression on his face. I turn a beer mat over and study its underside. 'That's the second one in three months that's vanished. Gone.'

'Teenagers like that are always going missing. Dozens disappeared during my time in the job. They run away. We catch them and take them back. They run away again. It's all a big game.'

'I haven't heard of these two being caught.'

Trevor sips on his beer and then passes a knuckle across his moustache, smearing a trace of foam into the bristles. 'And your thoughts on this are?'

I stare down at my drink then reach across to the neighbouring table for a fresh beer mat. 'There are these two men who turn up at the tip—'

'The Glen Hill site?'

There's an edge in his voice. I don't need to glance up to know his right eye will have narrowed. 'That's correct. This pair, they always show last thing on a Friday. It's like they wait out on the main road for the lorry that comes from the main processing site.'

'From Shawcross?'

I nod. 'Comes to pick up the waste-to-energy container. For the big incinerator they put in there last year—'

'You told me all about it. Enormous thing.'

I lift my gaze. His arms are crossed and he's examining the wall above me. 'Well, anyway. They were there again today. Same routine. Just before the container's winched onto the back of the lorry, they drop these packages in and are on their way.'

Trevor's now staring directly at me. The corner of his eye twitches. 'And?'

'Last thing on a Friday, Trevor. That's when staffing levels are at their lowest. Just me and the JCB driver by then – and as soon as the clock hits seven you can't see him for dust. The main processing site will be the same.'

'I'm struggling to see why you're so concerned.'

'They're up to something. It's not normal to have a regular routine for dropping off rubbish. Not domestic, anyway. The contents of that container will go direct into the incinerator – within hours, it's ash. Nothing survives the temperature in that thing. Not even bones.' I give him a meaningful look. 'I know the lazy bunch at the main site won't be inspecting it. Not last thing on a Friday. They'll all be clock-watching.'

'Peter, are you forgetting why you're now supervising the Glen Hill site and not the main one at Shawcross?'

I feel my teeth clench. I knew he'd bring this up. 'They were guilty. Just because I didn't catch them red-handed—'

'You accused your co-workers of taking back-handers. Formally accused them.'

'And they were.'

'But you weren't able to produce any evidence. You hid yourself on that site for how many nights?'

I say nothing.

'Not once did you witness them allowing commercial vehicles through. But you ignored me and went ahead with the accusation. Peter, if it wasn't for your circumstances, you wouldn't have got away with a formal—'

'They were doing it!'

The young man at the fruit machine glances over, eyebrows raised. Behind the bar, Dave pauses in the act of hanging up a wine glass. I see a reflection of myself in the mirror on the opposite wall. My temples and cheekbones seem to stand out more sharply than I remember them. There's a gap between the collar of my shirt and my neck. The knot of my tie looks too big. 'They were doing it,' I repeat more quietly, reaching to the next table for another beer mat.

'Peter, are you . . . have you been . . .'

'Taking my blood-pressure pills? Yes, thank you for asking. I have.'

'You seem agitated. Was Dr Phillips happy with this latest lot when you last saw him?'

'He was.'

'It's just that, when you change medications, there can be side effects. I know with my brother's blood pressure – when they tried him on a different one – it triggered off all kinds of things. Itching, insomnia, all sorts . . .'

'I'm fine, Trevor. I lost my wife, that's all. She had the medical condition, not me.' The pain of Linda suddenly going is back. 'Would that it was me,' I whisper, adjusting the mat's position on the table.

Trevor places a hand across my forearm. 'Peter?'

'I'm fine.'

He doesn't answer and I look up to see him regarding the table between us. At its centre are eight beer mats. I've arranged them in as near to a diamond shape as possible. But I need a ninth to complete the pattern. There are no more on the next table. It frustrates me, the fact my arrangement is flawed.

Resignedly, Trevor lifts his drink and slides his mat over.

'Thanks.' I fit it into place and some of the tightness in my chest recedes.

Trevor clears his throat. 'These two men who keep showing up. They're concerning you because . . .'

'You could check with your old colleagues, couldn't you? I noted down the registration of their vehicle.'

Trevor's shoulders sag.

'And there's this,' I continue, reaching under the bench to retrieve the plastic bag.

He sends an uneasy glance toward the bar. Dave is nowhere to be seen. 'What's in there?'

'They dropped it off this afternoon – in Oxfam's clothing container. I managed to pull it back out once I'd closed up.' Using the tips of my fingers, I open out the crumpled plastic so Trevor can see in. The muscle in the corner of his right eye is going off as he leans forward slightly, arms tightly crossed. 'What is it?'

'A men's top. Not men's – more a teenager's. The label says Super Dry. You can tell it's for a youngster.' I start to take it out.

'Leave it be,' Trevor hisses. His hands are still tucked firmly under his armpits. 'Put it back on the floor, for Christ's sake.'

'What would two men like that have a teenager's item of clothing for?' I can see he won't say another word until it is safely out of sight. I slide it beneath where I'm sitting. 'Do you want their vehicle's registration?'

The fingers of his left hand emerge from beneath his right arm. A forefinger taps against his jumper. 'I'm worried you're getting fixated again, Peter. Like with your colleagues at the Shawcross site.'

I immediately shake my head. 'They're up to something. It's bloody obvious.'

'Do you feel unsettled? How often have you been washing your hands lately?'

'The hand-washing is under control. This isn't about me.'

He drops a heavy glance at the beer mats. The slight crumpling in the corner of the third one on the right mars the diamond's appearance. Knowing he's now scrutinizing me, I fight the temptation to turn the mat over. But I know the underside will be nice and smooth. I know it.

'What was it then?' he sighs, reaching for his jacket on the next seat.

But I produce my piece of paper quicker. 'Here, I wrote it down earlier.'

Five to seven. Intently, I watch the approach to the main entrance. They're normally here by now. Rick is reversing the JCB into its corner and, as the diesel engine chokes to a halt, I hear the puffing hiss of a lorry applying its brakes. Harry, turning into the side road that leads to the site. No Cortina is ahead of him as the lorry comes into view and pulls up beyond the main gate. Where's the Cortina? Where is it?

'Boss!'

I blink and look to my right. Rick is leaning out of the JCB's cab, gesturing to the main gates.

I raise a hand in acknowledgement and extract my set of keys from the jacket behind the cabin's door. Why didn't they show? The local paper is open on page five. An update on the missing teenager. A possible sighting over in Liverpool, where his family was originally from. I can't help feeling irritated. By breaking their routine, the two brothers have disturbed mine.

As I stride down the ramp, I hear Rick's car starting up over in the spaces reserved for staff vehicles. With him setting off home, my Honda is the last car left.

Once Harry's driven the lorry through, I walk round to the public entry point. Even as I swing the barriers shut, I'm listening for the sound of their Cortina behind me. But it doesn't come.

Within minutes, Harry has winched the waste-to-energy container up on to the rear of the lorry. As he drives back out, I give him a farewell nod. He doesn't turn his head. His name was on the list I submitted to the regional manager.

After padlocking the main gates, I make my way back up the ramp to the cabin at the far end of the railings. The route takes me past the row of cages for car batteries, oil containers and hazardous chemicals. But it's the cages that draw my eye. The thick wire mesh and solid hinges of the doors it is now my duty to secure. A person could never break free once shut inside. Especially a young one. I wonder where the twins live: how private their home might be. Did they live alone, the two of them? At the end of an isolated lane like this one? Did it have outbuildings or cellars where a cage like one of these could be concealed?

I continue back to the cabin to get my jacket. The site is now quiet, everything packed away in its place. A group of crows have alighted in the tallest tree in the copse behind the rear fence. The containers have eliminated the problem of vermin, but there's nothing that can be done about the crows that swoop down the moment the place is free of people. Every dusk they appear, creatures of habit as much as any other. As much as me.

The interior of the cabin is nice and tidy. No plastic flowers in salvaged vases. No silly toys lining the windowsill. No decorations nailed to the walls. Just my new notice saying such items are not permitted. Looking over the restricted-access area one last time, I realize I've forgotten to tell Rick that his personalized number plate cannot remain in the JCB's cab.

'So.' I place my pint in the centre of a beer mat and sit back. It's obvious Trevor has news. There's a tenseness about him. Stored information that has to come out.

The young man at the fruit machine taps futilely at the plastic buttons before turning round. 'Dave, this bloody thing's just swallowed my money.'

The landlord frowns. 'What did you put in?'

'Two quid.'

He comes out from behind the bar and also presses a couple of buttons. 'Strange, thing's completely dead.'

I make sure no amusement shows on my face.

The young customer nods. 'Refund button, included.'

Dave's crouched down and is peering round the back. 'Bloody plug's come out. Cleaners, I should think.'

Trevor narrows his eyes at me and I sip innocently at my drink.

'I had a quiet word,' he murmurs.

'And?'

He crosses his arms and raises both shoulders in a slow shrug. It's his way of saying, I'm not sure. What's the best choice of saloon car? The slow shrug. Would he recommend the hotel he and Margaret booked in Tenerife? The slow shrug. Pros and cons. Advantages and disadvantages. Good news and bad news.

'What did you find out?' I ask.

Trevor gives me an unhappy look. 'Neither of the missing two lads were wearing a maroon top from Super Dry when they disappeared. Where is the thing, anyway?'

'In my garage. Safe and sound.' The news about the top isn't causing Trevor's glum expression. 'What about where they live? Did you get an address?'

He nods.

'Well?'

'I'll tell you on one condition, OK?'

'I don't know. You'll need to tell me first.'

Suddenly, he looks irritated. And tired. 'This isn't you playing bloody Miss Marple. If I tell you this, you agree to leave those two brothers alone—'

'So they are brothers?' My mind is like the fruit machine: connections lighting up. The police know about them. Why?

'Twins. Non-identical. Walter and Stanley Eggerton.'

'What have they done?'

He leans forward and lowers his voice. 'They've not done anything – which is why you must drop your . . . suspicions.'

I wait for more.

Trevor takes a good sip of his beer before continuing. 'They had an older brother called Cedric. Twenty-three years ago, he killed their parents at the farmhouse where they all lived. Up in Northumberland, it was. Walter and Stanley were eleven. Older brother was seventeen. The dad's Land Rover was found abandoned at the ferry port in Hull. A bloodstained axe was lying across the back seat. The older brother was sentenced in absentia.'

'My God.'

'Exactly. The twins moved to the place out near Glen Hill almost nine years ago. Only a few know about the family history – social services and the local police. You're not either of those.' He stares at me without blinking. 'Point taken?'

I fumble for a spare beer mat, pick it up and put it down. I want to ask where Walter and Stanley were when it happened. Did they witness the murders? How come the older brother spared them? But I know Trevor won't tell me any more, even if he knew. 'Where is this place they live?'

'It's a big cottage. Out past that mill. Very isolated.'

I look up, keeping my thoughts from my face. But Trevor is studying his drink as he adds, 'They don't lead the kind of life you or I would class as normal.'

From the battered old Cortina and their seventies clothes, I could tell that.

'It's just the two of them out there, for a start. And loads of dogs, apparently. They breed them in the outbuildings. They also take in waifs and strays. The RSPCA have visited a few times following complaints from walkers passing near the property.'

'Cruelty?'

He gives his slow shrug. 'Not malicious. More born of ignorance. They're just not very bright, according to the person I spoke to. The place is a tip. Very badly maintained. But they do their best by the animals; they certainly don't keep them in any worse conditions than they live in themselves.'

I think about how their wellington boots are always encased in a crust of dried-out muck. Disgusting.

'Now you know. And last thing, Peter – they buy bones, offal and the like from the two butchers out in Glen Hill. For their kennels. So, the packages they drop off could well contain bones and similar. I don't know. I just didn't want you retrieving one like you did that maroon top and jumping to the wrong conclusion.'

'Bones and similar? Are the kennels out at this farm commercial?'

He cocks his head. 'I don't know. Why?'

'Because if they are, they shouldn't be dumping refuse at a facility for domestic waste. That's illegal.'

Trevor's eyes close for a long second. 'Peter, you said it's just a few shoebox-size packages. Be reasonable.'

I want to say that is a fine attitude to take for an ex-police officer. Instead I adjust the positioning of the three beer mats before me. The triangle of space between them wasn't quite a perfect equilateral.

'So you'll let this go now,' Trevor states. It wasn't a question: it was an order.

I sit back. 'I have my responsibilities, Trevor. And ensuring the facility is used correctly is one of them.'

'You only bloody know what you do because I told you. And I told you on the condition you let it go.' Two red dots have formed high on his cheeks. 'That information was passed to me by an old colleague doing me a favour! You cannot act on it.'

I say nothing.

'White vans pull up outside the entrances to tips all the

time,' Trevor adds moodily. 'I've seen them on a Sunday. People unloading all sorts and carrying it up to the containers. Old sinks, broken tiles, all sorts. You know as well as I do that's commercial waste.'

'We're in the process of clamping down on that type of activity.'

'For Christ's sake, Peter. Leave the pair of them alone. Promise me you will.'

'I can't do that, Trevor.'

'You'd bloody better.' He seizes his coat and stands.

Over half his drink is still on the table. 'You've not finished,' I say, peering up at him.

He glowers down. 'Forget it. And forget next Friday, I'll make other plans.'

'But how will you get home?' I ask as he walks away. 'I drove you out here, remember?'

He waves goodbye to Dave and steps out of the door. I can't understand. That's a ten-pound taxi fare, right there. And no meeting up next Friday? That's over thirty years of tradition, that. Surely he didn't mean it.

A watched pot never boils, as they say – and Friday seems to take an age to arrive. When it does, the day starts with something that stops me in my tracks. One of the lads had left a copy of the local paper in the cabin and there it was on page two: another young person had vanished from the council home up near the mill. They'd included a photo of him – fourteen years old, black hair and pimples on his forehead. His eyes were older though. Like they'd watched things happen. Bad things.

The rest of the day crawls by, the arrival of each car a welcome distraction. Old mattresses, their secret stains exposed to the day. Rolled-up carpets, broken cabinets, warped buggies – over the railings they all go. Flocks of magazines, pages flapping as they fall. An aquarium with a tide-mark where the level of water once stood. What had lived and died in there? It shatters outwards on hitting the bottom of the container.

The levels of rubbish gradually rise up and every so often

Rick squashes down each container's contents, the vehicle's arms whining with the effort of supporting the sheer weight of the great bucket.

Finally, five o'clock arrives and the bulk of the day-shift make swiftly for their cars. Six o'clock and just the skeleton crew remain. Six thirty and they start looking hopefully to me for permission to leave a bit early. Only three cars had dropped off in the last twenty minutes. I survey the site. The restricted-access area has been swept. Everything is in order. The waste-to-energy container is three-quarters full, the exposed metal of its inner sides moist from where lobbed bags had burst.

All that refuse would be going nowhere tonight. Not if Tweedledum and Tweedledee arrived with their usual deposit. 'Have a good weekend, lads.'

They grunt their thanks and start filing across to their cars. I settle on to my stool in the cabin.

Five to seven and the Cortina appears. My heart gives a little jump. The lorry is twenty metres behind. The Cortina makes its way up the ramp and backs in towards the railings. I watch from the corner of my eye as they climb out. The one with the full head of hair opens the boot of the car and I can see a layer of boxes inside sitting on a sheet of plastic. Do they think I'm stupid? I make my way down to the main gates as they start dropping packages down.

'Evening Harry,' I say through the chain-link fence. 'Pick up for the energy-to-waste container is rescheduled. Tomorrow morning, now.'

His eyebrows lift. 'Since when?'

'About one minute ago.'

His jaw is set tight as he rams the gear into reverse. 'Could have let me know before I set off all the way out here,' he mutters, eyes fixed on the rear-view mirror as he backs away.

After closing the barriers for the car entrance, I turn on my heel and march up the ramp. Rick has just parked the JCB in its corner. He pokes his head out of the cab. 'Boss?'

'You can go,' I say.

The twins are standing at the railings, looking down at me with mouths half open. The lorry's engine roars as Harry trundles back toward the main road. 'Site's now closed,' I call out to them. 'Can you please leave the premises.'

They hesitate and I see the balder one's eyes shift to the boxes that are now lying on top of the bin bags some twelve feet below. Too far for you to reach, I think triumphantly. But not too far for me and my ladder. 'Please move your car, we're closed.'

The curly-haired one looks at his brother, then at the JCB, then at me. He is close to tears. They both are.

'On your way now,' I say, copying the tone Dave uses in the Rising Sun at closing time. The interior of the pub flashes up in my mind. Trevor has made no attempt to call me all week. And it's his turn to drive. Maybe there'd be a message waiting for me at home. Perhaps he'd just show up at the normal time like nothing had happened.

The boot of the Cortina bangs shut and, moments later, they drive slowly past, faces pale behind the windscreen. I watch the vehicle start down the exit ramp then unhitch the cat-ladder from the side of the cabin.

The crows are back, their hunched forms shifting impatiently on their perches. Rick's car starts up as I lay the aluminium ladder across the railings above the waste-to-energy container. I slide it outwards, letting the feet gradually drop closer to the bumpy surface of bags. I've judged it just right: the ladder's hooked ends fit over the uppermost railing, allowing me to climb across the narrow gap then down the sloping succession of rungs and into the container itself.

The smell seems to have pooled within the sheer metal walls – a heavy, cabbage-like aroma laced every now and again with the sharper notes of rotting meat. By the time I step off the final rung, the sky has been reduced to a rectangle of darkening blue above me. The boxes are to my right. Unsteadily, I make my way across the marshy surface. My foot sinks into a crevice and I have to place a hand on to a bin bag to keep my balance. On the other side of the thin plastic, something cold and lumpy shifts.

The uppermost box is now in reach and I remove the Stanley knife from my tabard. The blade slices through the wrapping of gaffer tape securing its end. I shake it gently and bones

cascade out. Not chicken ones; too big. And with ragged fragments of red meat clinging to them. The ends are bloody
stumps, sinew and tendons poking out like bad wiring. Cows'
bones? Sheep? As I open a second box and shake it, the sound
of the JCB starts up. Rick. I thought he'd set off home.

A clump of debris drops out. Clots of hair. Black hair. And
an ear. A human ear. Oh God. Oh dear God. I twist my torso
round, flailing desperately with my arms as I begin to fall.
My right hand makes contact with the edge of the ladder and
I'm able to drag myself across the slippery surface, kicking
and scrabbling with my feet all the while. By the time I make
it on to the lowermost rungs, my front is dripping with slime
and fragments of food.

Gagging, I climb up a few more rungs and the main part
of the site comes into view. Oh, thank God: Rick is still here
– back in the JCB. I'm about to shout when I realize he's
talking to a pair of people at the locked main gate. The twins.
Their Cortina is parked just outside. Their fingers are hooked
in the fencing and they're nodding eagerly as Rick continues
to speak down at them from the vehicle's cab. Then the
curly-haired one sees me and points. Rick looks over and
immediately grabs the wheel. The metal bucket rises up,
several hundred kilos of cast iron. As the vehicle rapidly
approaches the container I'm inside, the twins watch in dead-
eyed silence.

I would shout to Rick. Call the police! Those two are
murderers! Ring for help! But I know it's futile. My eyes
are glued to the registration plate propped behind the windscreen. I realize the letters spell a name. CD R1C. The family
resemblance is suddenly clear. The same pouting bottom lip,
the overhanging cheeks. And I cannot move. Even as he
manoeuvres the bucket directly above me and reaches for the
lever, I cannot move.

KATE ELLIS – THE FOX AND THE HENS

I can see them. Clucking around. Making a noise without a care in their little world. Hens. Prey.

They don't know I'm watching, aware of their every movement; every peck they take at the food and drink in front of them. I have hidden myself from view, pleased with my own cunning. Soon one of them will stray from the others then she will be mine. The special one. Marked for me.

'The countryside gives me the creeps. You can't see a thing outside.'

'Who cares about that? We're inside and we've got prosecco.' Janet giggled like the schoolgirl she used to be many moons ago; a lot longer ago than she ever admitted to the men she met on dating websites.

Annie sniffed and looked out of the window. Night had already descended, and the velvet darkness was quite unlike anything she'd known in the Leeds suburb where she lived with her idle husband and morose teenage son. She'd been looking forward to the hen weekend for months and she was determined to enjoy herself. It wasn't every day your best friend from school got married for the third time.

Although she did wonder why Sandra had chosen a cottage in the middle of nowhere for the celebrations. A nice hotel in the city centre – or even Scarborough – would have been better than the tiny hamlet of Lower Yarwood. But Sandra was the bride-to-be, so she was in charge.

There were to have been five of them – Annie, Sandra, Janet, Moira and Trish. Then Trish developed gastroenteritis and had to cry off. But, in Annie's opinion, everyone was a bit relieved, although they'd never have admitted it. Since the death of her daughter the previous year, Trish had walked

around engulfed in her own little cloud of misery. Not that
the others didn't sympathize, of course, but her presence was
bound to have put a dampener on things.

The cottage Sandra had chosen for her hen do was in a group
of converted farm outbuildings arranged around a cobbled
courtyard which was terrible for stiletto heels. There were six
holiday lets in all and Sandra had expected they'd have the
place to themselves: after all, who in their right senses goes
for a self-catering weekend in North Yorkshire in January?
They'd been surprised to see a light in the window of one of
the other cottages but nothing was going to put a stop to their
festivities. They were in a party mood so any other residents
would have to resort to earplugs.

If only they knew what was coming – if they had any idea
what I had planned, they wouldn't sound so cheerful. They'd
be screeching in alarm.

The secret is to take the hen by surprise so that she won't
suspect a thing as she clucks around in the dirt.

Moira had brought a karaoke machine, armed with suitable
music. The sort of tunes that guarantee a good time. 'I Will
Survive', the defiant anthem of all women of a certain age;
'YMCA'; 'Islands in the Stream'; 'Simply the Best'. All the
classics.

The bottles of prosecco were lined up in the little fridge
like soldiers on parade awaiting inspection. Once three bottles
had been polished off, the party began in earnest and the noise
level gradually increased.

By the time the bride-to-be Sandra was standing on the
dining table informing everyone within a half-mile radius that
she would survive, none of the women was in any state to
hear the mobile phone ringing. Then the music came to an
end.

This is my chance. She's now separated from her squawking
fellows. What a racket those hens make when something
excites them.

She leaves the safety of the group and I stalk after her,

waiting for the perfect moment. She struts along the cobbles and once she's round the corner it's time to strike. When she's least expecting it.

Sam Parsons, owner of the holiday cottages, studied his shoes, avoiding Inspector Jonah Westerman's eyes.

'OK, I was there last night. I had a complaint about the noise. Had to knock and ask them to keep it down.' He swallowed hard. 'The woman I spoke to gave me a right mouthful; got quite abusive, to be honest. Said it was a hen party so what did I expect. I told her I wouldn't have let the property to her if I'd known.'

Parsons, middle aged, beer-bellied and nervy, smoothed down his sparse ginger hair and Westerman knew he was lying. Times were hard and he would have let the cottage to the Devil himself and all his demons if they'd paid up front.

'You say you found the body first thing this morning. Remind me what time that was.'

'Just before six. I came down to check on the hens and she was lying there with her sparkly top all covered in blood. Didn't see her till I opened the hen-house door. Gave me a hell of a shock.'

'I can imagine. What do you know about the dead woman?' Westerman consulted his notebook. 'Moira Bateman.'

'Nothing. I told you. The cottage was rented to a Ms Sandra Beaufort. As for the others, I was never told their names.'

'What about the people in the other cottage?'

'That would be Mrs Jones and her daughter from Lancaster – over here to attend a relative's funeral. They arrived the day before yesterday and they're going home this morning. Nice quiet pair. No trouble.'

'One of my officers spoke to them first thing and they say they never left the cottage last night. They went to bed early so they didn't see anything suspicious. Although they did complain to you about the noise from Ms Beaufort's accommodation.'

Parsons nodded. 'They telephoned the farmhouse just after ten to say they couldn't get to sleep for all the noise. I came down straight away to sort it out.' He sniffed. 'That's the last time I let a place out to a hen party. Nothing but a damned nuisance. As if I haven't had enough trouble with that bloody fox who keeps having a go at my hen house. Lost one last night. My best layer,' he added as an afterthought.

It's done now and I'm sated. I have killed and, to my shame, I enjoyed it. The world has been put right and all the hounds in hell will never find my lair.

I am invincible.

It wasn't until the reality of Moira Bateman's death finally sank in that Sandra Beaufort and her friends truly sobered up. There was nothing like a brutal murder to counteract the effects of too much prosecco.

Moira, they remembered through their fading veil of alcohol, had received a phone call shortly after ten thirty. She told Sandra that she had to go out, mumbling something about urgent business as she staggered towards the front door, and the party had carried on without her. Even though the karaoke machine had been switched off when Sam Parsons had called to relay the neighbours' complaint, the drinking had continued and the giggling had grown in volume until just after midnight when someone noticed that Moira hadn't returned.

They'd all gone out to look for her, calling her name loudly and scaring off a fox who'd been lurking hopefully round the hen house. The hens, the feathered variety, had been making a terrible racket, Janet said.

There'd been no sign of Moira and the consensus was that she'd gone off to meet her ex who'd been begging her to go back to him. They thought he might have picked her up. They hadn't heard a car but by then they'd had so much to drink that a helicopter could have landed and they wouldn't have noticed.

According to Annie, there'd been nobody else about when she and her friends had gone out to conduct their half-hearted search. The only other occupied cottage had been in darkness so, presumably, Mrs and Ms Jones had gone to sleep once the noise abated, each giving the other the perfect alibi.

Sam Parsons, however, had nobody to vouch for him as his

wife was away at her mother's. Jonah Westerman knew that the person who finds the body is usually treated as the prime suspect. But this time he was keeping an open mind.

Westerman already knew that the call to Moira's phone had been made from an unregistered mobile, impossible to trace. And the call had come from nearby so the police were working on the theory that it had been made by her killer.

Then they made a breakthrough. The victim's ex-husband's car had been spotted by a traffic camera half a mile away at the appropriate time, so a patrol car was sent to bring him in for questioning. According to the other hens, Moira's separation had been bitter and her ex kept harassing her. Sandra went further, saying that the victim's ex was a vicious psycho.

But Jonah Westerman was a thorough man in his quiet way. He ordered more checks. He was always suspicious when things seemed too neat.

I'm leaving now. Moving on. Too many obstacles are being put in my way and the hen house is now as secure as Fort Knox. Besides, I've done what I came here to do.

Constable Chatterley stood to attention in front of DI Westerman's desk. 'The victim's ex-husband's denying everything, sir. Although he does admit that he knew where Moira would be. He says he drove out there intending to beg her to go back to him but he claims he changed his mind when he was half a mile away and turned back. Said he was in bed by midnight. Alone.'

'Believe him?'

The young officer shook his head. 'His story sounds dodgy to me. And I've checked on that other address like you asked.' He passed a sheet of paper to the inspector and paused as though he was about to make a dramatic revelation. 'There's no such place. It doesn't exist.'

'Are you sure?'

'Oh yes. I spoke to the local station. Then I found this. Report of an RTA last year. Hit and run.'

Westerman read the paper and looked up. 'Call a patrol car, will you?'

Half an hour later, Westerman and Chatterley were on their way to an address in a leafy Leeds suburb; when they reached their destination, Westerman instructed the constable to park round the corner and wait for him. His quarry had never seen him before and, as he wasn't in uniform, he would take her by surprise.

The door was answered by a woman. She wore a tracksuit and appeared to be in the best of health.

'Trish Bateman?'

'Who wants to know?'

He told her and produced his warrant card. 'You've recovered from your gastroenteritis, I see?'

The woman's face turned an unhealthy shade of red. 'To tell you the truth I didn't fancy the hen weekend, so I made an excuse. Why are you here?'

'Have you heard that one of the hen party was murdered? Stabbed?'

'Yes. Sandra phoned me.'

'I need to ask you some questions.'

'Why? I wasn't there.'

'Even so . . .'

Reluctantly she led him into the living room, where a young woman was sitting on the sofa, tapping away on a laptop.

'Your daughter, I presume?'

'Yes, this is Jane.'

His eyes wandered to the mantelpiece, dominated by a row of photographs of a smiling couple, on their wedding day and proudly holding a baby with a toddler standing by their side. In front of one photo, a portrait of a fair-haired young woman who bore a strong resemblance to Trish, a candle burned like an offering to a saint.

'Is Jane your only child?' he asked.

There was a long pause. 'She is now. I had another daughter. Liza. She died.'

'Did you and Jane enjoy your break in Lower Yarwood?'

'I've already told you, I never went there,' said Trish quickly. 'I told Sandra I was ill and stayed here.'

'So you said. But I'm sure Mr Parsons who owns the cottages will be prepared to identify Mrs Jones and her daughter. Mr

Parsons told us you paid for the accommodation in cash and arrived in a taxi so that your car wouldn't be recognized by the others. All you had to do was make sure you never left the cottage so you weren't seen by the hen party. Once you'd put a stop to the karaoke so that your phone call would be heard over the din, you phoned Moira to lure her out, no doubt telling her not to say anything to the others. Once you had her outside alone, she was at your mercy. And they were making such a noise they wouldn't have heard any call for help.'

Trish said nothing but Westerman saw that her eyes were fixed on the candle flame in front of the photograph.

'One of my officers has been doing some checks and he discovered that your younger daughter, Liza, was the victim of a hit-and-run accident. I've interviewed all the women who were at the cottage and Janet Wells told me something interesting. Last year Moira Bateman told her she'd been involved in an accident and needed to get her car fixed. She asked Janet if she could recommend a garage that would do the job without asking too many questions. Moira admitted she'd been drunk and talked about the incident as though it was something trivial she was hoping to keep from the police and her insurance company. But her accident happened around the time of your daughter's death and a witness saw a car just like Moira's speeding away from the scene. Moira's confession to Janet got back to you somehow, and you put two and two together.'

'The bitch murdered my little girl,' said Trish, clutching her daughter's arm. 'And she didn't care. Treated it like a joke – something naughty she wanted to get away with.'

Westerman cleared his throat. 'Patricia Fox, Jane Fox. I'm arresting you for the murder of Moira Bateman.'

He recited the familiar words of the caution. He'd always thought of himself as a hunter and he'd just cornered his fox. But on this particular occasion he didn't feel like celebrating.

The hens are making a racket again but there's nobody around to hear. I think of my cubs waiting for me, hungry. Sometimes a mother has to do what's necessary.

JOHN BAKER – AN
OLD-FASHIONED POISONING

Isabella went to the storage cupboard in which Miss
Bristow's materials were kept. She cut from a roll of white
linen a piece two yards long. In the kitchen, Lucy and
Louiscarl were laughing. Lucy had a black eye from their last
drinking bout the night before. Tonight they were drinking
cider and Louiscarl's laugh was as mad as Lucy's. Isabella
folded the linen and put it in a bag with a glass jar half filled
with vinegar. She understood the shortness of Louiscarl's life-
line. She knew why they had met and the part she had to play
in his destiny. In the last few days she had returned time and
time again to Grandmother Agnus's stories of death, and her
own knowledge of effective poisons. She left the mill by the
rear entrance to save herself the sight of her mother and her
lover.

It was late evening and the dew had begun falling. Isabella
felt the cold and wet on her feet. The moon was almost full but
misted over, and a handful of stars had the entire night sky to
themselves. Isabella walked away from the cliff, across Todd's
meadow, through the copse and over the stream to the place
where the ash were growing. There she inspected the leaves
and smaller branches of the young trees for several minutes.
But she did not find what she was looking for and eventually
picked up her bag and continued walking.

A bush of lilac on the edge of the stream was more fruitful.
She spread the linen on the grass under the lilac and set about
shaking the shrub, occasionally stopping to inspect the debris
that fell from leaves and branches.

She selected the bright, iridescent, golden green or bluish-
coloured bugs, all of them between a half and one inch in
length, and popped them into the glass of vinegar. Locally
they were known as blister beetles, but Grandmother Agnus

called them Spanish flies. At this time in the evening they were easy to collect, being dull and bedewed and unaware of what was happening to them.

From the first bush Isabella collected seven of the bugs, but before returning home she visited several other bushes along the stream. Her glass was full.

At the mill, Louiscarl and Lucy were already in bed, cackling away together at some huge vision the cider had bestowed on them. Isabella took her dead blister beetles from the vinegar and strung them together with thread. She hung them over the chimney breast and stoked up the fire to dry them as quickly as possible.

When they were ready, she put the beetles in a dry glass with a stopper and hid them away under her bed. It was the hour before dawn. The house was silent. She opened the door to Lucy's room and looked in at the couple on the bed. Alcohol hung in the air. They were both naked, lying across and over each other. Lucy slept with her mouth open, her arms thrown back on the pillow like a child. One of her teeth was missing, knocked out in the battle they called love. Louiscarl snored loudly. His face was a mask.

Isabella took over the cooking. Louiscarl did not complain about his portions. The Spanish fly, reduced to a fine powder by pestle and mortar, did not, at first, seem to stay his appetite. He wolfed his food and returned to the sawpit. During the next days he became lustful and wanton. He cornered Isabella in the woodshed after breakfast and squeezed both her breasts, panting heavily. She pushed him away and he stood back from her, stroking his erect penis through his trousers. He came for her again, lifting her skirts and tugging at her drawers. She stamped on his feet and escaped to the house.

Whenever he passed Lucy or Isabella, he reached out to touch them, caressing a shoulder or stroking the line of the neck. He pinched their bottoms and sometimes made a grab for a handful of buttock. On the third day he took Lucy over the kitchen sink in mid-morning, twisting her arm up her back until her eyes watered, had her again in the sawpit after dinner and dragged her off to bed in the evening while it was still light.

During that night he left Lucy asleep in bed and came for Isabella by the back door. She did not fight him but nor did she satisfy him. In the morning his erection was still present and at breakfast his eyes were dark and brooding.

'We should all go to bed together,' he said.

Lucy laughed.

Isabella went quickly to her room and locked the door.

She doubled the dose. Louiscarl spewed his dinner into the bucket while milking the cow. His shit turned to liquid and ran down his legs. His urine came in drops and at each drop he let out a loud shriek of pain. He shook. His teeth chattered and his eyes watered. He dragged his body upstairs and dropped on the bed. Isabella took him a bucket and a cup of water.

Lucy sat with him. Next day Isabella prepared food but he refused to eat. He fasted three days and regained some strength. He walked to the sawpit and gazed into it abstractedly for some minutes. Then returned to the house and sat in the chair by the grate. In the early evening Isabella gave him a slice of toast with potted meat and Spanish fly. He turned blue and there was blood in his vomit.

Lucy took him to her bed. Isabella cleaned up the mess on the wooden floor. In the vomit the shining elytra which make up the wing cases of the fly reflected the fading light of the day.

'He can't pee,' said Lucy from the stairs. 'He wants to pee but he can't. We should get a doctor.'

'No need,' Isabella assured her. 'He'll come round.'

During the night his lips became hot and painful and a series of small blisters appeared around his mouth. By morning the blisters had coalesced to form a large sac filled with fluid. Louiscarl was deformed and dejected. He wanted to vomit but his stomach was empty. He needed to pee but was unable to squeeze out a single drop.

'He's getting worse,' said Lucy. 'We *should* get a doctor.'

Isabella was sure a doctor was unnecessary. 'He'll come round,' she said. 'I think the potted meat was off.'

Louiscarl was dying, but very slowly. After a few days' fasting he made his way down to the chair by the grate. Isabella waited her chance and fed him more Spanish fly. He retired again to bed. He complained of pain in the region of his kidneys. He lost weight and the bones stuck out in his chest and shoulders. His eyes stared like great marbles in his head.

'I want to get in that sawpit,' he said at least once a day. 'I want to get well again, out in the sunshine. Back in the sawpit.'

On 8 October they heard of the death of Tennyson and Louiscarl dragged himself downstairs. He sent Isabella for a newspaper and she bought rat poison at the same time. The Spanish fly would work in time, but he had suffered enough.

'He died at Aldworth,' Louiscarl said, his head deep in the newspaper. 'His house, closely screened by plantations. And he's to be buried in Westminster Abbey on the twelfth.' He looked up from the newspaper. 'I want to be there. I want to be in London for the funeral.'

'You're not well enough,' said Lucy, shaking her head.

'We'll see,' said Isabella. 'Let's wait and see how you feel.'

'Listen,' said Louiscarl, his eyes fixed on the newsprint. 'With the splendour of the full moon falling upon him, his hand clasping his Shakespeare, and looking unearthly in the majestic beauty of his old age, he passed away on the night of the sixth of October.'

'Very nice,' said Lucy.

'Yes,' Isabella agreed. 'Very nice.'

Louiscarl smiled for the first time for weeks. 'He was reading *Cymbeline* when he died.'

Louiscarl did not attend Tennyson's funeral at Westminster Abbey. Isabella fed him the rat poison on 11 October and the strychnine killed him within half an hour.

A few minutes after eating the stew, he complained of stiffness about the neck and a look of terror came over him, as if he had a premonition of calamity. His head was jerked back and his arms and legs thrown forward. Lucy screamed. Louiscarl's chair overturned. Isabella leapt to her feet. Louiscarl was on the floor, his back arched. His weight resting only on his head and heels.

After a few moments he relaxed and Lucy bent to soothe his brow. The spasm returned immediately. While the women stood back and were quiet he relaxed, but at the slightest movement, or when one or the other of them touched him, he sprang back into the bow of his head and heels. The spasm and relaxation alternated rapidly for the next half-hour. He had difficulty in swallowing, his eyes were wide open and fixed, and his mouth drawn ugly aside.

When the symptoms passed he was dead. Lucy sank to the floor beside him in a faint. Isabella's face was wet with tears.

She sat on the edge of the bed, her hands gripping the counterpane. Lucy was moving around downstairs. Louiscarl's bookshelves lined one wall of Isabella's room and she cast her eye along the top row of books. The titles came into focus, into consciousness for the first time. Suddenly she could read them. *Confessions of an English Opium Eater*, *The Poetical Works of John Keats*, *A Vindication of the Rights of Woman*, *Childe Harold's Pilgrimage*.

Lucy's footsteps sounded on the stairs. Isabella felt a chill move up her spine but she did not move.

The Lady of the Lake, *Oliver Twist*, *Middlemarch*, *Erewhon*, *Dr Jekyll & Mr Hyde*.

The door opened and Lucy walked into the room. She carried the pestle and mortar. 'You done it,' she said.

Isabella looked away. *The Rubaiyat of Omar Khayyam*, *Huckleberry Finn*, *The Raven*, *Moby Dick*, *Faust*. She looked back at her mother. 'I'm going to read all his books,' she said.

'He shouldn't have hit you,' Isabella told Lucy.

Lucy laughed. 'That's what they do,' she said. 'They all do it.'

'He didn't hit me,' said Isabella. 'He was gentle. Always gentle.'

'No,' said Lucy, laughing madly. 'They twist your arms and blacken your eyes. That's what they like best.'

They carried him out to the sawpit. He was buried there with the remains of the rat poison and the Spanish fly, with the pestle and mortar and a copy of *Cymbeline*. 'He'll appreciate that,' said Isabella. 'All he wanted was to get back in the sawpit.'

In Mousehole people assumed that Louiscarl had grown tired of the women and left. There was a rumour that the gypsy woman and her daughter had done away with him. But it was just gossip, for he was still there. He roamed through the house. He sat in the chair by the fire, reading his books. Late at night, when Isabella was ready for sleep, he came slowly up the stairs and got into bed beside her. And in the early morning when she woke, she could hear him outside in the sawpit, cutting his timber.

MARGARET MURPHY – READ THE LABEL

L abels are for bottles; labels are not for people.
Take, for example: librarian; surgeon; nun; police constable.

Be honest, now – which of you read 'police constable' and *didn't* hear the creak of shoe leather? Or give the librarian a plump body cosily wrapped in a nice, warm (but slightly pilled) cardi?

You didn't? Well, good for you. How about . . . 'surgeon'? You're sitting in the waiting room, and the nurse says, 'Dr Higham will see you, now.' You walk through the door. What do you see?

Shirt and tie, obviously. Stethoscope, maybe. He's serious, confident, a brusque individual, used to being listened to, but not always the best listener. Certainly *not* a man to suffer fools. Right?

Wrong. When she isn't wearing scrubs, Dr *Sarah* Higham is rarely seen in anything more formal than T-shirt and jeans. She smiles, a lot, is occasionally subject to moments of uncertainty and (shockingly) will consult with even junior colleagues to decide the best course of treatment for her patients. She's a hopelessly assiduous listener whose clinics always overrun.

You assumed she was a man? Really? Did someone teleport me into an episode of *Dr Finlay's Casebook*?

Oh, come on, relax – I'm kidding . . . It's a natural enough assumption: surgeons are doctors and doctors are men, right? Well, no, of *course* not – let's not get too literal, here; this isn't about the way things really are, it's about *how they appear to be*. But it's still true in 2021 that two-thirds of senior doctors are male. So, hand on heart, did you see a straight-backed, sharp-eyed, smiling *woman* sitting in the doctor's chair, at the doctor's desk? You did? Well, yay you! Seriously – a round of applause for Enlightened of Utopia. But please, don't even *try* to convince me that it would *never* have crossed your mind – because that would be a flat-out lie.

OK. Here's a wholly (holy?) uncontentious prospect: nuns. Those quiet, contemplative, kindly souls whose vocation is to serve God and ease the suffering of others. Yeah, right. Try telling that to a fifty-something boyo who wakes screaming from the sweat-soaked nightmare that has tormented him for forty years: Sister Gabriel swooping down in the unforgiving night like a black-clad archangel to deliver retribution to his wicked flesh. Tell it to the Magdalens, those 'fallen women' condemned to a life of misplaced shame and shameful bondage by the very men who tripped them. Tell it to the schoolgirls subtly corrupted by a recurring homily on the sinfulness of wearing patent leather shoes. This from a Holy Sister who, though gowned and wimpled like the saints of old, was habited with unholy thoughts and for whom even the most innocent gesture was tainted with the reek of S . . . E . . . X . . .

You might ask why people like labels at all – the whistling postie, the jobsworth bean counter, the angel nurse, the tech nerd, the suit – since they're so unreliable. The labels are not the people, after all. Perhaps – but the clever metonyms and the well-worn stereotypes contain enough of Truth (capital T intended) to ease the problem of sorting the future BFFs from the fun-sucking emotional vampires, the soulmates from the stalkers.

And in a world that demands 35,000 decisions of the average Jack or Jill in a single day, labels save time and effort. You don't need to look beyond Miss Cardigan's napped wrapper; you *know* she will only ever marry the heroes in the books she reads. And when she's done with them, she will gather them to her bosom and shelve them tenderly for other lonely souls to find solace.

But what if the label doesn't show? Say you meet PC Plod in civvies or Miss C on a bus or a train, or in the frozen-food aisle of a supermarket? Not a problem; you'll find the label tucked in the gathering of Plod's brows, in the way he eyes the teenaged scallywags with the practised dead look of a seasoned law enforcer. You'll read it inked on the disappointed face of the librarian: 'Returned item. Not for reissue'. All resolved in the blink of an eye.

Because forming a first impression from that first glance takes just one *tenth* of a second – *literally* the blink of an eye. Don't take my word for it – Google it, you'll find the tenth-of-a-second rule is a stone-cold, documented, experimentally verified fact.

You might think, 'I'm not like that. I'm cautious, objective, a good judge of character. I'll take more time. Give me a minute – five, *ten* minutes; I'll modify that split-second evaluation, finesse it to a second, or even third opinion.'

Go ahead, take your time. But – spoiler alert – it won't change a thing. 'Cos when they say first impressions count, they're deadly serious. Give a sucker longer, they just use the extra time to confirm that first impression. To trust or recoil in horror, to befriend or run like hell – it's all settled in that first microsecond – fixed like flies in amber. And *completely* beyond your control. You see, it happens in the primitive part of our brain – some call it the lizard brain, but I like to think of it as the chimp brain. Two small, almond-shaped clusters of nerves called the amygdala, buried deep inside the skull. Trust me when I say the amygdala has nothing to do with thought and *everything* to do with instinct.

But we're *Homo sapiens* – wise humans – aren't we? We can reason, judge, change our minds – can't we? That's what our higher cortex is for. Isn't it? Isn't it supposed to apply reason to our irrational instincts, so we make rational, informed decisions?

In theory, yes. In practice, not so much . . . You see, the wiring from your chimp brain to the frontal lobes, where the coherent thinking happens, is – well – *dodgy*, to say the least. To put it bluntly, chimp you and human you are barely on nodding terms.

Imagine a conversation between scientists and the followers of a mystic who can heal ailments with a touch of his hand. What would they have to say to each other – what could they *ever* have in common? Why would a true believer try to communicate their joy in the presence of their Chosen One to scientists with their nit-picking arguments, quibbles, and fact-checks? Why waste time trying to explain belief to an unbeliever? Any self-respecting convert would want to keep the good news, pure and untainted by uncertainties, to himself.

And that's exactly what chimp brain does. So, that tenth of a second you spent getting to know your new friend – that fizz of excitement you experienced feeling a real *connection* – will stay right where it started, in the primitive nerve clusters buried deep in your chimp brain.

Add to that the fact that six million years of evolutionary instinct are embedded in our chimp-brained amygdala, whereas we've only been 'wise' humans for less than a thirtieth of that – we're practically *programmed* to trust our chimp instincts.

You might ask why we have higher brain function at all. I mean, what's the point of having executive higher-ups with their corner offices and their lofty views if they just get over-ruled by the plebs on the shop floor? Well, if you wind the tape back a bit, you'll see I didn't say that, exactly. It's *first impressions* I'm talking about here. For other stuff, the execs get their way. The wise chimp has a definite edge as far as learning facts and doing complex tasks go. You know, the reasoning and calculating, building and creating and all the other things that mean that we can live in heated and insulated homes and order in pizza, instead of shuffling from one miser-able feeding ground to the next in filthy weather. But in *this* scenario, you might say the *life-or-death* scenario, your rational brain is good for just one thing: supplying reasons why those first impressions were *right*. Which is all well and good if the look in the stranger's eye got your chimp-hackles up. Even better if you decided to walk away fast and tapped in triple-nine on your phone, just in case he followed you.

But what if you meet up with someone who is clever at disguising his true nature? One who camouflages anger as wit, covers a snarl with laughter, and presents animal lust as romantic love?

Then, my friend, you are royally screwed.

That split-second impression that convinced you it's a Good Thing to have this new person in your life is hard enough to shake, 'cos, you know – chimp brain/wise brain lines of communication are down. And then you go and make things worse by recruiting your wise-human higher cortex to prove you right. It's quite funny, when you think. You persuade yourself that you made a rational decision to trust the Narcissist, the Manipulator, the User, the Predator – and you keep adding more and more reasons to go on trusting him. Like a truffle pig, your wise brain will snout out examples of how kind/understanding/insightful/clever this monster-in-disguise is – and tell you how lucky you are that he actually *likes* you!

Even when he turns. Even when he sheds his camouflage as a snake sheds its skin. Then, you will find ways to excuse, or justify, or blame yourself. That's a lot of grief-making from one glance. From one, tiny electrical impulse.

I like that people like labels. But whatever the label says, it doesn't tell you who I am. What I am. It isn't the label that matters, it's what you do – not what you *say* you do. It's those things you do in the dark, when you think nobody is watching. – *Deeds, not words shall speak you.*

I should know.

I'm sitting opposite you on a train. Today, I've gone for a studious look: wire-rimmed glasses, a copy of *The Return of the Native*, broken-spined and well thumbed. A couple of rail tickets used as place-markers.

You read the label, see a man, youngish, good-looking (I've no patience with false modesty – I only lie about the important things, the things you can't see). We could avoid eye contact for two hours, I could pretend to read, you could listen to your iPhone. But I seem *nice*.

How do you know – that I'm nice, I mean? Because I'm attractive and tidy, but not over-groomed in a smarmy businessman way? Because my hair is slightly tousled and I don't seem aware of it, so I must not be vain? Yes, and yes. But also because I wear glasses, and that's always endearing – it hints at vulnerability. I'm a smiley fellow, too. If you were a guy, a whole different set of parameters would apply. I wouldn't smile so much, for one thing – because men don't trust other men who smile too much. If you were a *man*, I'd be laid-back. Cool – friendly, in an abstract, 'we can talk about football but not feelings' kind of way. Friendly, but not *chummy*. But you're not a man – you're a woman. And women *like* a man who smiles. Why? Because women are conditioned. Social programming makes them respond to a smile with a smile and smiling makes you feel good – so you feel good about me.

Here's a tip: listen carefully to what the other person says, then say it back to them. Psychologists call it mirroring. Of course, you'd need to change the words around a bit – you don't want to parrot them. Get it right, though, and they'll be flattered, credit you with a superior intelligence, just like their own – you've made a friend for life. Trust me; anyone who's lonely is just too damned lazy to lie.

Mirror a woman's smile for smile and she'll think she's found her soulmate. And here you are, smiling. Saying yes, why not? Let's go for a drink.

We'll talk about this and that. Mostly about you – I'll gently turn the conversation back to you whenever the chat strays too far in my direction. You'll think I'm fascinated by you and modest about myself. It's all about manipulation – of facts, expectations, emotions, beliefs. People are hard-wired to believe.

Read the label: I'm a teacher/doctor/librarian/policeman. What possible harm could there be in that?

The first impression of your chimp brain said that I'm safe, kind. Attractive. Attractive is very important. The clincher? I have my trustworthy face on: eyebrows higher in the middle than at the corners of the eyes for an open look, lips slightly parted, as though I might smile at any moment. People find trustworthy faces more attractive and less threatening.

I could tell you that I'm a surgeon – I have been, of sorts, on occasions. Or would you like me better as an explorer? I've done a deal of exploration in my time: unfamiliar terrain, a bit of climbing, camping out at night, covert ops, close observation; hunting, stalking, trapping. Best of all, I like to explore limits – of courage, of terror, of pain.

No matter how I label myself today, I've made that first impression on you – and you won't be able to shake it. So when I become suddenly negative, or rude, or aggressive, you'll probably blame yourself. You might even apologize – ask if you did something wrong. Which, of course, you did. In that tenth of a second when we made eye contact.

Read the label. Just don't trust it to tell you what's in the bottle.

KATE ELLIS – MY OLEANDER

One of the most memorable cases in Detective Superintendent Raphael Inigo Penhalen's forty-year career was the murder of Oleander Cordingly. It had been a baffling one but, even though he was a fresh-faced detective constable at the time, a flash of inspiration had made it the first triumph of many. It was certainly one for the memoirs.

He had always enjoyed locked-room mysteries, although he'd never imagined things like that happened in real life. Or real death. Most murders, in his experience, were commonplace and committed by rather stupid people. But this could hardly be said of Oleander's killer. The most intelligent thing any murderer can do is to fool everyone, including the police, into believing that it wasn't a case of murder in the first place. No murder, no investigation. No investigation and the killer gets off scot-free.

He sat at the little desk he'd set up in the shed at the bottom of the garden and, after reading through the notes he'd made all those years ago, he opened his laptop and began. His daughter had been nagging him to write his memoirs, an account of his most interesting cases. She swore that *The RIP Files* – his initials, RIP, being his nickname in the force – would become a bestseller. Although he put her optimism down to filial loyalty.

He knew he was no writer, but boredom had persuaded him to make a start. And it also gave him an excuse to escape Lavinia's constant nagging. It hadn't been so bad when he'd been working long hours, but things were different now they were spending twenty-four hours a day in each other's company.

In July 1978 the police were called to Byfleet Hall, not by the residents but by the ambulance crew who'd been summoned there to attend a sudden death – probably a suicide. At that time Byfleet Hall was home to the Cordingly family, as it had been for generations. The father, Henry, who spent most of his time abroad, was absent throughout the entire investigation. The mother, Clara, was an invalid – or at least that's what her son told the police. The son, Jonty, a child of the 1960s, was trying to run the place on the lines of a commune, along with his wife, Oleander, and her sister Jacoranda, known as Jack. Rip remembered thinking at the time that the sisters' parents must have been keen on flowering plants.

Oleander had been found dead in her locked bedroom, lying on the bed in a pool of vomit. When Rip and his inspector took their first look at the room, the corpse was still in situ, along with evidence of the failed attempts to revive her. A tape of Gregorian chants was playing and the burned-out ends of joss sticks protruded from a colourful vase on the bedside table. Beside the vase sat an expensive box of Turkish delight with a small wooden fork provided to spear the gelatinous cubes without risking sticky fingers. Half the sweet treats had been eaten and the dead woman had clearly been smoking a joint, because the stub lay in a nearby ashtray. The windows had been flung wide open, presumably to get rid of the telltale smell of cannabis before the police arrived. Rip's inspector suspected this was why the family hadn't called them right away.

As soon as they were outside, the inspector announced with confidence that the death was probably drugs related. The signs were all around if Rip cared to look. He muttered the words 'bloody hippies' under his breath and drove off, leaving Rip to take routine statements from the household. As far as the inspector was concerned, the case was closed.

Mrs Clara Cordingly, Jonty's mother, lived in a far wing of the large and shabby Georgian mansion and, whereas Jonty's quarters were filled with beanbags, dusty Indian throws and straggling pot plants, Clara's more conventional domain boasted antique furniture, threadbare brocade sofas and oil paintings of distant ancestors.

Clara denied all knowledge of what she described as the 'goings-on' in her son's part of the hall. Jonty had never been the same, she said, since he'd returned from a long stay in Italy with those two sisters in tow. Oleander and Jacoranda – odd names for a pair of odd women, in her opinion.

Although her manner was rather vague, Clara showed no sign of the frailty her son had spoken of when he was trying to persuade the inspector that she shouldn't be questioned. There was nothing frail about Clara's opinions either. The two sisters were always at each other's throats and she'd often heard shouting. She'd once heard Jack threaten to kill her sister and she suspected they'd been fighting over Jonty; her implication being that her son and the sisters were involved in some kind of *ménage à trois*. Although, as a mother-in-law, she knew it was best not to interfere.

Her only hope, she told Rip with apparent sincerity, was that one day the scales would fall from her son's eyes and he'd send both the sisters packing. As Rip listened patiently, he could sense the woman's desperation as she tried to hold back the tide of events like King Canute. Although, with Oleander dead, there was now a small chance that the tide might begin to turn in her favour.

His next interview was with Jack and he took an instant dislike to the woman, even though he knew a policeman should never make a judgement until he'd assessed all the evidence. However, from the very start of their conversation in the dingy drawing room, Jack's manner was hostile and defensive. When he asked her about the arguments Clara had overheard, she said that she and her sister had agreed to share Jonty but Oleander hadn't kept her side of the bargain. When the three of them had met up in Italy, they'd agreed on an open relationship, but all that had changed when Oleander and Jonty got married. Her sister had turned bourgeois, she said, as though it was the worst insult she could think of. She lit a cigarette and told Rip to leave. She didn't feel like talking to the pigs any more.

Rip resisted the urge to point out that pigs were highly intelligent animals, and went off in search of Jonty, who was lurking in the kitchen rubbing his shoulder as though he was in pain. The new widower at least had decided to put on a belated show of regret at Oleander's death – even though his emotional range didn't seem to stretch to full-blown grief. He seemed jumpy, and Rip wondered whether he was craving something to calm him down.

They sat down at the kitchen table and Jonty gave what sounded like a well-rehearsed account of events. Just after lunch his wife had gone into her room and locked the door, he said. She did that most days because she liked to meditate. Only, that particular day she hadn't emerged after a couple of hours as she usually did, so Jack had gone upstairs to check. Locked doors, of course, weren't in tune with the ethos of the house where all property was supposed to be shared. But when Jack had pointed this out to Oleander, she'd claimed she needed privacy for her meditation sessions and continued to lock herself in. This had caused more ill-feeling between the sisters although, Jonty added quickly, this couldn't possibly have had anything to do with Oleander's death.

Jack hadn't been able to get an answer when she'd knocked on Oleander's door, so she had called Jonty, who had rushed off to find his mother in case she knew whether there was a spare key. Clara, however, insisted that there'd only ever been one key to that particular room.

In the end she and Jack had encouraged Jonty to barge the door open, which he did, hurting his shoulder in the process. The key, which had been in the freshly broken lock, fell to the floor as soon as the door burst open, and Jack was about to rush over to her sister when Clara told them to stay where they were. Oleander was lying quite still, her eyes staring at the ceiling. It looked as though she was dead so it would be best if nothing was disturbed.

Jack became hysterical and Jonty was too stunned to do anything, so it had been Clara who'd entered the room on tiptoe to assess the situation. She'd ordered Jonty to call an ambulance. That was all he could remember.

When Rip asked about Oleander's drug-taking, Jonty's answers were evasive. She dabbled. Didn't everyone these days? Then Rip asked to have another look at the room where she'd been found dead.

It was a spacious bedroom and the grand bed where Oleander had breathed her last was a four-poster draped in cotton hangings decorated with embroidered elephants. The door frame bore the scars of Jonty's dramatic entrance and the windows were still wide open, letting in a chill breeze.

Rip was about to shut them when something stopped him. If there was a possibility this was a crime scene, it should be left untouched.

The tape machine was winking away on top of the chest of drawers and Rip yielded to the temptation to switch it on. Soon the ethereal sound of plainchant filled the air again. Music to meditate to – or to die to. He looked around the room, taking in his surroundings. Something was different, but he couldn't tell whether something had been taken from the scene or added. He hoped it would come to him in time. On the other hand, it might not be important.

Rip sat back and took a sip of the tea Lavinia had just left on his desk. He hadn't even noticed her come in and she hadn't interrupted him, which was unusual. Since his retirement he'd sensed her resentment of the time he spent in his shed, as though she considered it his duty to keep her company to make up for all the long absences during his working life. When he took a sip of tea he thought it tasted a little odd, but he had other things on his mind as he flicked through the pages of his notebook, stopping at a transcript of the next interview he'd carried out at Byfleet Hall; the one that had ultimately set him on the right track.

He'd spoken to Oleander's immediate family, but he suspected that four people couldn't run a place the size of Byfleet Hall on their own. They must have had help of some sort, even if it was only part time. He returned to the kitchen where he found Jonty still sitting at the table. Only now he was nursing a mug of coffee and Jack was sitting beside him with her hand resting on his knee. It might have been a gesture of comfort but, to Rip, it looked more like the first stage of a take-over. The queen is dead, long live the queen.

He asked them whether anyone else had been around at the time of Oleander's death and Jonty said that Old Pete had probably been in the garden somewhere. He usually was. Old Pete had been a fixture on the estate for as long as Jonty could remember and lived in the lodge by the lane. From the way he spoke about the old retainer, Rip sensed that, for all his vaunted New Age credentials, Jonty still retained a touch of the feudal overlord.

When Rip tracked Old Pete down in the kitchen garden, he was pushing an ancient wheelbarrow filled with compost. He was a wiry man with the walnut-like face of a smoker who'd spent most of his life out of doors. When Rip asked if he could have a word, he rolled himself a cigarette and settled on a nearby bench.

'You've heard about Mrs Cordingly? Young Mrs Cordingly, that is.'

'Aye. I've heard. Daft name that – Oleander. Oleander's pretty enough but it's bloody poisonous. Just like her. And the other one's poisonous too – Jacoranda. What were the parents thinking of, I ask you?'

'You don't like the sisters?'

'Not my place to say, is it.'

'You didn't see anything odd around the time she died?'

'Can't say I did. But if I was Master Jonty, I wouldn't have had them flowers in the house. Like I said, they're poison. Asking for trouble.'

He chuckled and Rip suspected that the flowers he referred to were the women. But when he asked, Old Pete shook his head. He wasn't saying.

'Do you have any help in the garden?'

'Only the mistress. It's a hobby of hers, gardening. Been at a loose end since the master buggered off abroad. Helps me in the greenhouse, she does.'

'I was told she's an invalid.'

Old Pete snorted with derision and took a drag on his thin cigarette. 'There are some who'd like her to be.'

'Who?'

'Not my place to say,' he repeated, as if to emphasize his loyalty and discretion. Not that Rip was fooled for one moment.

'Can I see the greenhouse?'

The gardener looked surprised but, without another word, he stood up and led the way to a large greenhouse standing in the corner of the garden.

'What do you use it for?' Rip asked once he'd caught up with him.

'This and that,' Old Pete answered as he opened the door.

Rip left Byfleet Hall that day wondering if he was letting his imagination run away with him. It wasn't until he was called into the inspector's office the following day that he learned that his suspicions had some substance.

Oleander Cordingly's post-mortem confirmed that she'd been poisoned, although the pathologist was puzzled about the exact nature of the toxic substance. Tests were ongoing.

It occurred to Rip that what they had was a classic locked-room mystery; the kind of mystery he'd loved as a teenager, devouring book after book by his favourite crime writers. But this was something he didn't mention to his superior for fear of sounding flippant.

The remains of the Turkish delight found beside Oleander's bed had been analysed and found to be perfectly harmless, so the source of the poison, whatever it was, remained a mystery. Unless it was something she'd come into contact with before she went to her room for her meditation session, although her husband and sister swore that she hadn't eaten or drank anything the three of them hadn't shared. Clara seemed to be out of the picture as a suspect because, according to Jonty and Jack, she'd been in her flat in the far wing of the house all morning, taking breakfast alone and not emerging until after her daughter-in-law was dead.

Jonty had been in the house with Oleander all morning, comforting her after she'd had yet another row with Jack over breakfast. Rip's inspector seemed to think this supported his suicide theory.

'Just think, Rip, taking some pills then lying down all comfy and half stoned with those monks singing away. She was probably depressed after falling out with her sister and she thought it was a good way to go.'

Rip pointed out that she'd shown no signs of wanting to take her own life; no empty pill packet and no note. It was then the inspector dropped the bombshell that, in Rip's opinion, made the suicide theory more unlikely.

'The doc's report said she was expecting. Three months gone. Maybe she couldn't face having the kid. Or maybe she didn't intend to go through with it. If her husband was carrying on with her sister, it might have been a cry for help – to get his attention.'

But Rip's thoughts were following a different track. He couldn't forget the look of smug triumph on Jack's face when she was comforting Jonty. A new baby was bound to have pushed her out of his affections once and for all. She was a woman with a motive.

But it wasn't until the burglary that he understood exactly how Oleander Cordingly had been killed.

The investigation rumbled on, as some investigations do. There was no definitive result from the lab and the inspector had been told it might take weeks to isolate the substance responsible for Oleander's death. In the meantime they had little apart from theories.

The burglary at a gift shop in the High Street a week later was a routine matter; one that Rip could safely deal with on his own in spite of his inexperience. When he arrived at the shop he saw that it specialized in tourist trinkets: tea towels, cushions, brightly painted ornaments, as well as local delicacies – packs of artisan biscuits, tins of toffees and locally made fudge. A plate of fudge pieces had been placed on the counter for customers to sample before they parted with their money and, as Rip waited for the owner of the shop to emerge from the back, he picked up one of the cocktail sticks beside the plate and speared the largest square of the brown crumbly treat, savouring the sweetness and resisting the temptation to help himself to more.

It was then that Rip suddenly remembered what had been missing from Oleander Cordingly's bedroom. When he'd first entered the room he'd noticed a small wooden fork beside the Turkish delight, but when he'd returned later it had gone. And he suspected he knew why.

But first he needed to visit the local library.

Rip sat at the library table flicking through the pages of a heavy reference book, searching for one entry in particular. When he found what he was looking for, he felt like punching the air and letting out a cheer, but he was in a library so he kept his elation to himself.

By a stroke of luck he'd been given the use of a patrol car and Byfleet Hall was only a short distance away. If things went his way he could be there and back in an hour.

He steered the car into the gates by Old Pete's lodge and continued up the drive, feeling increasingly apprehensive now that he was about to face a killer. Once he'd stopped in front of the house, he sat in the driver's seat for a while, planning his next move.

The decision was made for him when he spotted two people walking towards him, both carrying trugs brimming with newly harvested flowers and vegetables. Old Pete spotted him and came to a sudden halt, a guilty look on his face, as though he'd been caught doing something he shouldn't. His companion stopped too and stood there wearing an expression of mild interest.

Rip got out of the car and put on his hat. This was official.

'Mrs Cordingly, can I have a word, please?'

'Certainly, Constable.' Clara placed her trug on the ground and folded her arms while Old Pete hovered beside her protectively.

'I understand you're a keen gardener, Mrs Cordingly.'

To Rip's surprise Old Pete answered for her. 'I reckon missus knows as much as I do. More.'

He smiled at his employer, as though he expected the praise to please her. But she was wearing the same wary expression Rip had seen before on criminals who knew they'd just been caught out.

'When I visited your greenhouse I noticed some flowering shrubs.'

'That's right,' said Pete. They've been in there over winter. I'll move them to the front of the house now the risk of frost is over. Make a nice show, they do.'

'One of them is oleander.'

'Pretty flowers.'

'And highly poisonous. Every part. And lethal if you lick the wood. Was it you who swapped the little fork that came in Oleander's box of Turkish delight with a copy you'd made yourself, Mrs Cordingly?'

The woman looked around her, searching for a way out. But there was no escape.

Rip was in trouble. The inspector summoned him into his office and berated him for leaving the gift shop before he'd taken the owner's statement. His actions gave a bad impression to the public, he said. When someone's the victim of crime, they expect the police to at least make a show of investigating.

Rip stood at the desk with his head bowed, like a naughty schoolboy summoned to the headmaster's study, wondering how to mention that he'd just solved a murder.

'I've made an arrest in the Oleander Cordingly case, sir,' he said, deciding on the direct approach.

'We're still waiting for the results from the lab, so we don't even know whether it was murder yet. You're in danger of becoming obsessed, lad. Let it drop until we know for sure.'

'It was murder all right, and when I went to the gift shop and saw the cocktail sticks put there so customers could sample the fudge, I realized how it was done. Clara Cordingly hated her daughter-in-law and wanted her and her sister out of the way. When she discovered Oleander was pregnant, she knew she'd never be rid of her – so she had to die. Clara's quite a plant expert. She knew oleander wood would kill, so she made a little fork out of wood she'd obtained from the greenhouse and exchanged it for the one that came in her daughter-in-law's favourite box of Turkish delight. The Turkish delight itself was harmless, but the fork was highly poisonous. Once Clara had made the swap it was just a matter of waiting for meditation time.'

The inspector looked puzzled. 'Are you sure about this?'

'Yes. Thick rubber gloves, a craft knife and the remains of several twigs were found hidden in her wing of the house. Forensic will be able to confirm that it's oleander wood. She's waiting downstairs to be interviewed.'

The inspector said nothing for a while. Then he looked up.

'Good work, Penhalen,' he muttered grudgingly. 'Now go and clear up that burglary.'

'Raphael. Stop what you're doing and make those kebabs. Then you can light the barbecue. Hurry up. They'll be arriving soon.'

Rip looked up from his notes with a sigh, wondering how much longer he could put up with it. The idleness, the orders, the nagging; the bitter feeling of uselessness after a life filled with action. Their guests would be there any minute so his memoirs would have to wait.

As he left the shed, he fixed a smile to his face. At least he could enjoy the gardening now he had more time on his hands. The shrubs were looking good on the patio, their lovely deep pink flowers giving the place a continental feel. He'd first seen them as a child on a visit to Italy. Only he hadn't known the truth about them back then.

'I'll do those kebabs now,' he said.

His wife looked harassed. Old. She neglected herself these days. And to think she'd once been so pretty – and so proud of her appearance.

She grunted something that didn't sound like thanks before reminding him that she'd decided to become a vegan, so she wanted her kebabs made with no meat or halloumi – and she didn't want them to come into contact with any animal products. Once he'd reached the kitchen he began work, careful to keep the kebabs he was making for her separate from all the rest.

He glanced at the oleander tree outside the kitchen window and put on plastic gloves to handle one skewer in particular. He was sure it would work. And once it did, he'd be a free man.

ANN CLEEVES – THE QUEEN OF MYSTERY

At Malice Domestic they call me the Queen of Mystery. Of course I'm flattered by the description but I'd never use it about myself. Malice is a crime convention for true lovers of the traditional mystery novel, a celebration of the gentle art of killing. And I do kill my characters very kindly, without torture or the gratuitous description of pain. But we aren't brash or flash in Malice. Self-promotion is frowned upon. Unfortunately, some of the newer writers don't observe the conventions. I've seen T-shirts printed with jacket covers, giveaway candy, the blatant canvassing for awards. I'm Stella Monkhouse and I'm above that sort of thing.

I feel at home at Malice. It's *my* convention. When I walk in through the hotel lobby, I sense the flutter of the fans as they point me out to each other. I always dress my best to arrive. There are writers here too of course, and I wave to them as if we're tremendous friends, but really this is a performance for the common reader and the wannabe writer. I need those people's admiration and their envy more than the shared gossip over dreadful wine with fellow authors.

It helps that I was born British. Malice Domestic is always held in Bethesda, Maryland, but it celebrates the English detective tradition. Most of the regular attendees are ladies of a certain age, and the weekend always ends with afternoon tea. I came to the US when I was young to work as a secretary for a publisher in New York City. Perhaps I had ambitions to write even then; certainly I hoped to make a name for myself. My husband was a senior editor with the company and much older than I; we never had children. I thought then that was a good thing because it allowed me to focus on my work. Now I wonder what it might be like to leave behind more of myself than a pile of stories.

People sometimes mistake me for my series character; Molly Gregory is the gentle owner of a coffee shop in rural Massachusetts. She quilts, has a cat called Sherlock and solves murders in her spare time. I'm nothing like Molly, though I smile when readers ask me to send their love to Sherlock. One has a certain responsibility not to disappoint one's audience. But I've always adored living in the city and I wouldn't know one end of a knitting needle from another.

Publishers and other writers consider me ruthless, overly ambitious. They call me a monster behind my back, though they turn on the charm when I arrive. I'm the star. The multi-Agatha-award-winner. So why shouldn't I upstage them a little when we appear together on a panel? I'm a professional and this is a competitive business. Besides, I'm more entertaining than they are and it's me the readers have come to see.

There's no line to check in and the receptionist recognizes me. 'So glad to have you with us again, Ms Monkhouse.' This year I'm not guest of honour and I have to pay for my own room. That rankles a little, but someone else has to have a chance to shine, and next year they'll all be talking about me again. This year it's little Emily Furlow. She sets her books in Cornwall, though she'd never stepped foot outside Idaho when she started writing. She sent me her first book to blurb but I couldn't bring myself to comment. On my way to the elevator I see her surrounded by a group of readers, but I don't join them. I give a regal wave as befits the Queen of Mystery and move on.

In my room I unpack and hang up the dress I'll wear for the awards dinner. I've been nominated again for an Agatha, so I need to look my best. It's expected. The winner is chosen by readers over the weekend and I'm confident that their loyalty will see me through. The sight of Emily with her entourage has unnerved me a little though. It's essential that I end my career on top. Second best has never been good enough for Stella Monkhouse and it certainly won't do for this weekend. For a moment I feel something like self-pity. Or old age. Emily is at least thirty years younger than I am. In that moment I suspect that my recent books lack the wit and pace of the earlier titles and that she's a better writer than

I am. I ban the thought immediately and prepare to meet my fans.

There is nowhere for me to sit to do my make-up. The only mirror is the long one just inside the door where the light is appalling. My husband called the make-up my war paint, and today I need it more than I've ever done before. Clive and I were never passionate, but for a while we suited each other. Squinting in the gloom to fix my mascara, I wish that he were here, with me.

I sweep into the lobby just as everyone is gathering for the opening reception. There's a pay bar and I'm tempted to buy myself a large glass of wine, but today I need a clear head. I target members of the committee, hitting them with my special smile and the force of my personality. I need to dazzle them. These are the influential women who plan the convention and whose superb organization keeps it going year after year. Like a politician I can make them feel special. I remember the names of their husbands and who has a son or daughter looking for an internship in the business. Many of them do. I don't actually *promise* that my publisher will provide their offspring with work experience, but they're left with the impression that it's a real possibility. I haven't put this much effort into working a convention since I was a young writer struggling to make a name for myself with my first book.

When I feel at the top of my game, glittering, I head for Emily Furlow. She's sitting on the floor next to a group of women who sit on the bright red cubes of plastic that pass as seats. There's a glass of juice on the floor next to her – Emily, of course, never drinks alcohol. It occurs to me that I could slip an overdose of my medication into it and lose the competition for ever, but I know that Emily dead will be much more popular than Emily alive. Dead, *she* would certainly upstage *me*.

There's a stir as I approach. 'Stella,' she says. 'How lovely!' She's on her feet in one movement and we kiss on both cheeks. She's shorter than me and I have to stoop. 'I adored your latest book.'

I smile and murmur that she's very kind, then I turn my attention to the readers. The voters. There are a couple of women from Texas who come to Malice every year and I ask after their grandchildren. That's always a winner. We're called into the reception and the group walks along with me leaving Emily behind.

That night I struggle to sleep. The following evening will be the awards ceremony and I want to look my best. I think about Clive again. Before his death I thought I might enjoy living on my own with no distractions, but suddenly I realize I'm missing him dreadfully. I think of a possible parallel universe, a life cluttered with children and responsibilities, the demands of friendship. For a moment it has its attractions, but I know I couldn't stand it.

I wake to a beautiful Maryland day in late spring and decide that I'll go out to my favourite French café for breakfast. I can walk that far, despite the arthritis in my spine, and the fresh air will be good for me. In the far corner of the café, Emily Furlow is sitting quite alone, her nose in a book. My book. For a brief second I'm tempted to join her. I wonder what she really makes of it, whether she thinks it's up to my usual standard, but the moment passes and I find a corner of my own and pretend I didn't notice her. Because I'm in a strange mood. If she were kind to me I might be prompted to some sort of confession, and that isn't part of the plan at all. Not yet.

The awards dinner is just as it always is. The women have dressed in their finery and some of the men are wearing tuxes. Tradition is respected at Malice. The toast mistress is Catriona, another of my rivals, a Scottish woman based in California. She's witty and keeps things tight and fun, so we come very quickly to the announcement of the prizes. When the moment arrives, I wonder if I've lost the passion to win. Perhaps I could drift into retirement after all, take up knitting and quilting like my heroine. Bring a dog into my life. Perhaps it would be better if Emily took over my mantle. I hate to admit it, but she is a fine writer.

I pour myself a glass of wine; the other people at my table turn out not to be great drinkers. Catriona is opening the envelope. I fidget in my purse – after all, this mustn't seem to matter too much – so I'm not looking at the stage when the announcement is made.

It's me. I've beaten the record for the longest reign as Agatha champion. The glad-handing, the enquiries about grandchildren, the promises of internships that will never be kept, have all paid off. The people at my table rise to their feet and begin cheering. I grab my wine and walk a little unsteadily to the stage. There Catriona kisses me on both cheeks, though I sense her disappointment. She admires Emily's work. I sip the drink and take the microphone. The convention is that speeches should be kept very short, but this is an unusual occasion. As soon as I start speaking they will listen to me.

'This is my last time at Malice and I thank you all for making it so special. There will be no more Molly Gregory and no more Sherlock.' There are horrified boos and cries of *Shame!* I pause. I've always had a sense of dramatic timing. 'By tomorrow morning there will be no more Stella Monkhouse.' There's a sudden silence, a few embarrassed giggles, because they think I'm making a tasteless joke. 'In my fiction I take research seriously. I know about poison, the prescription meds that can kill.' I lift my glass in a mock toast. 'In here there's more than enough to finish me off.' I'd taken the pills from my purse while Catriona was speaking, and I drink the remainder of the wine with a very unladylike gulp.

Ironically, I've never felt more alive. Not even when I was holding the pillow over poor Clive's mouth to kill him. He asked me to do it – after the stroke he knew he was holding me back – but he never expected me to agree. When I can't sleep, I'm haunted by his pleading eyes, begging me to let him live. However, this isn't a time for regrets. This is what I've always wanted: to be the centre of attention, to shock and thrill with my words. And I know that when I'm dead my books will shoot to the top of the bestseller lists, for a while at least. Articles will be written about me. The obituaries will tell the world that I died as a champion. I couldn't have borne to be a woman who once *was* the Queen of Mystery, who slid into obscurity as her writing lost its power. Now, I'll reign for ever.

CHAZ BRENCHLEY – FOR KICKS

N ot difficult to trace her path across gravel and grass, to read the story of her passing. Not difficult, no – but God, it was hard.

Hard just to stand and look, to do it privately in his head. Harder still to do it all aloud, to make it real for others as it was already far too real for him.

To say, *Look, here is where she was kicked the first time. Kicked and kicked, just here.* And, *See this, see? This is where she crawled to, before he came back and kicked her again.*

God knows why she didn't die, he said, *she was meant to. But oh, she's tough,* too tough, he thought, *brilliant girl, she hung on somehow. Look, see, here she grabbed the railing, hauled herself up. Forgot where she was, maybe. Saw the river and just dropped back, though,* and who could blame her? No blame if she'd wriggled under the railing and gone head-first into the water. *When she moved again she went the other way, up onto the bank there, you can see the trail she left,* blood and bent grass and the red stone deeply stained. *That's where we found her,* unconscious, seven or eight hours after she'd first been kicked; and she hadn't woken up since and wasn't likely to, the doctors said, amazing that she was still alive at all. Only their machines to keep her so, to do her breathing for her.

And she was seventeen years old, and that was the story of her night out, as far as they could piece it together from the waymarks that she'd left; and Christ, but it was hard to tell it.

He sent them off then, these young constables, to make their enquiries door-to-door; and one word of advice he sent with them. 'Don't make a mystery out of this,' he said. 'Don't expect it to come out like the books. It won't. Nothing clever,

no smart boys wanted. It's drudge-work will solve this one.
The better you do it, the quicker we can wrap this up and get
warm again.'

Oh, he was cold and getting colder: exposed now, with the
youngsters dispersed and the forensics team peeling off their
coveralls and packing up their sheeting, giving back the
land. He stood and watched them drive away, and thought
he should be going too. Nothing useful he could do here,
plenty to do elsewhere. But the wind's bite couldn't move
him yet.

Someone had set a sculpture here, between the housing
estate and the river: a sandstone archaeology, inherent with
contradictions. It was a ruin recently made, the broken eroded
shell of an old house to set against the hard finished angles
of the new. This was where the girl had crawled to. Looking
to find help, perhaps, all she'd found was some thin shelter
from the weather, not enough.

Once there'd been shipyards all along this bank. That's what
he remembered. Cranes' shadows stretched further than height
and sun would suggest; the hooter's blast still echoed in his
head at least, though the last of the yards was gone.

History was important. You couldn't escape history, and you
couldn't defy it. There'd been housing here before the shipyards
were ever built; one demolition followed another, and none of
them mattered in the long run. What goes around comes around.
History moves in cycles. Pointless, even wishing to frustrate
an inevitable machine . . .

As he rubbed with his thumb at a sandstone picture on a
sandstone mantelpiece, a little piece flaked and fell away. He
snatched back his guilty hand, absurdly feeling that it was
history itself he was diminishing here; and was almost glad
to let his eyes find that darker stain again, where the girl had
bled on the stone.

The father sat at the bedside, hunched and trembling. His skin
was grey, his eyes watered; his hand reached constantly towards
his daughter, reached and reached and never quite made it.
Shaking fingers rested on the sheet just an inch short of her,
too afraid to touch.

A restless tide had carried the mother over to the window, then ebbed and left her stranded. Narrow hips perched on the narrow sill, she stared out through the blind, not to see again what an ungentle world had made of her only child.

Better for them if she'd died outright, he thought as he watched them, as he watched the damage happen. Better that than this, waiting endlessly for an end to hope, far too long delayed.

Pulling up a chair beside the father, playing detective, he said, 'One thing, if we could just get this sorted. The doctors say she's got other marks on her – older, five or six days old. Wouldn't know how she got those, would you?'

'Marks?'

'Bruises, mostly. Been knocked about a bit, she has.'

'You want to ask her boyfriend about that.'

'I'm asking you.'

The father turned his head then, looked at him, looked away. 'You want to ask the boyfriend.'

The mother said nothing at all.

Always come back to what you've got, they used to tell him. So here he was, walking the riverside again. The wind had changed; it was at his back now, pushing and nudging but cold still, bitter still. *Plus ça change*, he thought wearily. Here it came again, that feeling of inevitability. Enough to make anyone cold, the sense of being only a fleeting ghost in the machine, too quickly gone and changing nothing.

Still, as well to make his body work a little. He wouldn't like to have things too easy, here where it had gone so hard with her.

Down in the dock, yachts rubbed keels with fishing boats, and he wondered how much damage a man could do with a pair of deck shoes. Not enough, at a guess. They were talking boots here, they were surely talking boots. What did fishermen wear on their feet?

Past the dock, past the housing estate was an office development with clever gates, whimsical gates designed to look open when they were shut and locked. They should have been shut and locked well before the girl went out looking for kicks,

but that needed checking. If someone had been working late
– some young man, say, with fashionable boots – then someone
else would know.

He looped back around the unfinished estate, where some
houses were only breeze-block shells with bricks growing up
for cover, red to hide the grey; and grey was the colour of her
father's face and red was the colour of her blood, and could
it have been the father did this thing? Fathers had done worse
before. Maybe that's why he was shaking.

No constable on guard now, no gawking civilians, no one
to show where they'd found her. Nor any need. She'd made
these stones her own, signed them with more courage than
blood. And she was only a little thing, and he admired her so
much; and couldn't say so, he could only hold it as a secret,
a private pride in a client who had done marvellously better
than anyone had any right to expect.

He tried to think of her coming along here alone and in the
dark, and couldn't do it. Few enough reasons for a hard-booted
stranger to be doing that, none at all for her. So she'd come
with someone. Statistically likely candidates, father or boyfriend,
and boyfriend surely more likely; a girl didn't often go out
walking with her father. Not at night, not at seventeen.

The boyfriend was all cropped hair and tattoos, no surprise;
and the father must have looked just the same when he was
younger.

'Knock her about a bit, did you, lad? Last week, I mean,
not last night?'

'Nah, not me.'

'Someone did.'

'That'll be her dad,' he said. 'On her all the time, her dad.
But so what, anyway? What about the bastard did her over,
that's your job.'

*I think all you bastards did her over. Over and over, that's
how I think you did her . . .*

Talking to a girlfriend:

'Yeah, they did, they beat her up. Both of 'em. Not together,
like, but they both did it.'

'Why did she put up with it?'

'Nowhere else to go, was there? Home's home.'

'She could have stopped seeing her boyfriend.'

'Aye, she said that. She said she was going to finish with him, maybe.'

'Uh-huh,' and another motive, another reason to get kicked, if she wanted to kick him. If she told him. 'Have anyone else in mind, did she?'

'There was this lad, yeah. Don't know if she ever went out with him, like, but she wanted to . . .'

Not hard, to find the other lad. The girlfriend had his name. Feed that into the computer, and bingo: an address, a record, a brand-new theory.

And a sad sigh, a shake of the head, *Oh, lass, lass. Why did you keep doing this to yourself? Why do it over and over again?*

Because she was seventeen, of course, and she thought she would always heal. She thought she was immortal. Didn't they all?

The record said here was another guy who knew how to use his feet, all the way from common assault to GBH. Nine months in prison for that one, and he'd only been out for three; and the address was a flat just over the road from the new estate, only five minutes' walk from where they'd found her.

So a hard knocking, fist on wood, and then a foot in the door as soon as it opened; and because he was watching his feet, he saw this lad's feet as well.

Saw big shiny paratrooper boots, excellent for kicking but not a scuff, not a mark on them; and swore silently as he flashed his ID.

The lad bridled without conviction, flexed his tattoos uncertainly.

'Nice boots, son. New, are they?'

'Yeah. Yeah, they are. Got 'em in the market. Good, eh?' And he wasn't challenging, he wasn't confrontational, he wasn't right at all.

'Terrific. So what have you done with the old ones, then? Have a look at them, can I?'

'Nah, they're gone. Put 'em out with the rubbish, like . . .'

Uh-huh. That meant a happy day or two for a vanload of constables, sifting through shit on the council dump. And all a waste of time, because those boots wouldn't be there, they'd be in the river. If they went in at the right time, just at the turn, they'd be halfway to Norway by now.

He took the lad in anyway, on general principles and utter personal certainty. No chance of charging him without a confession, and no real chance of that; but a man could dream. And he had it in his dreams that if by some fluke this ever did come to court, he'd want to say to the judge something that judges had all too often, all too outrageously said for themselves:

She was asking for it, your honour, he'd want to say, and would never have the chance. *That's why she got herself into this. For kicks, for the kickings. It's all she knew, you see, it's the only way she had to measure affection. Everyone who ought to love her beat her up. That's what love was, what it meant. So the worse she caught it, the better she was doing. The more the bastard loved her, do you see?*

Taking a break from the interview room, from the sound of his own voice hammering against a sullen silence, he walked through the story one more time. The wind threw a hard rain against big signs as he passed, *Development Corporation* and *European Funds*, all the machinery that kept a battered city breathing against the odds.

What goes around comes around, he thought, like bad music snagged in the head, repeating and repeating. History marches with its boots on, and always in circles. Why kick against it?

Walking in circles, he came to that sculpture again, red stone more deeply stained with red. Weather would see to that, he thought, no need for scrubbing brushes. Weather was time's tool, and irresistible. Some day too soon there'd be nothing left of her bar the husk of her body in a hospital bed, maintained by vigilant machines.

And one of these days – when it was politic, when it was advisable – they were going to turn off the machines.

encounter with Sheehey had filled her with excite-
iveliness.

ub that evening I had just rung the service bell, my
y the drinks, when there was a great hullabaloo
y of murder went up and near the whole establish-
to crowd into the back alley, gawking to see and
John Crowther and he had been cut and his collar
s were dark with blood.

da who raised the alarm and she had smears of blood
ds and her face and when the policemen came they
n interest in her. I was bound to say my piece and
might speak in private to an officer and there was a
ering among my fellows, all keen with curiosity.

dlord's parlour was given over to us and I told the
about Ada and Donal Sheehey, and I described
dalliance and how John Crowther beat his daughter
erhaps Crowther caught them and the Sheehey lad
him in self-defence.

vengeance for the beating?' the officer supposed.
spiracy to get rid of the man? Did the daughter put
p to it?'

ould she call for help if she were party to the deed,'
hereby setting herself up to be pilloried? Find
I urged the man. 'See if he can give a true account
f.'

y was discovered at the station waiting for the milk
with no baggage. He told them he was innocent but
would be blamed for his association with Ada.
claimed innocence. And begged for Sheehey's life.
l was only twenty, surely his youth would be a
ion.

al was held in Lancaster. Sheehey was tried alone
found him guilty. Much was made of his butchery
Crowther's neck was slit wide open. Sheehey was
to hang and the appeal for clemency was denied
hanged him at dawn on the last day of August.

rowther gone the family faced hard times indeed.
decided to ask her sister-in-law in Halifax to take
Leonora could barely look at Ada or say her name,

CATH STAINCLIFFE –
TWO BIRDS

The trouble started that Easter, in 1871. That's when John Crowther caught sight of his eldest girl, Ada, walking out with the Sheehey lad, Donal. When Ada came home, John was waiting, the poker in his hand, ready to knock some sense into her. I could hear the ructions through the wall, Ada screaming and John shouting, 'No daughter of mine will be seen dead with a Fenian bastard like Donal Sheehey,' and Leonora wailing in the background, imploring him to stop.

Our Violet began to cry, 'Dada, Dada,' and I set down my whittling and took her on my knee and jiggled her about and by-and-by she quietened. She was too little for me to explain why they were fighting next door. It was times like that I missed Betty most keenly. We would have shared our thoughts on the matter and near enough always saw things in the same light. But Betty had never recovered after her laying-in and I was a widower and Violet motherless.

Next time I saw Ada, walking up to the mill, she was in a sorry state. He'd blacked her eyes and broken her nose. The bruising would heal but with her nose spoiled she had lost her looks for good. Seemed to me the beating had hardened her, for she did not hide the wounds but walked with her chin up, mouth set tight.

He was a pig of a man, Crowther, no gainsaying that, but I did wonder how I would act once Violet was of age and looking for a sweetheart. If she took up with some shyster or ne'er-do-well, what would I do? Not that Sheehey was a shirker, he worked at the abattoir, but Crowther could never see beyond the colour of his religion.

I would not beat my girl, I was clear on that. My own father had been quick with his fists and vicious with the birch. It

taught me neither respect nor obedience but only a fierce
loathing of the man and, when I was old enough, I burnt the
birch and told him if he raised his hand to me or anyone in
the place I'd make my own way and he'd not have a farthing
of my wages for the house. By then I was already working as
a bobbin maker, a better position than he had ever had.

He nearly burst at my bare-faced cheek, his face like beetroot
and knives in his eyes. Then he tried to smile, wriggling like
a spaniel, and said, 'Even your mother?' 'Even my mother,'
I told him. Three weeks he lasted. Then he belted my mother
and tried to tell a tale about it and I left. I sent for her, for
her and the rest, when I had found a couple of rooms to rent,
but they stayed with him. So after that I had no family around
me to speak of.

I asked Ada to sit in with Violet some nights when there
were meetings I wished to attend or a lecture at the Reading
Rooms. I left her bread and cake and tea in the pot. Her hair
was the colour of wheat, silken in the firelight, and her eyes
the palest blue, like a glaze on fine china. We made small talk,
nothing of consequence, and I gave her a little money which
she always refused at first but took at my insistence. When I
saw that poor misshapen nose it made my gorge rise. Not at
the sight itself but at the manner of its destruction, John almost
twice the size of Ada and mad as a bull and her defenceless
and at his mercy.

Wakes Week was in June, as usual, all of the town out on
holiday and the looms still and silent. Near enough everyone
went to Blackpool. I took Violet. We always stayed in the same
guesthouse along with other folk from hereabouts. Whole streets
in Blackpool you could name what mill or factory the visitors
were from.

The Crowthers were in my place, on the ground floor.
Leonora was always pleasant, petting our Violet and passing
the time of day. John and I would exchange a nod, no more.
I had scant regard for the man and I assume the feeling was
mutual. He probably found me weak natured, the way I
attended to Violet by myself instead of lodging her with rela-
tions or finding a new wife to do it for me.

When I was at work, Violet went to my neighbour on

the other side, Mabel, who had eight of
others. Mabel and her gang were two do
and she would enjoy the rare treat of l
bed of an evening knowing the landlady
them while all us parents could make

That first evening, we had a knees-up
was full to the rafters, the waiters fighti
trays of mild and stout and port and
man too with his tray. I troubled him f
sour with vinegar and tasted of brine an
with sand. I'd a moment's loneliness t
liked them.

Pushing my way out to the privy, I
Crowther going through the side door
swear to it, was Donal Sheehey. The
him round our way since Easter and
had found some other girl to tip his
of her, carrying on with him, and un
well.

I spied them most nights, Ada sli
wondered that John had not. Though S
into the midst of the saloon but waite
and Ada stole out to meet him. And
the hour, at nine. I thought I should
to their liaison, surely I was not the

Tongues would tattle.

On the Thursday, as I was leaving
her but she was not in any of the roo
outside, the yard and all about, and
against the far wall, I saw two fig
heard a woman's moan and I was s

Our last day on the beach was fir
When the donkeys came, Violet w
ride on the smallest animal but as
she bawled her head off. The wo
back.

All the Crowthers were at the be
and Ada seemed carefree, laughir
wondered if I had mistaken her th

Or
ment
At
turn t
and th
ment
there
and cl
It w
on her
took a
asked
lot of
The
policer
the nig
and tha
had kil
'Was
'Or a c
Sheehe
'Why
I said,
Sheehe
for him
Shee
train an
feared h
Ada
The
consider
The t
and they
skills, f
sentence
and they
With
Leonora
them in.

for had Ada not been making mischief with Donal Sheehey then John Crowther would still be walking God's own earth. And it was clear that there would be no place in the Halifax house for Ada.

I put my solution to Leonora first, to test the water, and she became weepy with gratitude. Ada less so, though biddable. I would marry the girl and so grant her respectability though no doubt some would mutter that I was an old goat and that she was damaged goods. Violet would have a new mother and a woman's touch would warm my home again.

She sits now, smocking by the fire, her hair glints gold. She spends too much time wool-gathering. I suspect she daydreams of her Fenian boy, of those stolen moments. But I have her now. That steeliness she showed after Crowther broke her face has been curbed. The loss of father and sweetheart has, I think, left her reeling. I am a rock she may cling to.

She will not talk to me about Donal; she wants to keep her secrets.

As I keep mine.

That Thursday night in Blackpool, awake all the hours, imagining her up against the wall, the moan she made. Dog-tired and punch-drunk on the beach the next day, watching her in the waves, the flush of her cheeks as she splashed her sisters, her costume close fitting, her hair beneath her cap whipping as she twirled, her giggling a tickle in the pit of my stomach.

Later, watching the clock at the bar, knowing he came at nine. Buying Crowther a drink and a second, listening to him whining about his lot. Then I go to the privy, spying Ada still in the snug with the women as I hoped, and I fetch John Crowther. Ask his help, one of the lads is in a bad way, puddled with drink. Crowther has no suspicion.

I walk around the alley to make a show of looking about. 'The sot has vanished,' I say. Soon as Crowther's back is turned, I grab him from behind, one hand clasping his forehead and with my knife I slit him. It's quick like that and only a little blood on my hands which comes off in the old horse trough.

Minutes later I am ringing for drinks, the life and soul, while Ada keeps her assignation and finds her father and comes running in. And the commotion sends Sheehey haring like a dog from the traps, setting in motion his downfall.

Two birds, one stone.

I lay my palm upon her golden hair, feel the heat beneath, and she follows me upstairs.

She will learn to moan for me. And me alone.

MARGARET MURPHY – BIG END BLUES

The moment I clapped eyes on her I knew she was trouble. So what did I do? You guessed it – I took a few steps back, broke into a run, and did a flying leap into her arms. That's me all over: always hitching my cart to the wrong pony. Thing is, she's got style, has Jemma. They say imitation's the sincerest form of flattery – well, with us it wasn't so much imitation as co-ordination. We wanted to make an impact, and since Jemma's eye for colour and texture is more refined than mine, and she's a little older than me – twenty-three years of wisdom to my nineteen – I tend to follow her lead. So, I went along with her choice. I mean in *every* detail. Skirt, blouse, jacket, shoes – even those little extras that fashion shops call 'accessories'. If Jemma bought it, so did I. We shuffled the colours around a bit – you don't want to look ridiculous, do you? But in all essentials we were identical.

It was Jemma came up with our showbiz name. We were in a shop. Hers was a black denim jacket, red skirt, white scooped-neck T-shirt. Mine was red jacket, black skirt – the tops were the same, as I recall. She looked at us, a glory of patchwork side by side in the mirror and said it straight off: 'The Harlequin Twins'. It was a joke of course. You had to see us to get it. I sometimes wonder what folk make of us, her a tall, willowy blonde and me, a short, well-stacked brunette.

She has a good length of stride, does Jemma – pretty impressive in stilettos. If you've ever worn them, you'll know what I mean. She glides, I wobble, but only a bit, and very fetchingly, I'm told.

We do a double act – on and off stage. Country and Western mostly – and when the mood takes her Jemma can work the Mississippi Delta into her everyday chat like she was born to it.

We were having a bad day. A grey December afternoon in the north of England is depressing enough, but our transport was well and truly knackered, and it looked like we'd have to cancel our gig because we didn't have the wherewithal to pay for repairs. A grey December afternoon in the north of England with no escape route – that's death on wheels – except our wheels weren't rolling.

'Big end's gone,' the mechanic said, slamming the bonnet and wiping his hands on a filthy towel.

'Why, thank you, honey,' Jemma said, fluttering her eyelids and twanging all over the place. 'All that dieting's been worth the while.' She slid her hands over her perfectly toned buttocks just to hammer home the point, but he wasn't having it. She was wearing the white denim skirt – thigh length (just) – and the fringed nubuck jacket in red. Shoes to match the jacket and morals to match the skirt – at least that's the gist of what she was trying to put over to him.

He just narrowed his eyes and carried on wiping his hands. Must've been gay. It's always worked before: she gets the job done on the promise she'll make it up to him after we've got the van back – well, she can't very well have him handling the goods with those grimy palms, can she? Of course, by the time he arrives at The Dog and Duck, all spruced up in his best jeans and trainers, we're halfway down the M6, twenty minutes from our next gig.

We were set up for a theme pub in Birmingham. All the staff dress up as cowboys and cowgirls. Four slots over two nights. The pay's all right, if you can manage your money, but Jemma's got a hunger for shopping and we wouldn't be the Harlequin Twins if I didn't keep up, now, would we? Besides, on the road, you've got other expenses, like food and drink, make-up, equipment, but Mike the mechanic wasn't playing, and it looked like our motor problem would be the big end of a beautiful partnership.

We decided to think about it.

When Jemma needs to think, she walks. So we walked. Every few steps I had to run a bit just to keep up. We fetched up a couple of miles away, near the docks. Empty warehouses on one side of the road, a flattened plot on the other. Someone had put up a billboard: *Industrial land with outline planning permission.* Some hope.

Jemma stopped at the bus shelter and wiped the seat with a paper tissue, parking her bum carefully on the edge of the narrow yellow strip of plastic. Which made me think.

'Plastic,' I said, sitting next to her.

'No.' Jemma has a rule, kind of a code of honour – never upset your credit-card companies. Why? Because they pay for your clothes. We were already up to our limit on account of the Birmingham gig demanding a new outfit each. 'No plastic,' she said.

I shrugged. They would probably have checked our credit-worthiness anyhow.

Just then, a big, wheezy old removals van pulled up at the kerb, throbbing with pent-up bass rhythms. A bloke got out – well, I say 'bloke'. He was more simian than *Sapiens*. Bloody huge, fat and all, but enough muscle so you wouldn't be tempted to call him names. He opened the cab door and the music boomed out, loud enough to rattle your teeth loose. He jumped down with a wrench of some sort in his hand. Big wide thing it was, with handles both ends, like a plane propeller – a device with wings, to avoid embarrassing slippage – only for men.

Jemma looked over at him and said, 'Hey, love, you couldn't turn that shit down, could you?' No offence in it, just a polite request.

He growled – no, seriously – he really *growled*, like a dog, only bigger and meaner. And twice as dangerous. He started towards us with that bloody great wrench in his hand and I think, *there's nobody between us and the river.* This bloke could do whatever he wanted and we wouldn't be able to raise a minor quibble, never mind an objection.

We ran. God knows where we thought we were running *to*, but when someone as ugly as that looks at you like that, you don't think, you just run – anywhere, so long as it's *away*. He lobbed the wrench and I got it between the shoulder blades. I went down hard, about halfway across the road.

I'm winded and crying. I see this shadow over me like in

some horror flick and I roll over, so at least I can see what's coming. He bends down and lifts me by the front of my jacket and I think, *I'm dead*. Then I hear Jemma, like her voice is coming from far off, but it's clear.

'Pooky,' she says, 'Now don't you be a grizzly old bear. You know we didn't mean no harm.' Where she got Pooky from, I don't know. She's always coming up with names like that – she thinks they sound authentic Southern USA.

The big bastard drops me, and I fall on my back, whooping, trying to get my breath. Jemma's standing the other side of me, smiling, swinging that shiny wrench back and forth between her legs. Her image doubles, quadruples, on and on, like a thousand tiny images in a glitter-ball and I think, *Oh, God no – Jemma don't—*

She pays the mechanic in cash, not wasting a smile on him this time, just completes the transaction and leaves. I'm driving. The van's never sounded so good. We motor for a while with the radio turned down low.

'All right?' she asks.

I'm not, but I nod anyway, gripping the wheel tight to stop my hands shaking.

She sorted everything. Got him off the road, over to his lorry. I helped her drag him on a piece of tarp we found in the back. It was empty aside from that one piece of ratty tarp. I said a prayer he had finished for the day, that someone wasn't waiting on a doorstep, checking the time, anxious for the removals man to arrive. We draped him over the engine and closed the bonnet over him. He looked like one of those joke dummies you sometimes see, halfway up a wall – Santa with a sackful of goodies, that kind of thing.

'It won't fool anyone, you know,' I say.

'Correction,' she says. 'It won't fool anyone *for long*.' Just long enough for us to get away, she meant. I suppose she thinks I'm being ungrateful. 'In the meantime . . .' She digs into her handbag and fans a handful of cash. 'Enough to be going on with.'

I nibble my lip and she sighs. 'Cherise, honey, I'm gonna say this one more time.' She doesn't often turn the Southern charm on for me. My stomach lurches – because when she does, it means trouble. 'But this is the *very* last time.' She checks off the points on her fingers. 'Nobody saw us. We left no finger-prints. Not one bitsy clue. And it's not like he knew us. Who's going to suspect two sweet little ladies like you'n'me?' She bats her eyelashes and looks at me all innocent.

She's making me nervous, but I've got to admit she'd been thorough. Insisted on walking back into the city centre, rather than get a taxi, despite my bad back. She wore a disguise, so when she tried the numbers he had considerately written on a scrap of paper alongside his credit cards in his wallet, she was unrecognizable. I wouldn't have known her – her own *mother* wouldn't have known her in that get-up. Dark glasses, I would have expected, but she also wore a woolly hat – not a strand of hair showing – she even bought some cotton-wool balls and stuffed them in her mouth to fatten her cheeks. I was impressed. Jemma is vain: she doesn't make herself look plain without a damn good reason.

'They take pictures at cash-tills these days, you know,' she told me. Proud of herself.

I'm proud of her, too. Me – I'd've walked into the nearest cop shop and made a tearful confession. Ruined the rest of my life. Not Jemma. Still, I *am* nervous – kind of in awe of her.

'Pull over.'

I do as I'm told. A quick glance around and then she drops Pooky's wallet down a drain at the side of the road.

'Untraceable, see? And that's the end of it.'

I want to believe her, honest I do. But she's got that look on her, like the day she gave us our stage name, and I know that this is only the start. For Jemma and Cherise read *Thelma and Louise*. It's only a matter of time.

MARTIN EDWARDS – BAD FRIDAY

'*I want you out of my life! I just wish you would die!*'
Like a chisel ripping through flesh, the woman's voice pierces the hubbub in Coach U. I'm wedged in the carriage entrance as a morbidly obese businessman blocks the aisle while trying to squeeze his bulging suitcase in between two seats. The woman swears, and I wince as hot rage pours from an unseen mouth into the sweaty air.

The first off-peak train on a Friday evening from Euston to Liverpool Lime Street is always jam-packed. To make matters worse, the previous train has been cancelled – leaves on the line, or the wrong kind of rain, or some other excuse, I don't know – and this one teems with specimens of exhausted humanity desperately seeking unreserved seats.

The fat bloke abandons the unequal struggle, and disappears down the train, matching fat suitcase in hand. As people push forward, I lean against a luggage rack and catch my breath. I've not felt so exhausted since the last weeks of my pregnancy. There is nowhere to stash my bag, but at least I can keep hold of it. Anything rather than the embarrassment of finding I'm the victim of a thief.

The train lurches forward, and I catch sight of the woman who wants someone dead. She's lucky enough to have bagged a seat, but is staring at her iPhone with the sort of concentrated disgust that only a faithless lover can inspire. I can't tell whether she's hung up on him, or he's hung up on her. She is in her mid-twenties, with luxuriant dark hair and lips whose default expression is a spoiled-brat's pout. Because she has over-indulged in fake tan, and under-dressed for an October evening, a great deal of orange flesh is on display. If Josh were here, he'd find it hard to resist ogling. But I must stop thinking about him. Josh and I aren't together any longer.

The orange-skinned woman stabs the dialling pad with a purple fingernail, and screeches, 'It's me!' at precisely the moment we enter the tunnel outside Euston. Losing the connection provokes her into a lurid bout of swearing, and this prompts the old chap sitting next to her to bury his head in the *Evening Standard*. I read the headlines on the other side of the paper – *Stock market plunges, Celebrity couple split, Hoxton minimart stabbings: 'no arrest imminent', Chelsea striker suspended* – and, shuddering, avert my eyes. A young couple in the seats opposite Ms Orange murmur to each other in a foreign language I can't identify. I find myself hoping their command of English isn't good enough to enable them to understand what she is saying.

As we emerge from the tunnel into the evening gloom, the train manager announces that the shop and buffet car are open and, after apologizing for the overcrowded conditions, he offers a sweetener: a few free seats in the first-class carriages are being made available for the common herd. Those of the common herd (sorry, customers) who still haven't found seats stampede towards the rear of the train, and they are joined by the elderly man next to Ms Orange, who grabs his ancient bag and dashes for freedom with an unexpected turn of speed.

Quick as a flash, I thrust my own case into the newly created space on the luggage rack, and plonk myself down right next to Ms Orange, where I can keep an eye on it. At once I discover that her perfume is as pungent as her voice is loud and her manners vile. Never mind; after a long and dispiriting day of foot-slogging around Hackney, I'd rather endure an unpleasantly close encounter for two and a quarter hours than stand for one more minute.

I glance at the *Evening Standard* that the man abandoned in his haste to escape. Opinion pieces about the quest for a kinder, gentler politics – good luck with that – and the fact that our police are no longer wonderful. I'm not tempted to read them. It's been a bad, bad Friday – and it's the thirteenth of the month; perhaps there's something in the old superstition. The weekend offers minimal prospect of rest and recuperation. I'm dying to sweep Barnaby up in my arms, of course, and at least the sight of his tousled hair and big brown eyes will more than compensate for the pain of encountering Josh and Erica again. I have a recurrent nightmare that one day I'll go back to Aigburth to see my son, and he won't recognize me. Mum says it's my own fault, and I hate to admit it, but she's right. She's even hinted that Barnaby is starting to care more for Erica than for me.

I'm ashamed I'm not looking forward to staying with Mum, and not simply because Archie is an old bore. I'm the child of a broken marriage, perhaps it's in the genes, and I'm destined to see my own relationships forever falling apart. Or perhaps Mum's also right when she says I love my work more than I do any of the men who have flitted through my life. Archie is a tedious old sexist who treats Mum like a servant, but at least he's hung around for the past ten years, and grows tasty vegetables in his allotment for her to cook.

Ms Orange indicates with a graceless shuffle of her thighs that she wants to get out of her seat, and I stand up and move aside to let her past. Neither of us speaks. Is she, too, destined for the first-class coaches? Somehow I doubt I'm going to be so lucky. I offer a politely conspiratorial smile to the foreign couple opposite, but they are wholly preoccupied with each other, their mutual devotion a stinging reminder of what I've thrown away. I close my eyes, but I can't get Josh's sad face out of my mind. The sadness in his eyes when he said enough was enough will haunt me to the grave. How could I not have realized I'd made such a mess of everything?

I'm still scarifying myself mentally when a loud noise rouses me. Ms Orange is back, bearing a paper bag crammed with smelly train food. I'm betting her knack of conveying impatience and bad temper is the product of years of practice. I haul myself to my feet with an insincere smile of apology, and resist the temptation to stamp on her toes as she shoves past me. I regret my self-restraint instantly, as she pokes a sharp elbow into my midriff in the process of sitting down.

After watching her take out of the bag a burger with onions, a KitKat, and a small bottle of Shiraz, I resort to eye-closing once more, trying in vain neither to inhale, nor visualize her chomping away with her mouth open. The sound effects alone are graphic enough to demand a health warning.

She's just started slurping down the wine when a rap music ringtone hits me like a cannonball. My eyes are forced open as she starts bellowing into the iPhone to someone called Sheena about the awfulness of her ex, but my attention isn't really roused until, ten minutes into a rant studded with obscenities, she mentions his name.

'I told him, I'm never going to help you out again, no matter what. You treat me like a slave, Josh, I said, and I'm not standing for it no more.'

For a wild, fantastic moment, I wonder if she's talking about my Josh. Or, at least, the Josh who used to be mine. Could he be two-timing Erica? Suppose he'd met Ms Orange on the rebound, and decided he wanted someone crude and curvy as a replacement for a tall, thin, twitchy workaholic. Might he have an unsuspected craving for implants and neck tattoos? You can't put anything past a man, that's for sure. But it makes no sense – the world is full of Joshes. Including that other Josh, the one who these past few days has crowded even my ex-husband out of my thoughts. I'm still not sure whether that's a good thing, or bad.

A brief period of respite follows. Ms Orange's complacent smile tells me that Sheena is reassuring her that she was wasted on Josh anyway. But then we enter another tunnel, and she bangs the iPhone down on the table separating us from the foreign couple. Predictably, this cracks the screen, prompting another fusillade of obscenities as she inspects the damage. The pair sitting opposite don't turn a hair.

The rapper returns as we speed through the Midlands, giving me my cue to get up and amble off in search of a cup of coffee. I take my time, only to find on my return that Ms Orange is deep in conversation with yet another friend. This time it's Kayleigh who is being treated to an exhaustive account of Josh's offensive habits and profound unworthiness. Unfortunately, it seems that in happier times Ms Orange acquired a Josh-related tattoo on an intimate part of her anatomy. Kayleigh once had a similar problem, apparently, and they debate the drawbacks of laser treatment.

Why do people talk so loudly about personal stuff on train journeys? I suppose they think it doesn't matter – people within earshot don't know them, and their paths won't ever cross in future. I try to shut out her furious East End tones, but it isn't easy. There's no escape; on my foray to carriage C for coffee, I passed several people sitting on suitcases, who no doubt presumed that those spare first-class seats would all be filled by the time they made their way to the other end of the train. At least we're not far from Stafford now. Anyway, I suppose I'm a professional nosey parker.

The foreign couple are stroking each other's hands. It's sweet, but also excruciating, if you've messed up pretty much every relationship you've ever had. I take refuge in the Closed Eye Ploy, fantasizing that the train will get stuck in an unexpected snowdrift in the middle of nowhere, and that Ms Orange's ranting will provoke all her fellow passengers (sorry, customers) into a joint enterprise murder plot. Before long, images from a different movie, an old black-and-white thriller about strangers on a train, start floating through my head. How about offering Ms Orange a deal – I'll kill your Josh if you kill mine?

But no. Not a good idea. Apart from anything else, I wouldn't trust her not to mess up. She might even try a spot of blackmail, in preference to murder. Besides, I don't really want Josh to die. He's not a bad man, even if he did move in with my sister a matter of weeks after our marriage finally broke down. I suspect most people blame me and my obsession with work for our break-up, and I'm certain that Erica chased him rather than the other way around. All the same, the day he left me in London to go back to Aigburth, taking Barnaby with him, I could have killed him – possibly with my bare hands. If I hadn't been out on a job, that is. Call me a lousy mother – plenty of people have – but I'm still not confident that I'm ready to look after our son on my own, two hundred miles away from domestic back-up. I'd have to ask Mum to be there for him when I'm working away. Or, even worse, beg Erica for help. I don't wish her dead, either, but we're not on speaking terms right now. She's always been a bird of prey, but I never expected her to catch my husband. How long will it take for her to chew him up and spit him out? It's what she always does. You could call it her m.o.

A patch of countryside with poor mobile coverage kills Ms Orange's latest conversation, and the moment her signal is restored, the rapper heralds a call from someone wanting to make an appointment with her. Apparently, Ms Orange is a mobile hair stylist. There are plenty of them around, of course, just as there are plenty of Joshes. Even so, my ears prick up as Ms Orange takes careful note of the new client's address in Hackney, and when she gives her own email address, I commit it to memory. No longer am I quite so desperate for her to pipe down.

The appointment fixed, we arrive at Stafford, and Ms Orange rings another friend, Pixie. From the frequent references to an ailing mam – evidently in hospital at Arrowe Park at the moment – you don't need to be Stella Gibson or Sarah Lund to deduce that Pixie is her sister. I suppose it's a point in their favour that she and Pixie seem much closer than Erica and me. Their mother had a heart attack, I gather, while on a pilgrimage to Liverpool to visit John Lennon's birthplace. As for Pixie, far from wanting to snare Josh for herself, she seems to be egging Ms Orange on in her denunciation of her ex. Not like Erica at all; after dumping her own husband, she never made any secret of her interest in mine. Do I believe that they only got together after Josh and I split? Probably it's true, and anyway, who cares? I never thought Erica was Josh's type, one more mistake in a long line. Water under the bridge.

'I lied for him,' Ms Orange says. My eyes remain shut, but now I'm agog, 'I risked my own neck, when Mam was hovering between life and death. And you know what? He didn't even say thank you.'

The diatribe goes on and on, giving me plenty of time to reflect on human nature's oddities. Ms Orange complaining about discourtesy? Pot, meet kettle. But for all her loudness, rudeness, and sheer unpleasantness, I'm starting to warm to her. Is it possible she could improve my day?

'You're right,' she tells Pixie. 'He deserves what's coming to him.'

I send a text to Andrew, asking him to remind me of a name. Within a minute a reply pings, and I sneak a glance. *Daniella Blyth.*

All the way to Crewe and beyond, I keep willing Ms Orange to explain herself in words of one syllable. But she enjoys insulting her ex too much to say anything worthwhile. Not to worry. Instinct tells me I'm on to something. And then I remind myself that my instinct is hardly infallible.

This is different, though. It's business, not personal. I'm hoping for more information, but by the time we reach Runcorn, she's announced that she never wants to think about him again. She just wants him out of her life. As she said before.

Well, it might just be I could play Fairy Godmother, and grant your wish.

We're slowing down on the approach to Edge Hill, close to our destination in the heart of Liverpool, when I steal another look at Andrew's text. This time, I put my phone down on a small patch of the table untouched by the mess made by Ms Orange's meal. It catches her eye.

She turns her head, and stares at me. Something flickers in her expression. Yes, there is outrage, but also I recognize fear.

'What's going on?' she demands.

I gaze straight back at her. 'Daniella Blyth?'

She squints at the foreign couple, as if suspecting them of working undercover. 'Who wants to know?'

The train slows. In a few moments, we'll pull in to Lime Street. Like a conjuror plucking a pigeon from his sleeve, I take out my warrant card.

'Detective Sergeant Leanne Wood, Metropolitan Police.'

The orange cheeks redden as the horror of what she's said begins to dawn. 'You've been earwigging, you nosy bitch.'

'Hard to avoid hearing what you had to say, Daniella.'

She launches into another volley of obscenities, but I see in her fuddled eyes that she can't recall exactly what she's said out loud. Probably she thinks she's given more away than she did. That's the trouble with a guilty conscience. It's not compatible with a big mouth.

I soak up the abuse for half a minute before saying, 'It's not you we're after. It's Josh.'

And then I watch as dismay gives way to calculation. She's been caught out. She knows as well as I do that she's facing a charge of perverting the course of justice in a double murder case. But she's also streetwise enough to realize the advantage of playing a 'get out of jail' card. So often doing justice depends on changing loyalties. If Daniella wants Josh to die, she may be more than happy to help us to arrest him on suspicion of murdering Saeed Anwar and Begum Anwar at Hoxton in London seven days ago. All she needs to do is to withdraw the alibi she gave him when Andrew interviewed her.

The story was that the pair of them had been occupying each other in bed in Daniella's flat at the time a man in a crash helmet tried to rob Anwar's minimart in Hoxton, and when the owner and his daughter refused to hand over the takings and rang an alarm, stabbed them both in a panic before fleeing the scene. Saeed suffered a ruptured liver and died at the scene. Begum's throat was cut; she only lasted forty-eight hours. The incident took less than two minutes from start to finish, and was captured on an ancient CCTV, but the images were too blurry for us to identify the killer beyond doubt. Our top five suspects included a local petty criminal called Joshua Hughes, but Andrew couldn't crack his alibi, and our attention turned elsewhere. Not that I or my colleagues have got very far. My own inquiries have amounted to one dead end after another. So it's been a tough old week, though a thousand times harder for the grieving widow and mother.

'All right,' Daniella says, as we pull into the station. 'But you'll have to do me a deal. I'll want to call a lawyer. You lot aren't to be trusted.'

I stand up and pull out my case, trying to disguise my exultation. I've even figured out why I didn't recognize her from the photo pinned to the whiteboard in the incident room. She's changed her hairstyle and colour, as well as going over-board on the fake tan.

'I trust you to co-operate, Daniella. After all you've said about him.'

She glares, before giving an *easy-come-easy-go* shrug. We get out of the train together. I don't want to let her out of my sight, but I doubt she'll try making a run for it. She probably thinks I've recorded everything she's said, all the way up from Euston.

We walk along the platform, side by side. At the barrier, I glimpse two familiar faces. Josh – *my* Josh – and Barnaby. What are they doing here? It wasn't in the script. Barnaby's waving excitedly, and Josh is wearing a sheepish grin and flourishing a bunch of red roses. No sign of Erica.

Don't tell me that he's dumped her?

For a mad moment, I forget that I'm a woman police officer, just as Josh has so often wanted me to forget my work. I drop my suitcase, and run to the barrier, arms outstretched. For a moment, I even forget about Daniella.

I swerve Josh's attempted hug and embrace Barnaby. It'll take more than a bunch of flowers to make amends. But even as I clutch my warm little boy and hear my ex's stammered words of apology, I remind myself that it takes two to screw up. Let's see how the weekend goes. I'd better not say too much. So often it's a terrible mistake.

We walk out of the station together, with Barnaby between us, chattering nineteen to the dozen. Almost like old times. Who would have believed? It's finally Good Friday.

CHRIS SIMMS – THE PASSENGER

K ay Wilson surveyed the items on the baked asphalt and sighed. Heat crashed onto her from the blue sky above. 'Terry, I'm not being funny, but how the hell are we going to carry all this?'

Her husband closed the boot of the car and turned round. He had a large sun parasol in his left hand. 'We'll manage, doll, don't you worry.' He propped the parasol against the rear of the car and lifted a picnic bag by its long shoulder strap. 'Put your head through here. You can wear it across your back. That leaves your hands free for the deckchairs. I'll carry the rest.'

'Why can't we just do two trips?'

'I'm not trudging all the way back. Prefer to leave the windbreak in the boot than do that.'

'We can't leave the windbreak.'

'How about that massive bag with your stupid Lilo in?'

The main thing she'd been looking forward to was floating in the shallows on the Lilo. Just like she'd have done if they'd actually gone on their proper holiday to Spain. 'Oh, pass me the bloody chairs and let's get going.'

With each step, the sand shifted beneath Kay's feet. In less than a minute, she could feel the thud of her heart. A trickle of sweat teased its way into one eyebrow. She felt like one of those refugees off the telly. 'Won't here do?'

Terry glanced back. 'Look – we get beyond that lot with the blue and white windbreak. Not a soul! Beach to ourselves.'

That was easily another hundred metres. Her calf muscles were aching. It wasn't all that crowded where they were. Two young couples, one of them with a toddler in a sun shelter. A solitary man who looked fast asleep. Ever since the bloody COVID thing, Terry was like a man on a mission. Social distancing, in his book, meant going to the supermarket late at night. Wiping down every letter the postman delivered. Opening doors with his little finger. Needing to get her breath, she plonked the deckchairs down and turned to the beach behind her.

Further along, the pier jutted out into the sparkling sea. At its far end, a steep ramp dropped straight down into the water. She used to sit on the beach for hours with Gavin, waiting to see if the lifeboat would be launched. Maybe that was the start of her son's interest in boats. To think of him now in the Navy. Amazing.

A whiff of curry almost made Kay sneeze. The smell was heavy and cloying. Enough to turn her stomach on a hot day like this. She turned to the blue and white windbreak a little way in front. She could hear a lot of different voices coming from behind it and none of them were speaking English. One of them straightened up and she clocked his jet-black hair. Fuck's sake. Could they not just settle for sandwiches like normal people? She picked up the deckchairs, now happy to walk on.

'How's this? Not bad, hey?' Terry announced. 'Bit of effort and it all pays off.'

He'd dumped their stuff on the far side of a knee-high groyne, the gnarled timbers peppered with white barnacles. 'And an extra, ready-made windbreak, too.'

'Just happy we're upwind of the lot back there,' she muttered, dropping the chairs down. 'It's not even midday and they're cooking that muck.'

He briefly scowled in their direction. 'There was method in my madness. Right, let's get set up.' Unfurling the windbreak, he nodded at the smaller bag. 'Mallet's in there, love.'

Once everything was in place, they slumped down in the deckchairs with their legs stretched out before them. Kay kicked her flip-flops off, dug her heels deep enough to feel cool sand and closed her eyes. 'Who needs the Costa Brava when we get days like this?'

She heard the rustle of the newspaper as Terry opened it out. Moments later, he tutted. 'Six boats made it across yesterday.'

'Six!'

'The country's full to the brim. Where the hell will they go? There's no more bloody room.'

'No idea.' She glanced at the chiller bag, reminding herself that, when it came to lunch, she needed to give the tomatoes a decent wash. On this programme the other day, it had shown the sort of people who picked the stuff out in Spain. Black as the ace of spades, the lot of them.

'And the bloody French are just waving them over. It's a total disgrace.'

Better stop him before he gets going, she thought. 'Terry, be a star and blow the Lilo up, would you?'

'Now?'

She tilted her head to the side and gave him one of her looks. 'Please? Before you get into that paper.'

'I've just sat down.'

'I know. But I want to have a little bob about before I sort out lunch. Please, Tel, you know I love you.'

He folded the paper in half and threw it on her lap. 'Bloody mug, is what I am.'

'You're not, you're gorgeous.'

She reopened the paper and began to flick through as Terry started to expel lungfuls of air into the slack expanse of shiny plastic. Something about Brexit. They were bringing all that up again. Hadn't we already left? She was just glad the lot they'd voted in weren't going to let Europe push them about. Her eyes crossed the page. Someone in Birmingham who'd been roaming the city centre stabbing people. Grainy CCTV of a dark-skinned bloke with a bushy beard. No surprise there. Probably in the country claiming asylum. She cast the paper aside. It was all just too depressing, it really was.

Far out to sea was a line of wind turbines. She watched their long rotors as they slowly revolved. Terry hated the things, which was a shame; when he'd lost his job in the car plant, she'd suggested he retrain as a wind turbine engineer. There was a future for him in that industry, surely? She found their clean white forms elegant. Plus, the way the world was going, being a country that generated your own power was a good thing. Being self-sufficient. Not letting some foreign power have a hold over you.

She focused on the structures, not wanting to let her thoughts about the state of things ruin her day. Round and round the blades went. Just like windmills, weren't they? And someone sees a windmill nowadays and what do they think? Oh, a windmill. How quaint. People just needed time, that was all.

'Christ almighty, I need to sit down.'

She looked across; Terry's face was bright red and his eyes glassy. She giggled. 'You been at the vodka?'

'Feels like it.' He groped for the deckchair. 'Seeing bloody stars here.'

The Lilo was now a rigid rectangle. 'You're the star, Terry Wilson. That's what you are.'

'Just pour us a cup of tea before you go off on your little paddle,' he replied, flopping into his chair and letting his head tip back.

Kay uncoiled the Lilo's green plastic cord and buried the end of it just beyond the water's edge. Little wavelets were flattening themselves against the sand. The sea wasn't cold. Not quite as warm as Spain, but not far off. Cancelling their two weeks away hadn't turned out so bad, she told herself. Not when you thought of how much they'd saved on flights and a hotel. Feeling self-conscious in her swimming costume, she laid the Lilo in the shallows and checked both ways. No one was watching. This bit of beach really was all theirs. Terry's head was still back, plastic mug of tea in the sand beside his chair. Bless him. He'd put on a fair bit of weight during lockdown. They both had, if she was being honest.

She loved the coast. That sense of being right on the edge of the nation. She surveyed the sea stretching away before her. British waters. Once the Lilo was in shin-deep water, she climbed gingerly on, relieved only a trickle of water managed to snake into the grooves near her feet. This is gorgeous, she thought, lying back and letting her hands hang over the side so the ocean could lick at the tips of her fingers. The tinkle of the funfair carried on the gentle breeze. Seagulls called from off towards the pier. Every so often there was a gentle crunch as the bottom of the Lilo nudged the sand.

*   *   *

Kay found herself in the supermarket once again. A part of her knew it was a dream, but that didn't mean she could stop events from playing out. It was always the same. Back when things were first locking down and the shelves were being stripped of everything. But this supermarket wasn't Asda or Tesco; it was the Indian one that had opened down their road last year. None of the labels made sense; everything was printed in an alphabet she couldn't understand. She needed eggs and flour and pasta. Terry wanted teabags. Which aisle was it all in? The people crowding around her were speaking a different language. Up and down, up and down she hurried, futilely scanning the shelves as brown hands grabbed the last few packets and tins . . .

It was water washing across her feet that woke her. Terry playing a bloody joke. Was he yanking the Lilo's cord from side-to-side, too? Idiot. She opened her eyes, but rather than her husband's grinning face, all she saw was torn grey cloud. She half-sat up; rank after rank of little waves were marching across the open sea before her. She turned her head and saw the row of wind turbines. They were still a long way off, but now they were slightly behind her. Twisting her head further, she realized with horror that the shore was little more than a yellow band stretched thin across the horizon. The water separating her from it wasn't the pleasant pale blue of the shallows; this stuff was dark and forbidding. Almost black. The wind was a lot stronger, too. Cold enough to be raising goosebumps on her upper arms. She shouted in the direction of the distant beach. 'Terry! Anyone, help!' The wind was blowing directly into her face; no one was ever going to hear her. Suddenly, the Lilo felt very small. She lay down on her front and desperately tried paddling towards the shore. Tips of waves broke against her face, soaking her hair. She closed her eyes and kept going until the pain in her shoulders made her stop. Raising her chin, she saw with dismay the coast was even further away. The wind was carrying her out to sea.

She lay back down as a voice in her head announced that she might die. No, she said. You're only a mile or so out. Terry will be awake by now, surely. He'll have called the police. The coastguard will be on their way. Ours is the best coastguard in the world.

Spots of rain started hitting her. She raised herself onto her elbows to look around. The shore was now obscured by a shifting veil of grey. The sea and sky seemed to have merged. Directly above her, the sun reduced to a ghostly disc before fading completely. The first sheet of rain hit her moments later. She pressed herself against the Lilo and gripped its sides as the sea began to buck and writhe beneath her. If I come off this now, I will drown.

There was no way to tell how long she clung on – twenty, thirty minutes? – before she heard a raised voice. Her eyes snapped open. Was that really someone shouting? More words. Indistinct, but these from a female. She lifted her chin. Huge raindrops lanced down, raising countless little crowns in the water surrounding her. Squinting, she made out a dim shadow away to her left. A new voice bellowed something.

'Help!' She screamed. 'Over here! I'm here! Help!' She risked waving one arm back and forth above her head. 'Here! This way, I'm here!'

The voices went silent as the object grew more solid. Details developed. Two rows of . . . what were they? Hunched heads and shoulders? She realized the wind was pushing her directly towards what was definitely some kind of boat. But it was so small. So low in the water. Were there really that amount of people crammed inside? The swirling rain thinned for a second and she could see it was a RIB. A Rigid Inflatable Boat. While in the Sea Cadets, Gavin had done some of his training in one. 'Help me. Please, help me!'

Faces were looking in her direction, eyes wide with confusion and fear. They were all black or brown: Africans, Arabs and everything in between. But they had a boat.

At the back, a man the size of a heavyweight boxer half-stood. 'Here!'

He lobbed a coil of rope towards her. It unwrapped itself in the air, slapping into the water just beyond her reach. Now she was afraid she'd be carried straight past them before he could throw it again. On his second attempt, the end of the rope landed across her legs. She grabbed it and felt herself being pulled towards the vessel.

'Give me your hand.'

Wiping soaked hair from her eyes, she reached towards him.

Another voice shouted something and an argument broke out. The man withdrew his hand to gesticulate angrily. They were, she realized, quarrelling over whether to let her on. Keeping her grip on the rope, she used her other hand to cling to the casing of the dead outboard engine mounted on the boat's rear. Please, for Christ's sake, don't push me away. A wave burst across the prow and a child briefly screamed as the shouting match continued.

Eventually, English was spoken again. It was the man who'd thrown the rope. 'Here, come. Take my place, here.'

Powerful hands gripped her and she was dragged over the side, falling into the bottom of the boat. Even in the wind, what a smell. Just like the doorways where homeless people had left their blankets. Faces peered down at her. She registered both curiosity and hostility. Less than half of them had life jackets. Bags and suitcases were jammed between people's feet. A small girl paused in the act of scooping water from the bottom of the boat.

The big man finished looping the Lilo's cord around the base of the engine then started to climb out. 'Sit there!' He pointed to the space he'd vacated.

'What are you doing?' she gasped.

'We are changing places. It's fine.'

'Really?'

'I have this.' He brandished the soaking length of rope. 'I will—'

The boat lurched as another wave hit. He lost his balance, half-landing on the Lilo. She saw the rope splash into the sea beside them and slowly sink from sight. Now all that connected the boat and the Lilo was its thin cord. He scrabbled on to the narrow expanse of plastic and grasped the engine's casing. 'It is not working,' he said. 'The man in France did not fill it with fuel!'

A flicker of lightning illuminated the sky and the wind increased in strength. Something was yelled, and the children crammed into the middle of the boat began scooping water more quickly. Kay saw they were using empty ice-cream containers. The woman next to her vomited over both their feet as the boat pitched forwards. She heard herself scream. Opposite her, an old man fixed her with a beady eye, his face deeply etched by criss-crossing lines. The boat started to tilt sharply and the man clinging to the engine grunted with the effort of holding on. A geyser of water shot up as the Lilo slammed into the back of the RIB, then the cord snapped tight as a narrow gap reappeared.

Kay looked at his fingers; the tendons were standing out as he fought to keep his grip on the engine's slippery surface. The sequence repeated itself again and again, each time more force-fully as the waves grew in size. She glanced about. Most of the passengers were oblivious; too busy taking full containers from the children and emptying them over the side. The water inside the boat was now above her ankles. The woman beside her had started to feel slack and heavy. She'd fainted, head lolling forward, drool hanging from her lower lip. A young man further down the vessel started rocking back and forth, a keening howl of terror coming from his lips. A meaty slap as another wave smashed against them. Water hit the side of her face like shrapnel.

The man on the Lilo started to cry out. 'I cannot, I cannot!'

Kay turned to look. Oh Christ, he was trying to climb back on board. There was no bloody room! The thing would capsize or sink. Kneeling on the Lilo, he got one arm into the boat, fingers scrabbling for something to grasp. She moved her leg clear. No way was he grabbing hold of her. The RIB reared up and he slid back on the Lilo. She saw the plastic cord was starting to turn white as it neared breaking point.

The old man opposite produced a small knife. But his fingers were shaking as he tried to get the tip of the blade beneath the cord.

The man on the Lilo shouted again. 'Help me!' He lunged at her. 'Help me!' Fingers caught in her hair. His eyes were wild, teeth bared.

Shoving his hand away, she snatched the knife from the old man. With one quick motion, she severed the cord.

*   *   *

The squall started losing strength about fifteen minutes later. As the wind calmed, the thick layer of cloud began to break up. Patches of sunlight settled on the ruffled sea. Not wanting to, she looked briefly in the direction the Lilo had been carried. Nothing. The woman beside her groaned quietly and wiped at her face. She could sense the old man watching her with a quiet intensity. There, still in her hand, was the knife. She reached over the side and let it fall from her fingers. Then a siren blared out. She looked over her shoulder. That distinctive orange and blue: a lifeboat! Dark waves were disintegrating into brilliant foam as it swept across the sea towards them. She could see faces – white faces – at the bridge windows. Her whole body began to shake and she found herself on her feet with the rest of them. 'Here! I'm here! Oh thank Christ, I'm here!'

'Kay Wilson?'

She nodded eagerly in reply. 'Yes! I'm Kay.'

The lifeboat had drawn up alongside, protecting their smaller vessel from what remained of the wind. The man who'd spoken had a neatly trimmed beard. He signalled off to the side. 'Radio in – it's her! And tell them we're going to need police and immigration for this lot.'

A ladder was lowered down.

'Up you come, love. Are you OK to climb?'

She grabbed the rungs and began to struggle the short distance up. Once more, strong hands helped her. As she flopped gratefully onto the deck, a foil blanket was draped over her.

Something was thrust before her face. 'It's OK, you're safe now. Here, get this eaten – it'll give you energy.'

She took it with a trembling hand.

'Right!' His voice was harder now. Authoritative. 'We can take the children. Them, the little ones. Understand? Those ones. Only them.'

Kay moved to a sitting position and tore the wrapper off the snack bar. The RIB was out of sight but she could still smell the thing.

Another crew member appeared with a box. He started

tossing small packets over the side. 'Foil blankets! For warmth. Blankets, yes.'

The first of the children soon appeared. A shivering boy of about seven, expression blank as he shuffled to the side. She ate her food as the rest of them appeared. The silent line was led away to the cabin.

The man with the beard spoke over the side again. 'We'll tow you to shore, yes? Pull you behind us. It's OK. It's safe.' He turned away from the railing and looked down at her. 'Mrs Wilson? Would you like to come inside?'

She took his hand and got unsteadily to her feet. Now the RIB was in view. There was the old man, staring up at her with knowing eyes. An arm was wrapped about her shoulders and she was guided towards the cabin door.

'How did you end up on that boat?' the crew member asked.

'The storm carried me towards it.'

'Bloody lucky, that was. And the Lilo? What happened to that?'

She thought about the man who'd given her his place. How the swirling grey simply swallowed him. 'Not sure,' she mumbled. 'The wind must have taken it.'

KATE ELLIS – THE CONFESSIONS OF EDWARD PRIME

E dward Prime was a nuisance.

This was the third time that month he'd presented himself at the front desk and asked to see Detective Constable Janet Crowley. And she felt she'd had enough.

'I've got to get it off my chest,' he said, leaning towards her. She could smell something rancid on his warm breath and she edged her chair back a little. 'I've got to make a clean breast of it.' He lowered his eyes to focus on her chest and she raised her hand instinctively to make sure her shirt was properly buttoned.

He began to fidget with the empty plastic cup in front of him. They always gave him a hot drink in the interview room. Maybe that's why he came, she thought. That and a feeling of self-importance.

'What are you talking about, Mr Prime?'

'The woman on Howdale Road. I killed her.'

She took a deep breath and opened the file that lay on the table in front of her. 'That's as well as the post office you robbed in Bucknell Street and the man you stabbed to death outside that nightclub last week, is it?'

'Well, er . . . I've been busy.'

'So I see. In the past six months you've confessed to no less than eighteen crimes.'

'Like I said, I've been busy.'

She looked across the table at him. He was skinny with greasy brown hair and a long face that glowed with perspiration. The cheap yellow T-shirt he wore stretched tightly over his midriff riding up to reveal a not-so-tantalizing glimpse of pasty flesh. She could smell his sweat. She wished his mother had taught him to use deodorant.

'Look, Mr Prime. Edward,' she said. 'We know you haven't

done anything. We could charge you with wasting police time, you know.'

He lowered his eyes, a small, secretive smile on his thin lips. 'I know about the locket.'

Janet Crowley looked up sharply. Up till now Edward had been so predictable. 'What locket?'

'The one I took from Paula Sloane when I killed her. The one with the picture of the kiddie inside.'

Janet stared at him, lost for words. They knew from Paula Sloane's friends and family that she'd always worn that locket; never took it off. They'd kept the fact that it was missing from the press. There was always something they held back. Just in case.

'Do you know where the locket is?'

Edward shook his head.

'But if you killed her, you must have taken it.'

Edward frowned, as though the logic of the statement was too much for him to take in. If it hadn't been for the mention of the locket, Janet would have sent him on his way by now. But she had to find out more.

'How did you hear about the locket?'

Janet watched as new hope appeared in his eyes. 'Aren't you going to arrest me?'

Janet considered the question for a moment. 'No, Edward. We know where to find you if we need you. You go home to your mum, eh.'

There was no mistaking the disappointment on his face. He was twenty, she knew that from the file, but he looked like a child denied a promised treat. 'But I did it,' he said in a whine.

'You find the locket and we'll have another chat.'

It was the best she could offer. And as she watched him shuffle from the room, she knew it wasn't enough.

As soon as Edward unlocked the front door, his mother was there in the hall. He could tell she'd been cooking from the smell of burning that hit him as soon as he walked in. She'd never been much of a cook.

'Where have you been?' She stood there, arms folded, a plump vision in velour tracksuit and carpet slippers.

'Nowhere.'

'You've been to that police station again, haven't you?'

Edward could hear the exasperation in her voice. He closed the door behind him and bowed his head. 'No. I never. I've just been out. Walking around.'

His mother turned away and began to shuffle back into the kitchen. 'I'll put the kettle on,' she said.

Edward wasn't listening. Paula Sloane was dead but he knew her secret. He knew who she was.

The DCI stood in front of the white board and gave Janet a disapproving look as she slipped into the room. She was late for the briefing. If the DCI knew why, she knew he'd tell her to charge Edward with wasting police time. But somehow she couldn't bring herself to do that to him. Perhaps she was becoming soft.

'Paula Sloane. Aged forty-five. Divorced. Lived alone. Found stabbed in the kitchen of her house in Allerton the day before yesterday. No weapon found. No enemies that we know of. No suspects. Nothing appeared to be missing apart from a locket she always wore: according to everyone who knew her, she never took it off.'

Janet began to put her hand up, nervous that the DCI would make some cutting comment. She was certain that he thought she wasn't up to the job any more; that she was a middle-aged woman marking time till retirement. She knew she couldn't keep up with the young men and women on the team with their gym-honed bodies and their hungry ambition tinged with a soupçon of callousness. When she spoke they all looked round, and she felt her face burning.

'Sir, I've just been talking to Edward Prime. He comes in to confess to any local crime that's been on the news.' She glanced round at the sceptical faces. 'Anyway, he confessed to Paula's murder. Normally, I would have taken it with a pinch of salt but he mentioned the locket. He knew it was missing. Is there any chance the information could have leaked out somehow?'

The DCI was staring straight at her. 'Is he still down in the interview room?'

'I told him to go home. He lives with his mother and we can pick him up any time if necessary.' She held her breath, expecting a public dressing-down for letting a potential suspect go.

But the DCI shrugged. 'Any chance he's our man?'

'I wouldn't have thought so, sir. He seems harmless.'

'As long as we know where to find him.'

Janet exhaled. She'd said her bit now and it was up to the senior investigating officer to decide what to do about it.

The DCI continued. 'One thing you should know about our victim is that twenty years ago her baby was abducted. It was a boy called Adam, aged four months. She left him in his pushchair outside the post office on Allerton Road, and when she came out the pushchair was still there but there was no sign of the kid. There was a major hunt for him, of course, but he never turned up. According to Paula's family and friends, she never really got over it and her marriage broke up as a result.'

A stick-thin young woman with long blonde hair raised her hand. 'Any chance the kid's disappearance is connected to her death, sir?'

'Good question, DC Parker. Truth is, we don't know, but it's an avenue worth exploring. She'd recently hired a private detective to try and trace the kid. We've spoken to him and he claims he didn't get very far. However, she rang him on the evening she died and asked to see him the following day. I said I'd send someone round to take a statement.' He looked straight at Janet. 'DC Crowley, can I leave it to you to have a word?'

Janet saw that all eyes were on her again. But this time she felt a small glow of triumph. 'Of course, sir.'

The evening was the only time Bradley Temple, the private detective, was free to see her, but at least that gave her a chance to have something to eat at home before she drove to his flat at the Albert Dock for their meeting.

Her son, Russell, greeted her when she arrived home. The house seemed to be in chaos. It always was when he was home from university.

'Hi, ma. How's crime?' he said as he propelled his lanky body off the sofa. His accent was still decidedly London, but that was hardly surprising as they'd only recently moved up north.

Janet didn't answer. It was a question he always asked, an automatic response to her arrival. After a brief conversation about his day, which had been mostly spent in front of his computer screen, she cooked some pasta for them both and Russell wolfed it down as though he'd not seen food for days. Then, when she said she had to go out, he kissed her on the top of her head and told her to take care. She told him not to be daft, she was always careful. But she appreciated his concern.

Throughout her police career down in London and now up in Merseyside, she'd had very little to do with private detectives, and most of what she knew about them came from the pages of novels. But she thought Bradley Temple was a good name for someone in that particular profession and her mind conjured up a dark, handsome gumshoe in a belted raincoat tramping the mean streets of inner-city Liverpool.

She drove into town from the suburbs, through streets of fine Georgian houses, eventually ending up at the waterfront. It was still light when she arrived at the Albert Dock, but there was a chill breeze blowing in from the river and it had started to rain. Bradley Temple lived on the second floor of an old warehouse building, now transformed into luxury apartments. And when he greeted her at the door, he proved to be as disappointing as the weather. He was stocky and bald and he wore a shiny suit that had seen better days, but he invited Janet in with scrupulous politeness and offered her a cup of tea which she accepted gratefully.

'Terrible about Paula,' he began. 'She seemed a nice woman. And she hadn't had it easy. Not since her kid was snatched like that.'

Janet smiled sympathetically. 'I believe she called you shortly before she died. What did she say?'

He paused as though he was about to make a dramatic revelation. 'She said she thought she'd seen Adam; her son who went missing.'

'Where did she see him? And what made her think it was him?'

'She was walking down Allerton Road when she saw a young man going into one of the bars. She said he was the spitting image of her ex-husband so she thought . . .'

'That's hardly conclusive.'

'That's what I told her. But she was convinced it was him. She asked for a meeting but she died before I could find out what else she knew.'

'She said she had more information?'

'Yes, but she wouldn't tell me what it was over the phone.' He hesitated, as though he was deciding whether to break a confidence. 'But when I'd called on her a couple of days earlier, I'd noticed a young man hanging around. I had the impression he was watching her house.'

Janet leaned forward. 'Can you describe him?'

The man closed his eyes. 'He was around five ten; brown hair that looked as if it needed a good wash; greasy skin; long face; T-shirt that looked a size too small for him. Unattractive character but he didn't look particularly dangerous.'

'Have you seen a picture of her ex-husband? Could there be a resemblance to this young man you saw?'

He shook his head. 'No, I never saw a picture – she said she'd destroyed them all after the divorce. But I don't think that matters too much. I think it was all in her imagination. Clutching at straws – it's what people do when they're desperate. And she was desperate all right. Poor woman.'

Janet took a sip of tea. Surely the man Temple described had to be Edward Prime. Now all she needed to do was to get a confession. Which, given his track record, should be simple.

Edward sat in his bedroom, turning the locket over and over in his hand. He'd taken it from her as a keepsake. After all, it was his by right.

He pushed back the threadbare rug beside his single bed and lifted a loose floorboard before plunging his hand down into the space where he kept his treasures. He could feel the book down there. He'd collected everything together; all the evidence that he wasn't who they said he was. He had kept it hidden from his mother – or the woman who called herself his mother – because he didn't want her to discover that he knew the truth.

He was sorry about Paula. There had been blood all over her nice dress, which had been white with red flowers, and the stain had looked like a massive flower that had spread like some evil weed to engulf the others. He'd wanted to do something to save her but it had been too late. Since then he'd dreamed about it every night. The blood and Paula's dead, staring eyes.

He took out the book and opened it. The whole story was there in yellowing newsprint: 'Child missing'; 'Where is baby Adam?' And then there was the article that appeared in the *Echo* last month saying that Paula had never come to terms with her loss. That was how he'd come to realize that his mum had taken him from outside that post office. That she'd carried him off and left the empty pushchair. When he'd found the cuttings in her dressing-table drawer he'd confronted her. And he'd known she was lying when she said she'd only kept them because Paula used to live in the next road and she was interested in the case.

He'd decided to go to Howdale Road to find his real mother. He'd watched her for days and when she'd left the house to go shopping, he'd followed her. He felt he must have killed her although he couldn't quite remember doing it. But he felt guilty. He always felt guilty.

He remembered bending over her body and unfastening the locket. And when he'd opened it he'd seen a picture of the baby which must have been himself. He'd taken the locket away with him because it was all he had of hers. He knew that if he took it to the police to prove his story, they'd take it off him. And he didn't want to lose it, so he'd lied about knowing where it was. But a lie was a little sin compared to all the others that crowded in his head.

He heard the woman who called herself his mother calling him from downstairs, telling him tea was ready. He'd have to think carefully about his next move.

Janet slept on the problem and, after a sleepless night, she came to a decision.

Russell was still in bed so she grabbed a slice of toast and shut the front door quietly behind her. After what Bradley Temple had told her, she knew she had to bring Edward Prime in for questioning. She had no choice.

As soon as she arrived at work, she hurried to the DCI's office. She could see him there behind his glass partition. Busy as usual and half hidden behind heaps of paperwork. She knocked on the door, waited a token second, and then pushed it open. He looked up and, from his expression, she knew her interruption wasn't welcome. But she stepped forward and stood in front of his desk like a schoolgirl reporting to the headmaster.

'Last night I went to take a statement from the private detective Paula Sloane hired. Bradley Temple, he's called.' The DCI put down his pen and appeared to be listening so she carried on with new confidence. 'He thinks he saw a man watching Paula's house. And the man he saw fits Edward Prime's description.'

'Then pick him up.'

'Right, sir. I was going to, but I thought I'd better let you know.'

'Take someone with you in case . . .'

'I know Prime, sir. I can manage on my own.'

He returned his attention to his paperwork. It was up to her now. And she knew what she had to do.

Prime lived in one of the streets off Smithdown Road. Most of the terraced houses were occupied by students and the Primes' stood out from the rest with its hanging basket beside the front door, its fussy lace curtains and its cat ornaments on the windowsill. Most of the students had gone home for the summer so the street seemed deserted as Janet rang the doorbell and waited.

She had been dreading an encounter with Prime's mother. Like all mothers she was bound to be a fearsome defender of her young and she couldn't face the thought of a confrontation. She was relieved when Edward himself answered the door, opening it a crack and peeping out.

'Edward. I need another word. Shall we do it here or shall we go down to the police station?'

Edward's eyes lit up. 'You believe me then? You believe I killed her? I'll come down to the police station.' He suddenly looked disappointed. 'Mum's out at the shops.'

'You can let her know later,' Janet said quickly. 'It won't take long. We just need to talk to you, that's all.'

There was a spring in Edward's step as he walked to the car and Janet tried her best not to feel sorry for him as he sat next to her in the front seat, gazing out of the window like a child on a day trip. He looked proud and excited. He was important now. The police were going to hang on his every word.

'Where are we going?' he asked as she turned onto the road that ran beside the river. 'This isn't the way to the police station.'

'There's no hurry so I thought we'd take the scenic route. It'll give us a chance to have a chat if that's OK.' She had reached Otterspool now and, after negotiating the roundabout, she brought the car to a halt on the promenade. She could see the expanse of churning grey water to her right as she opened the window to let the odour of Edward's sweat out of the car.

She turned to him and smiled to put him at his ease. 'Somebody saw you watching Paula Sloane's house shortly before she died.'

'I've told you already. I was there.'

'You admit you killed her.'

He suddenly looked unsure of himself. 'She was lying on the floor and there was blood. I must have killed her, mustn't I?'

'Did you take her locket?'

He nodded. 'It had a picture of me inside,' he said almost in a whisper. 'I wanted to keep it.'

Janet saw the tears in his eyes and she felt an almost maternal urge to comfort him, to tell him that everything was going to be all right. But she knew there'd be no comfort from now on.

'A picture of you?'

'When I was a baby.'

'Think carefully. Did you see anyone coming out of the house before you went in?'

A secretive smile appeared on his lips and his eyes met hers. 'Yeah. I did see someone.'

'Who?'

He looked away. 'I'll put it in my statement.' He said the last word with relish, as though making a statement meant that the police were finally taking him seriously. He was going to be a murderer. A kind of celebrity.

Janet opened the car door. 'Would you like some fresh air, Edward? You're going to need it if you're going to be cooped up in a cell for the next few years.'

'Yeah. But I need to tell Mum where I am.'

'You can phone her when we get to the police station.'

Janet looked round. Because of the bad weather the promenade was empty except for a solitary runner, oblivious to everything except the music from his headphones. She waited till he was out of sight then she walked round the car and opened the passenger door.

The body was washed up at Crosby two weeks later. And because the river had done its worst, it had to be identified by DNA and dental records.

Of course his confession to Janet had no witnesses so it wouldn't stand up in court, but the police weren't looking for anyone else in connection with the murder of Paula Sloane. The discovery of the locket in Edward's room had clinched it.

Mrs Prime had sworn that her son's belief that he was the missing baby, Adam Sloane, had no basis in fact. Edward got these ideas in his head, she said. He'd always been the same. She had been willing to take any tests they wanted to clear her of Adam's abduction and the DCI had taken her up on her offer.

The results confirmed that she'd been telling the truth. Edward had been her son all right. She had only kept the newspaper cuttings because Paula had lived in the next road: it had been a bit of local excitement, that's all. Maybe if Edward hadn't found them, he would still be alive.

When Janet saw the DCI emerging from his office, she began to study her paperwork, trying to look busy. She was aware of him approaching her desk. Then she heard his voice.

'Have you finished with those witness statements?'

Janet picked up a cardboard file and handed it over.

'I've just had Mrs Prime on the phone . . . Edward's mother. She still can't understand what happened.'

'I've been through it time and time again, sir.' She sniffed. 'Edward wanted some fresh air, so I parked at the promenade. We were walking along chatting when he suddenly took it into his head to run off. I did my best to chase after him but . . . He just jumped into the water. I threw a lifebelt but there was no sign of him.'

'There'll be a thorough investigation, you know that.'

She nodded meekly.

'What I can't understand is what you were doing there in the first place.'

'I didn't think it'd do any harm to have a stroll and a chat before we came to the interview room. He was unlikely to see the outside world for years if he was convicted and I felt a bit sorry for him, if you must know. I suppose I'll be disciplined.'

'Undoubtedly. You screwed up.' He paused. 'You should know better at your age.'

She looked round and saw the young blonde DC smirking into her coffee.

'I suppose Paula's murder was playing on his conscience and he couldn't face life any more. But if he really believed she was his mum, why kill her?'

'Who knows, Janet? Maybe she laughed at him. He's hardly the son of most women's dreams. I don't suppose we'll ever know for sure.'

The DCI walked away, barking an order at one of the others. Janet returned to her paperwork, trying to ignore the stares and sniggers. As far as they were concerned, she'd miscalculated badly.

That evening she managed to get home at a reasonable time, but she found the house empty. Russell was out. He'd left her a note saying he'd gone round to a friend's house and wouldn't be back till later. He couldn't have timed it better because there was something she had to do.

As soon as she'd changed out of her work clothes, she took her collection of old photograph albums from the bottom drawer of the sideboard. It was the early ones she was looking for, the ones containing pictures of Russell when he was very small. She knew she should have destroyed them years ago, but she'd been down in London then and it had all seemed so very far away.

It had all been planned down to the last detail. The day after she took him, she travelled to London, where she stayed with her cousin who'd been completely unaware of her deception. She hadn't told her about her late miscarriage: instead she'd let her believe that she'd had the baby and was struggling as a single mother.

After the miscarriage the need to replace her lost child had become so urgent that she'd searched round for a child to take; a child who would become her own. She'd watched Paula Sloane, sick with envy that she had a beautiful baby when hers had never lived. She'd seen Paula ignoring her baby's cries and leaving him alone in the cold outside the post office. And she'd seized her opportunity.

She began to take the photos of the smiling baby from the album. They were so like the picture in Paula's locket, now in the exhibits store at the police station, that anyone seeing them would guess the truth at once. She carried them over to the grate and lit a match, turning away because she couldn't bear to see the image of the innocent child licked by flames.

Everything had been good down in London: she'd enjoyed her work in the Met and she hadn't even minded when they'd teased her about her Liverpool accent. She'd rented a small apartment that had suited her and Russell just fine. And she'd nursed her secret so closely that she'd almost forgotten its existence.

Then years later she'd had to return to Merseyside to care for her elderly mother because there'd been nobody else to take on the responsibility. By the time her transfer up north came through, Russell had started at university and her mother had died six months later. But all had been well until she'd spotted that piece in the newspaper – the article about Paula Sloane's shattered life – and the reality of what she'd done all those years ago had struck her like a hammer blow.

Everything came to a head when Paula spotted Russell one day and noticed his strong resemblance to her ex-husband.

For twenty years Paula had scanned every face in every crowd for that resemblance, and all her instincts had told her that she'd finally found the one she'd been looking for. She'd followed Russell home and pushed a note through his door which Janet found. She knew she should have ignored it, but she'd needed to know how much Paula suspected. So she'd paid her a visit.

Paula had reacted hysterically, screaming and threatening to report Janet to the police, saying that she'd go to prison for a long time. And, worst of all, she'd threatened to tell Russell – or Adam – what kind of monster had brought him up. Janet had realized that even if she threw herself on Paula's mercy, there'd be no calm reconciliation, no embrace of forgiveness. And, faced with Paula's wild fury, she had been forced to pick up a knife and defend herself.

When she'd realized the full horror of what she'd done, she'd dashed from the house, praying that she hadn't been seen. Being in on the investigation, she knew there'd been no sighting of a fleeing woman, so she'd imagined she was safe. Until Edward Prime made his confession. And when he hinted that he'd seen her leaving the crime scene, she knew she had to act.

She was sorry about Edward. She'd always remember the look of terror on his face as she shoved him into those grey, inhospitable waters. It would be there with her for ever, preying on her conscience.

The last remnants of blackened paper glowed and curled in the grate. The pictures were burned now. She was safe. As she straightened herself up she saw a car drawing to a halt outside, and when the doorbell rang she brushed the ashes from her fingers and hurried over to the bay window. The DCI was standing at the front door with the smirking blonde. Only this time she looked deadly serious.

When Janet opened the door the visitors said nothing and, as they stepped inside, she knew it was over.

'A witness has come forward,' the DCI began almost apologetically. 'He was running on the promenade and . . .'

Janet bowed her head. Perhaps it was time she unburdened herself. She had so much to confess.

STUART PAWSON – ULTRA VIOLENT

There's a saying about a man needing to do three things in his lifetime before he can feel fulfilled. Trouble was, he couldn't remember them. 'Father a son' was almost certainly the first one, but the others had gone. Something about planting a tree or ploughing a field, perhaps? Ah well, it would give him something to think about as he lay on the sunbed, before he started the serious planning.

The eight-tube, high-output sunbed had been a good buy, he decided. It was Aristotle Onassis who said that the first essential for being successful was a tan, and he didn't do too badly for himself, did he? His first wife, the opera singer, wasn't anything special, but Jackie Kennedy was. Once his tan was up, he thought, he'd fetch the Bullworker down from the loft, start working out again. But seriously, this time.

He examined his reflection in the big mirror on the wardrobe door, looking for evidence of colour-change. There were red patches on his shoulders and knees, and his back itched where he couldn't see it, so it must be working. He raised the leg of his boxer shorts for a before-and-after comparison. Yes! No doubt about it – there was a difference!

He hated boxer shorts. These had little Santa Clauses on them, interspersed with sprigs of holly. He'd bought them for when he went to spend last Christmas with Auntie Joan, hoping that they'd create some amusement when he finally bedded his cousin Jennifer. Good lovers always have a sense of humour, he'd read in one of his magazines. It hadn't come to that, though, and the hilariously funny shorts had remained within the perpetual darkness of his cavalry twills. Jennifer liked him, he was sure. Maybe even fancied him. But he'd gone at a bad time, before her exams, and she was studying hard every night, round at her friend's house. Next time it would be different.

Thirty minutes front, thirty minutes back, the instructions said. Not a second more. He made sure the goggles were tight, flicked the timer fully over and slid under the ultra-violet tubes as they popped and flickered into life. He'd decided to wear the shorts under the sunbed so that later there would be a contrasting line showing next to his new Speedo swimming trunks when he started going to the baths at the sports centre.

They were wrong about the three steps a man had to take to fulfilment. For a start, he hated children. The sex bit would be OK, but the skill was to avoid having kids. You only had to go down to the precinct to see how easy it was to have them. And any idiot could plant a tree. Trees would plant themselves quite happily if humans didn't interfere. As for ploughing a field, it was hard to imagine anything more boring than driving in slow-motion circles until it was done. Yes, they'd definitely got it wrong.

And, of course, the most important one had gone unsaid. Why did men join the army? Why did Americans, even the women, carry fancy little handguns and then wander, late at night, into areas where they shouldn't go, secretly hoping that a mugger would dare to try it with them? Why were the SAS everybody's heroes?

He knew why. When you looked into your own mind, followed the tunnel right to the end, kicking aside all the junk that countless teachers and priests and probation officers had piled up along the way, not to mention parents and set books and hymns and all that crap, you came to a stone. A big flat stone, lying face down. He'd made the journey, dumped the debris, found the stone, dared to turn it over. The message underneath was simple. It said: A man is not a man until he has killed someone.

The click of the timer switching off startled him, and the temperature started to drop. He reached out, turned it back to maximum and rolled over, to go through his plan to commit perfect murder. That would be the finishing touch in the reinvention of himself. After that he would have the inner confidence, the serenity, plus that indefinable air of mystery, to go with his new physical appearance. Two hundred miles was the magic distance. Drive two hundred miles, kill someone you'd never met before, drive home without leaving a trace behind. Easy. You'd be safer than a doctor at an inquest.

Sunday he polished his car. He'd bought it two weeks ago – a second-hand Ford Escort – and was determined to keep it immaculate. Next week he would put his plan into operation. Tuesday was the ideal day, he had decided. Tuesday was the low point of the week for most people. Nothing ever happened on a Tuesday.

Ideally, he would have liked to have a conversation with a policeman. Ask him a few questions, test his theories, but he didn't know one socially and he could hardly breeze into the local nick and start asking questions about murder enquiries, could he? He threw the wash leather into the bucket and drove round to the filling station to top up the tyres and the petrol tank.

Parked in the schoolyard was a huge articulated caravan, with the emblem of the local police force on the side. 'There's a thief about' said the posters showing a fleeing youth, and 'Don't let him get away with it. Call in for advice.' He decided to do just that, after he'd been to the garage. Car thieves worried him. They were lowlife; should be exterminated.

Fifteen minutes later he climbed the four steps that took him inside the caravan. 'Morning, sir,' the policeman in charge of the exhibition greeted him, his voice filtered through a black moustache.

'Er, good morning.' He wandered around, looking at the displays of photographs and charts, conscious of the policeman's eyes following him.

'Anything you need any help with, sir?' the officer asked after a decent interval.

'No, not really. Well yes. I have an Escort, and was wondering . . .'

'Let me tell you what's available for cars. Top of the range are microchips . . .' He droned through his spiel, explaining about concealing electronic implants that cost more than the Escort was worth, about tracking devices and silent alarms.

'And finally,' the policeman concluded, 'we have these.' He
held up what looked like a fat fibre-tipped pen.

'Oh, what's that?' the visitor asked.

'Secret marker pen. Simply write your postcode on everything that is removable, then, if it ever turns up amongst stolen
property, we can identify it. It shows up under an ultra-violet
light, but otherwise it's invisible. One pound fifty to you, sir.'

'Gosh. Just your postcode?'

'That's right. A postcode identifies the owner to within ten
or fifteen houses. After that, we knock on doors.'

'Right, I'll take one.' He retrieved his purse from the inside
pocket of his parka and offered a fiver to the policeman.

'Thank you, sir. I'll just find you some change.'

His confidence was growing. He felt he'd struck up a small
rapport with the officer. 'Thank you.' He placed the coins in
the purse. 'Have you been doing this long?'

The policeman blinked, taken by surprise. 'About six weeks,'
he said, because he couldn't think of a reason not to.

'Just at weekends?'

'That's right. We're slowly working our way round the county.'

'It's a good idea,' he told him encouragingly. 'So you're a
proper policeman the rest of the week?'

'Yes. Traffic.'

He noticed the 'sirs' were absent from the last few exchanges.
'Do you prefer being with Traffic to, say, catching murderers?'
he asked.

The Velcro moustache was decidedly down-turned at the
ends. 'A death's a death, *sir*,' the policeman told him, the *sir*
laid on like cheap margarine. 'And for every homicide in this
country there are ten fatalities on the road.'

A young woman with two children clumped into the caravan.
'Right,' he agreed. 'OK.' He waved the pen. 'Thanks for this.'
Cocooned in the Escort again, he threw the secret marker into
the glove compartment and embraced the steering wheel, his
body shaking with silent laughter. 'What a plonker!' he giggled
to himself. 'What a flipping plonker!'

Tuesday he drove north. The A1 took him into Yorkshire, and
when he had 210 miles on the trip recorder, with the signs

indicating Leeds off to the west, he took a slip road and headed east. It was agricultural land, with areas of woodland and still plenty of hedgerows. He drove methodically, turning on to narrower lanes as they occurred, looking for the ideal spot.

A Citroën estate was parked in a bald patch of ground at the edge of a wood. It was an unofficial car park for people out for a walk. Or dumping rubbish, his eyes told him, as he scanned the scattered bin liners and their spilled contents.

A dog, a nondescript terrier, came bounding towards the Citroën and then turned expectantly, waiting for his master to appear. The man was middle-aged, wearing a chain-store padded coat and carrying a stick for the dog to chase. He changed his shoes and opened the rear hatch to let the dog in, like he probably did every day, unaware that on this occasion he was being watched. 'Perfect,' the observer whispered to himself, noting the exact time. 'Just perfect.'

One week later, but two hours earlier in the day, he did the long drive north again. It was a bind, but that was the whole point. Most murderers are careless, can't be bothered travelling too far. They work on their own doorsteps, and pay the penalty. The police mark the places where the bodies are found on a big map, and the killer almost always lives somewhere in the middle.

The next time – and he was sure there would be a next time – he'd come up here again, but to somewhere different. This first one would be put down to a random killing, but when there had been two or three . . . He'd have to wait, of course. A year would be about right. Not exactly a year; more like eleven months, or fourteen. Unpredictable, that was the key.

He felt good, seeing the world about him with a renewed clarity. There were voices, a choir, singing in his head. Last night he had purified himself. A man was about to die by his hands, so it was only right that he should be in a state of grace when he performed the act. He'd had beefburger steak and egg for tea; the meat to signify death, the egg for new life. *His* new life. He wouldn't eat again until it was over. Then he did the colonic irrigation, to rid his body of toxins, followed by ten minutes' meditation. After that he watched videos of famous serial killers from his collection, nodding approvingly at their deeds, shaking and smiling at their mistakes, until he knew he was ready.

He parked the Escort in a gateway to a field about two hundred yards from the unofficial car park. A week earlier, after the man in the Citroën had departed, he'd made a reconnaissance of the area, studied the lie of the land. He knew exactly where the act would take place. From the boot he removed a long bundle wrapped in a blanket. He extricated the shotgun that had belonged to his step-grandfather and opened a brand-new box of cartridges. Fifteen minutes later he concealed the gun under a bush in the hedgerow, alongside the path the man had to take, and waited.

So far, he'd been detached, almost clinical, and had marvelled at his own coolness. But as soon as the intended victim hove into view, something else took over. He breathed deeply, controlling his excitement. Not for a single second did he doubt that he would do it. Today was the day that he would move onto a loftier plane than that inhabited by the fools and no-hopers who plagued his everyday life. Today he would play with the gods.

When the man was twenty yards away, he stepped from the bushes, the gun held behind him. The man hardly noticed him, then smiled a greeting. At ten yards he levelled the shotgun. A puzzled look crossed the man's face, as if to say: 'Look here, you shouldn't wave that thing about.' At five yards he braced the butt into his body and stiffened his grip. At three he pulled the trigger.

The dog was leaping around the prostrate body, yapping and whining, so he shot that too. Then he dragged the pair of them off the path and concealed them in the undergrowth, where they wouldn't be seen by passers-by, but would soon be discovered by a search party, after the alarm was raised. But by then he would be a long way away.

He found his way back to the car through the woods, ready to drop the gun into the undergrowth should he meet anyone else, but he didn't. The car started instantly, removing his last major worry, and he slipped the gear lever towards first and eased the clutch. The gateway was rutted where tractors had removed the harvest a few weeks earlier. The rear wheels of the Escort slid sideways into the depression and he side-swiped the gatepost.

'Hell!' he cursed, then remembered he had front-wheel drive and pulled out into the lane. A quarter of a mile later he stopped. There had been a murder somewhere in the Midlands a few years earlier, and he'd just remembered how the murderer was caught. He'd left flakes of paint from his car on the branch of a bush. The police identified the make and the model from the paint, and many months later an alert copper with not enough to occupy his mind had noticed a car of the right type with a scratch at exactly the right height. He shook his head sympathetically. That was bad luck, but he wasn't going to rely on luck. He climbed out to look for damage.

The bodywork was unmarked, but the rear wheel trim was partially dislodged and would have fallen off in the next few miles. He was calm, thinking rationally. Professional, that was the word. The trims were nothing special, not even the original ones fitted by Ford, and one found down the road half a mile from a body could hardly be considered a clue. There was even a spare one in the boot, so he wouldn't have to buy a new one. He kicked the trim back onto the wheel and was opening the car door when a thought occurred to him. It wouldn't be much of a lead to the police, but there was a way it could be a *mis-lead*. A colossal mis-lead. He grinned at the thought of it, and congratulated himself on his clear thinking. Already he was in that lofty place where the eagles flew but the turkeys never ventured. It would always be like this from now on.

During the planning of the murder, he had wondered about providing a red herring, to direct the police down a wrong avenue, but had eventually dismissed the idea as an unnecessary complication. 'KISS' said the poster on the hospital notice board – Keep It Simple, Stupid. But one of the marks of greatness was the ability to adapt to changing circumstances; to be constantly updating the action plan. This was one of those times.

He took the secret marker pen from the glove compartment, where it had lain since he purchased it, and opened the Escort's boot lid. Wearing his driving gloves, he scrupulously cleaned every possible vestige of a fingerprint from the spare wheel trim. Then, working right-handed, which was unnatural for him, he wrote a Leeds postcode in small figures near the inside edge of the trim. He knew Leeds was LS, so he wrote LS15, making it look as if it could be 16, followed by a 7 that might be a 1 and a WN that could have been almost anything. He drove back to the gateway and left it propped against the post he'd hit. After a comprehensive look around he drove away for the final time.

He'd done it! He donned his Ray-Bans for the drive home, towards the afternoon sun. It was going to be all sunshine from now on. The engine of the Ford purred effortlessly as he cruised down the A1, well inside the speed limit, singing along with the tunes on Radio 2. During a lull in the music he did an impression of a country bobby saying, 'We think the killer lives locally,' and giggled at his own joke until he had to find a tissue to blow his nose.

Next day he put the car through the car wash. At home he polished it until it hurt his eyes, paying extra attention to the wheels, removing every grain of foreign dirt from them. To a forensic scientist dirt was as distinctive as a fingerprint, so it was important to get rid of it all. On a whim, while the trims were off, he secret-marked them with his own postcode, using his proper hand and bigger, sloping letters and numbers.

After lunch he had a sunbathe. Maybe tomorrow, if he looked brown enough, he would consider visiting the swimming baths. It was relaxing on the bed, the warmth from the UV lamps penetrating the skin, reaching deep into his bones. God, he felt good. Eleven months was a long time to wait before he did it again. Maybe he'd have a rethink about that.

Thirty minutes front, thirty minutes back. That was the maximum safe dose. As the lamps clicked off after an hour, he was wondering how soon the police up in Yorkshire would examine the wheel trim under a UV lamp. First of all, they'd test it for fingerprints, but they'd find nothing there. Experts would check the size and manufacture, and find that it could have come from any one of ten million cars. No problem in that department. Then they would examine it for any dirt that might lead them to its original location, but again they'd draw a blank. It might be a day or two before they tested it in ultra-violet light.

Ultra-violet, he thought! Just like his sunbed. Would the secret marker pen show up under his sunbed? He quickly dressed and went out to the car. Two minutes later he was back in his bedroom, armed with one of the wheel trims. He fitted the goggles to his eyes and wound a few minutes on to the timer. The tubes, still warm, instantly burst into life. He bent over, holding the trim underneath them. Something was there, but it was indistinct. He raised the goggles, defying the instructions that came with the bed, and squinted at the plastic disc.

Somewhere outside he heard a car stop and the double slam of its doors, but it hardly registered in his brain. And he never noticed his own postcode that he'd neatly written near the edge of the trim, for all his attention was grabbed by the huge block capitals emblazoned across the middle, glowing like a neon sign. One letter, three numbers, three more letters. It was a registration number. His number. The number of the Escort, inscribed there by the previous owner. Outside, the hinges of his front gate squealed as it opened, and he heard the crunch of gravel underfoot as someone came to his side door. He sank to his knees, oblivious of the short-wave radiation burning into his retinae. What was it the plonker of a policeman had said? 'We're slowly working our way round the county.' That was it. And, more chillingly, 'After that, we knock on doors.' He turned around, waiting for the sound of knuckles against woodwork.

CATH STAINCLIFFE – PERFECT STORM

They were calling it 'The Ogre from the Polar'. Dennis didn't know why they bothered naming the snowstorms anymore. Not like they were exactly a rarity.

The forecaster was talking about 'The Beast from the East', decades back. How that had been a harbinger of the winter storms to come, the gale-force anticyclones that, along with all the other extreme weather, formed most of the news these days. Interspersed with warnings of the latest plagues. Lists of no-go areas. Additions to the roll call of cities that were little more than mass graves.

Dennis glanced out of the window. Whiteout, still. Though the roar of the wind had weakened to a moan. The radio was growing faint. He'd wind it up later.

He moved to put another briquette on the fire. The Ogre from the Polar didn't work really, did it? Not like The Beast from the East. Logically it should be The Ogre from the Pole – but they'd messed about trying to make it rhyme. How about The Polar Ogre? The White Shite? He grinned at that one. The Troll from the Pole? Depended on your accent whether that worked.

Day three and – like the forecast had predicted – the end was in sight.

Well, he reflected, nothing was actually in sight. Not out there. Fatalities would be counted once it was safe to venture outdoors. Some would only be found when the snow had melted. Frozen to death or crushed by collapsing structures or falling trees (in those places that still had any trees).

No trees around these parts. Not even in the valleys. Centuries ago the uplands had been cleared for farming and grazing. None of that now since the grass and bracken, the heather and winberry, had baked away. Yorkshire Dales to

Yorkshire Desert. The lead mines were already long abandoned, and back in the 2020s the quarrying had finished. No
call for stone when no one built anything any more. Just
patched up the empty places left standing.

He reckoned he'd be able to get out tomorrow. Go check
on Bessie and her hens.

Raise the alarm.

Dennis wondered if there had once been an actual object
that was lifted in times of crisis, like a flag, or maybe a bell,
or a column of smoke. Times when the ancient tribes were
crossing the hills to trade, and buried their dead in burial
mounds covered in stones.

In his grandparents' days when he was a little kid, a simple
phone call, a 999, brought help. Imagine that.

Now it would mean reporting 'the incident' the next time he
went into Settle for trading. They kept a tally in the town hall,
a big old book for births, marriages and deaths. Accident, he'd
tell them. I'll sort out the burial.

He smiled at the thought of all those eggs, all those hens.
Enough to barter for oats and oil and to stock up on briquettes
as well. Some booze even. In fact, if he played his cards right,
expanded Bessie's operation, by rearing pigs, he'd soon
generate enough valuable capital to have a shot with the most
lucrative markets. Tobacco, booze, drugs.

People would give an arm and a leg for a bundle of cheroots,
a bottle of 40 per cent or a packet of powder promising a few
hours of oblivion. Even more for painkillers and antibiotics.
Amazing someone still had the means to produce any medi-
cines. How did they get the raw materials? Original stocks
were long gone, a looter's paradise. He imagined sheds in
Darlington or Kendal, security guards at the gates. Guns and
dogs. Signs with skulls on.

Could be risky though, throwing his lot in with people like
that. High stakes. Probably safer to stick to his plan to build
on what Bessie had started and diversify.

The roof of the cottage creaked under the weight of snow.
Dennis's stomach rumbled. He should eat.

He cut up a potato and a wedge of hard white cabbage,
adding it to the last of the chicken stock he'd made from a

carcass last week. He set the pan to boil over the fire and threw in a pinch of salt. He was running out. Another item for Settle, unless Bessie had any he could take.

She wouldn't be needing it now.

He ate quickly; the potatoes were bitter and chalky but the stock was sweet enough. He added another speck of salt. He dreamed of what he'd be able to eat when his plan came good. Salty bacon, chops rimmed with fat, peas and carrots. Real bread. Cheese even. There had been cheese at the market on occasion. And dark fruit cake, honey-sweet and thick with dried apple and pear and strips of orange peel. Costing a fortune. Auctioned to the highest bidder.

Fish, Dennis thought. Once there'd have been fish. There was a picture in the old family album. His grandfather with a fat brown trout in one hand and a rod in the other. A lakeside somewhere. Dennis had never tasted fish. Toxic, even if you could find any. He had seen eels a few times, in pails in the marketplace. They turned his stomach.

Beggars can't be choosers.

Oh, sod off, Mam, he muttered.

He had asked Bessie once what fish tasted like and she tried to explain there were lots of flavours; some tasted of the sea, others like steamed chicken breast, a light taste. And tuna, extinct now, had been red, dense like steak. Turned pinky-grey when it cooked and tasted meaty.

Dennis couldn't imagine it. Same with bananas and choc-olates and melon and coffee. Just words. Like all the dishes she had in her old books. Chilli con carne and balti, falafel and macaroni cheese, guacamole and strawberry cheesecake. Bessie would ask him to read them out to her. The list of ingredients, the recipes. Hotpot, she'd say, or paella. Minestrone, brandy snaps, lobster bisque. Her eyes no good for reading any more. She could find her way around her cottage and out to see to the hen house and the crops in their polytunnel. Scrawny fingers stretched out at her sides, checking for the landmarks on the way.

I can see, she'd say, but it's all blurry, smeared together. Still, I manage, and when I'm gone you can take it all on.

But her going had been a long time coming. Far too long.

A thick blanket of snow slithered from the eaves and fell at the eastern side of the cottage. Dennis went to the window and looked out. The drifts came up to the sill more or less, stretching off down the dale, covered deep. Nothing visible. No old dry-stone wall or gatepost. No gully or outcrop, not even the scar that ran along the summit of the hill like a long grey spine.

In a day or two, as the snow thawed, all the old channels that ran from the peaks would be frothing with snow melt. The valley floors flooding afresh. Water turning the dust to mudflats. On the slopes, here and there, long-dormant seeds would crack and sprout, unfurling green, bursting with hope. Only to crisp and wither in the pitiless sun or burn in the next sharp frost, or shrivel, harrowed by gales.

Bessie had been in bed for two weeks straight back in the summer, riddled with fever, and Dennis thought his wait was over.

Then she rallied. Life in the old bones yet, she'd said, when he'd pitched up at dawn one day to find her mucking out the hen houses. No one went outside in the middle of the day any more. Boil your lungs.

He'd tried talking to her before that, about expansion and partnership, pigs and the like. He'd put feelers out in Settle about weaners and what they cost. Working out how long to feed them up until they were ready for sale.

I'm too old for any of that, she said. I like things as they are. All I need is what I can grow in the tunnel and what the hens give me. And there's always enough eggs to swap for fuel and the odd treat. Besides what would we feed pigs on?

You, he thought. Angry at her dismissal.

He tried once more after thinking it through. Telling her that if half the potatoes went to the pigs, the scheme might work. And the cabbage stalks, he said.

The chickens need the stalks.

Not all of them.

She'd given him a look, like he was worthless, a disappointment. The same look his mother always had for him. And in the same cold, hateful tone, Bessie said, Dennis, this is my land and those are my chickens and that'll be the end of it. Your time will come. You're young yet.

But it hadn't. Not soon enough. And how much longer would he have to wait? Another five years? Ten? More? She'd had a long life and she was only going to get weaker, like a hen that couldn't lay any more, so it was a kindness really. Better than months of decline with nothing to help with the pain, nothing to ease her breathing or soothe her to sleep.

This way, it would have been quick. She wouldn't have suffered. He'd soaked the briquettes in linseed oil, sacrificing a good half-pint of the stuff, then sprinkled them with saltpetre. He'd made two trips to Settle to get the saltpetre. None to be had the first time. It came all the way up from Worcester. Made from bird shit – they still had pigeons and crows there. Dennis wondered whether anyone had tried making it with chicken shit. He should find out what was involved, experiment sometime.

Outside, in his own yard, he'd almost taken his eyebrows off when he struck the flint to test one of the doctored blocks. The briquette catching light and shattering, flaming fragments flying through the air.

She wouldn't have known what hit her.

The thaw began with sunrise. Once the sun had started to descend again, Dennis judged it would be possible to walk the half-mile to Bessie's.

While the storm had howled and the snow kept him cabin-bound, he had passed his time making a list in his head, like the list of ingredients in Bessie's old books.

1. Check what could be salvaged. Pans, the kettle, other metal bits.
2. Move stuff into the old barn. (It had been refurbished once as a home. Had an upstairs as well. Empty for years but still sound. He could fix it up.)
3. Clear the well.
4. Feed and muck out the hens.
5. Feed and water the crops. Pick anything that was ready.
6. Bury Bessie. (That would have to wait till the ground was soft; even then it would be hard to dig. The lime-stone was close to the surface, only three or four inches

of thin dirt most places. An old mine shaft might be
better, or a cave. The hills were riddled with them. He
thought fleetingly of the polytunnel, the compost with
cabbages and potatoes and herbs. But that wasn't
respectful. And, practically, he needed every inch of
ground for crops. Anyway, he didn't want to be
unearthing a skull or a hand by mistake. Give himself
a shock.)

The snow was blinding as he made his way along the track,
pulling the sledge, his snowshoes skidding now and again.
The snow squealing underfoot.

He wore his sunglasses. The plastic lenses were scratched
and one arm bent so they hung lopsided, but they served to
shield his eyes from the worst of the glare. You saw plenty of
people sunblind, feeling their way like Bessie did with anything
unfamiliar. They would sit destitute in the market square, too
daft or too poor to have used protection. Bessie swore she'd
always worn shades, as she called them. Even had a spare pair.

They'd be nothing but a pool of plastic now.

The snow was turning to slush where he crossed a beck,
but hard packed elsewhere. He hauled the sledge up the rise
to Bessie's place and stopped on the crest of the hill, bracing
himself for the sight.

A thump to his gut when his eyes fell on the cottage. Snow
still thick on the roof, windows intact. No sign of damage,
not smoke nor fire.

His mind stumbled over explanations. Something had killed
her before she could stoke the fire? A heart attack, a bleed in
the brain. Or had she fallen asleep, let the fire die? Froze
before she could act. Cold-sickness, hypothermia, stealing the
heat from her body then the sense from her brain. People often
stripped naked, feeling unbearably hot, so they shed their
clothes and hurried death along.

It wasn't the end of the world, he told himself. In fact, if
she had just pegged it, then he could make use of all the things
in her cottage which would otherwise have been lost. Exchange
what he didn't want. He could live in the place while he did
the barn up. Then use the cottage to house the pigs.

He slid down the slope to the yard, the sledge skidding alongside him and fishtailing to a stop on the level.

The big old key was still in his pocket, so she couldn't have got out and gone off anywhere. And the snow still rose a couple of feet all around the cottage.

Dennis called out as he began to scoop the snow away from the door, making as much racket as possible to cover the sound of unlocking it. Just in case.

When his way was clear he pushed the door open and stepped inside.

The room was cold. Stone cold. Colder inside than out. His breath made clouds in the air.

Everything looked just as he'd left it, except the fire was dead in the grate. Curls of ash and cinders, black and white.

The basket of briquettes he'd brought and readied for her, untouched to one side.

Bessie?

He stole towards the sleeping area in the alcove, her bed hidden away behind the curtain.

Drawing the curtain aside, he saw a heap of bedding, quilts and blankets piled high. Was she under there?

Bessie? He put a hand to the hump and jerked back when it moved.

Bessie threw back the covers.

Dennis. Voice croaky. She smiled, teeth grey and stubby. We made it.

Why didn't you light the fire? he said. It's perishing.

It hurt to breathe, the air a knife in his lungs.

Has it stopped? she said.

He nodded. It's thawing.

Bessie climbed out of bed, still smiling. She slipped on her sunglasses, pulled one of the blankets round her shoulders then walked slowly to the door and opened it. Her face tilted up to the sun. Baked Alaska, she muttered. Boeuf bourguignon.

She was losing her marbles, Dennis thought. That would explain it. He looked at the flint beside the hearth, the crumbs of dead ash.

I'll feed the chicks, fetch the eggs, she said, still facing away, they'll be ready for it. You light that fire.

He stood, hands clutching for answers. Heart in his throat. Stupid bitch.

He could substitute the briquettes, tell her these were damp or something, fetch more from his place.

Pigs are very greedy, she said. That's what I was told. Had you thought about that?

What? No. I, erm . . . I don't think these briquettes are—

He heard the snick of a flint. The unmistakable smell of a cigarette.

Bessie turned from the doorway. Only a couple left, she said, holding up her hand. I have one every birthday. But this is a special occasion, wouldn't you say? She took a drag and blew a smoke ring, which stretched and billowed above her head.

Outside the world was white and still, glistening. The shadow of the sledge, a bruised blue, reaching across the ground. Nothing moved except the drift of smoke. The only sound a tick-tick from the corner of the roof where the snow was melting.

Bessie took another drag.

I'm half blind, she said, but there's nothing wrong with my sense of smell. Sharp as a tack, believe you me. Linseed oil. Stinks of fish. Someone could do themselves a serious injury messing with stuff like that.

And she flicked the burning cigarette to fly in an arc from the doorway and land in the basket of briquettes beside him.

Dennis raised his palms, opened his mouth, but whatever he was about to say was lost in the thunder of the explosion that ripped through the cottage, hurling him to the floor while sheets of flame, hungry for fuel, licked over his skin, devoured his clothes and hair.

Ears ringing, hip and shoulder throbbing from the impact of being blown over, Bessie got to her feet and walked back to the cottage. The door was still on its hinges, key in the outside. She shut and locked it. The heat from within already matching that of the sun above.

Greedy, she said to herself. Smoke was curling from the chimney and smuts fell like black snow. The smell of burning meat on the air. Sticky barbecued ribs, she murmured.

She gave a sharp sigh, a shake of her head, then made her way, the snow crunching beneath her feet, to see to the chicks.

CHRIS SIMMS – GAFFED

'I did the right thing?'

'Yeah, Malcolm, you did the right thing.'

'I don't know . . .' Hunching forward, he rubbed at the fine hair on his head as if massaging shampoo into his scalp. 'Christ.'

The man in the other armchair watched. This guy, he thought, is wound so tight, he's liable to snap.

Malcolm's hands dropped and his head came back up. He blinked away the beginnings of tears and sucked in air with such force, a tremor went through his lower lip.

'Sit back,' the other man urged. 'You need to get a grip here, OK?'

Malcolm's brown eyes flitted nervously towards a small window set deep in the timber wall. Outside, the light was beginning to fail. A gust of wind sent huge flakes of snow against the glass, and the sound they made was like moths, trapped in a jar.

'You're safe here,' the other man insisted quietly. 'Don't worry. Try not to worry – you did the right thing.'

Malcolm kept looking at the window. 'Then, where are they?'

'Coming.'

'You called over an hour ago.'

'Malcolm, we're in a cabin in the middle of fucking nowhere. There's a blizzard blowing outside. Give the poor bastards a chance.'

Malcolm sank back in his seat and surveyed the cramped room, eyes moving like those of a cornered deer. 'Do you always see your informants here?'

The other man grinned for a moment. 'Only if they ring me with something worthwhile.' He glanced at the memory stick sitting on the low table between them. 'I don't like giving up my weekends for any old shit.'

Malcolm's gaze stayed away from the diminutive object. 'Yeah well,' he murmured hoarsely, sounding like he was about to retch, 'it certainly isn't that.'

'I believe you.' The man slowly climbed from his armchair and bent stiffly before a wood-burning stove. Opening its door, he tossed a log onto the glowing embers and clanged the heavy door shut. Squatting inside, the hunk of wood appeared almost as if it was trying to decide what to do. Then smoke started rising from its flanks, followed shortly after by the first flickers of flame. The man limped around the little hut, drawing a purple velvet curtain across each small window. 'This is the end of your life – as you know it. I won't bullshit you with fake promises. It'll be hard. Witness protection programmes aren't a ticket to an easy life.' He made his way back to his armchair and sank into it with a sigh. 'It'll be an apartment somewhere to start with – shared with a couple of detectives who'll fart a lot, scratch their nuts and generally wish they weren't babysitting you. Then, after the trial, you'll be found mundane work in a mundane office. No contact with your friends and family—'

Malcolm let out a bitter snort.

'What?' the other man asked.

'I have no friends,' Malcolm muttered. 'And now Mother's gone, I have no family, either.'

The man tilted his head to the side. 'Is that why you made your move?'

'Yes,' Malcolm stated sadly. 'He doesn't know she's dead. It was so sudden, so out of the blue.'

The other man began to nod. 'I get it. With her gone, Slater's hold on you is broken.'

Malcolm's eyelids fluttered slightly. 'You knew . . . you knew about my . . .'

He waved a hand dismissively. 'We've been watching you for years.' In fact, he said to himself, several people have suggested we should try and flip you.

'You've had me under surveillance?'

'Not just you. Plenty of other . . . reluctant recruits in his empire. You must have realized that.'

'Well, yes. But there were always precautions in place. In

case you guys had bugged his offices, tapped the phones. And, of course, the computer systems had to be completely secure—'

'Which was down to you,' the other man cut in. 'And a damn fine job you did, too. One time, we even asked the Feds to try and get past the firewalls you built.'

'And could they?'

'Nope.'

What satisfaction the answer gave Malcolm didn't last long. His shoulders slumped once more as his eyes dropped to the memory stick. 'Well, now you've got everything you need to bring the whole thing crashing down.' He licked at his lips.

The other man waited, half-knowing what the next question would be.

'When . . . when did . . .' Malcolm stumbled over his words. 'How did you discover about me?'

'You being homosexual?' the other man asked matter-of-factly.

'I wouldn't necessarily describe myself as that,' Malcolm replied, eyes still downcast.

The other man shrugged. Hanging about in men's wash-rooms, he thought. That's not homosexual behaviour? Driving a hundred miles to wander the West Hampton dunes on a weekday afternoon? You don't even have a dog. 'Some places you were observed in the vicinity of,' he said, 'the fact you lived with your mother, no sign of any . . . significant other.' He stopped short of saying: your choice of pastel-coloured cardigans, the bird-like way you move, how fastidious you are with your appearance. Even now, he thought, you're checking to make sure your hair isn't ruffled where you were rubbing at it just now. 'Can I ask when exactly your mother passed away?'

Malcolm swallowed, and the hand that had been smoothing his hair fluttered at his throat. When he tried to speak, only a croak came out.

'Do you want a drink?' the other man announced abruptly. 'A splash of bourbon?'

Malcolm looked uncertain. 'Is that sensible?'

'Well, no chance in hell I'm driving anywhere tonight. And neither will you be. The car you came in? That's not yours any more. None of your old life is. You'll be driven to a secure house. Everything's changed, you do realize that?'

'Perhaps a drink would be good.'

'Absolutely.' He reached to the sideboard next to his chair, pulled the stopper on a square-shaped bottle and poured two generous measures. Holding one of the glasses out, he said, 'Here's to the one that got away.'

Malcolm's fingers shied away from the proffered drink. 'Sorry?'

'The one that got away,' the man repeated.

The trace of a smile appeared on Malcolm's lips as he took the glass. 'You think,' he said tentatively, 'I have?'

Returning his smile, the other man clinked his glass against Malcolm's and almost drained his drink in one gulp. 'Good stuff,' he said fondly, swilling round what was left of the chestnut liquid.

Malcolm lowered his glass, breathing out as he did so. 'That burns the throat.'

'Should do,' the other man replied. 'It's a dozen years old. Now, you were telling me when your mother passed?'

Malcolm took another small sip and ruminated a moment longer. 'I found her this morning.'

'This morning?'

'Yes.'

'But driving out here – that must have taken five hours, easy.'

'She's still there,' Malcolm blurted.

'Still where?'

'In her bed.'

He regarded Malcolm for a second. 'You discovered her and . . . drove straight here?'

'No.' Malcolm sipped again, more deeply this time. He tilted his glass at the memory stick on the low table. 'I copied the files first then I started driving.'

'Wait up.' The other man's voice now had an edge to it. 'You had my number, that much I can understand. It's probably in Slater's files somewhere, along with a photo of my face.' He jabbed a finger at the floor. 'But how did you know about here?'

'I didn't – I just set off and rang you from the first gas station I got to. When I told you I wanted out, you gave me directions. Remember?'

The answer seemed to relax the other man. 'God, yes. For a minute there, I thought you knew about this place.' He finished off his drink. 'Only one or two in my team know about this place. And Slater won't miss you until Monday morning? You're sure of that?'

'Certain. After you gave me those sat-nav coordinates, I just drove . . .' Malcolm's voice trailed away as he smiled. 'For the first time in – oh, as long as I can remember – I felt free. Mother gone. Slater too – I hope. It was a feeling of immense . . . release.' He drained the last of his drink and settled lower in his seat.

The other man reached for the bottle and poured them both another decent splash.

'We need to make arrangements for Mother,' Malcolm said, watching the flames in the wood-burner. 'She's just lying there in her bed.' He blinked. 'That . . . that damned crucifix above the headboard. Him, staring down at me from it.'

'It's fine, don't worry. We'll take care of her, OK?' The other man stretched his legs out and crossed his ankles, tumbler positioned on the swell of his stomach. 'You really didn't take any chances, did you? Just got the hell out.'

Malcolm gave a nod. 'Slater's threats wouldn't work any more. The . . . the film he had of me. How could he show that to Mother if she was dead? I knew it was my only chance: so I took it.'

The man lifted his drink. 'Here's to you.'

There was now a flush in Malcolm's cheeks as he raised his glass and drank again.

Both men sat listening to the sound of the wind moaning under the cabin's eaves. Something collapsed in the wood-burner and the log rolled to the side, gently thudding against the metal. A cluster of sparks darted up and vanished.

'It's nice here,' Malcolm stated, looking at the sheepskin

rug on the floor and the framed displays of colourful fishing flies on the wall. 'Cosy.'

'Thanks.'

Malcolm placed an elbow on his armrest and leaned his temple on the back of his fingers. 'The one that got away.' His voice was so faint it was almost inaudible.

The man's head moved. 'Mmm?'

'The one that got away,' Malcolm repeated more loudly. 'What you called me earlier. Has no one got away before?'

'You know they haven't. Or we wouldn't be sitting here.'

'Actually, you'd be surprised at how little I know. Slater's very good at compartmentalizing things. The only person with an understanding of his organization's true extent is him. And maybe you, Detective Mulligan.'

The man pondered the comment. 'Believe me, his empire goes in all directions.'

'And have many tried to . . . escape from him? Obviously I've heard the odd rumour. People vanishing, trusted people.'

'Plenty of those. We've sometimes found a body – what was left,' he glanced up, saw the trepidation creeping across the other man's face. 'But that's not important. What is important is you. And what you've got for me on that memory stick.'

'No,' Malcolm said, taking a small gulp of his drink. 'I'd like to know. Those stories; I was never let in on them. Tell me about some of the ones who failed.'

'There's not much to tell,' Mulligan replied despondently. 'Remains would turn up, sometimes at the very rendezvous point we had arranged. Another avenue of investigation would close down.' His voice suddenly came to life – but with bitterness, not enthusiasm. 'There is one who gets away. Who keeps getting away, again and again. But not from Slater: from us.'

'I'm not sure I follow you . . .'

'He'll probably still be beyond our reach, even after you testify.'

'Who do you mean?'

Detective Mulligan stared down at his glass. 'The person Slater employs to make people disappear. Now, that's someone who'll endure. His type always do. Slater will be locked up – for the rest of his life – and this man will simply find another employer. He's a true pro.' He put his glass on the table. 'Could you use some food? I could use some food. There are two rainbow trout in the kitchen, ready filleted. I've got some nice bread, as well. I know it's nothing much . . .'

'Sounds like the Bible,' Malcolm said with a lopsided grin.

'Sorry?'

'When Jesus fed the five thousand?'

The detective looked lost.

Malcolm shook his head. 'Mother would read to me from it when I was young. Doesn't matter. The food sounds delicious. But what if your team get here?'

'They can sit outside in their SUVs. Besides, this storm? We've got more of a wait yet, if you ask me.' He struggled out of his seat and hobbled into the kitchen. A pan clattered.

Malcolm placed his glass alongside the detective's and stepped surreptitiously across the tiny room. At the window to the side of the door, he lifted the corner of the curtain and peered out. Night had now fallen. Beyond the flakes ghosting down the other side of the glass was unbroken black. His eyes went to the heavy wooden door. Seeing the bolt was well-oiled, he slid it silently across. Just to be safe.

On the adjacent wall there hung a photo. A woman, her back turned to the camera, watching two children playing in the shallows of a lake. The lake beside which the little cabin stood. Mulligan's boys, he thought. Now grown-up. One a sergeant in the New York police department, one a teacher in Boston. Mulligan's wife, Jenny, died eleven years before. Malcolm knew all this because he'd been ordered to learn it. Know your enemy, Slater had said to him. And Detective Mulligan headed up the team whose mission it was to bring Slater's empire down.

Nestling between two roof beams above the photo was a glass case. Mounted within was a large, stuffed, trout. Its crooked mouth was parted slightly in an eternal sigh.

'So this person,' Malcolm called out as he retook his seat. 'Does he never leave any evidence behind?'

Mulligan's voice floated through from the other room. 'Nope. He's forensically aware, as we say in the job. Probably goes about his business wearing a scene-of-crime suit. Some of the boys think he's Chinese – one time a single hair was found on a body. Far Eastern origin, according to DNA taken from the follicle. But that's about it. The boys have given him the nickname Fu Manchu.'

'Who?'

Mulligan poked his head round the door, a spatula in one hand. 'The oriental killer from that old film? The sinister one with a long, wispy moustache?'

'How do you know it's the same person that does all the dirty work?'

But Mulligan had vanished back into the kitchen and a sizzling sound broke out. He reappeared a minute later carrying a chopping board. On it were several rough slices of thickly buttered bread. As he placed the board on the table he said, 'You really want to know?'

Malcolm inclined his head. 'I want to, yes. Knowing about what Slater has ordered will make it easier to testify against him.'

Mulligan had returned to the kitchen and Malcolm picked up a slice of the bread and began to eat it.

'This guy has a signature – like a calling card.' The sizzling noise died down. 'The same method each time.'

'Which is?'

Mulligan walked back into the room, bringing with him a smell of lemon and seared fish skin. In each of his hands was a plate, a length of fish across the middle. 'He tortures them first – using a scalpel or a razor. Something extremely sharp. Precise cuts, methodical. I should think to glean everything they had on Slater.'

Malcolm's fingers trembled slightly as he took his plate. 'That's probably enough detail about his methods.'

'Yes, probably,' Mulligan said. 'The other infuriating thing is how he always seems to anticipate our next move. Like our ops room has been bugged or he's hacked into our computers to snoop on our emails and reports.'

'Really?' Malcolm sat up a bit. 'Your system could have been compromised? That would take some doing. This smells amazing, by the way.'

'Well – it's only simple, as I said. Fresh fish, that's the secret.'

Plates balanced on their knees, they both began to eat, heads bowed over their food. After another minute, Mulligan spoke again, his mouth half-full. 'The other suspicion is this guy's had medical training.'

Malcolm put his cutlery down. From under the cuff of one sleeve, he removed a handkerchief and dabbed at the corners of his mouth. 'Why do you think that?'

'The victim has always been drugged. A powerful muscle relaxant, probably mixed into a drink. Enough to turn their limbs all floppy. Another reason to think the guy is oriental – or of a slight build. Rather than overpower his victims physically, he does it chemically.'

Malcolm chewed on his piece of bread in silence.

'Sorry, I didn't mean to make you feel uncomfortable,' Mulligan said. The last of his fish was now gone and he put his plate on the table. 'That hit the spot.'

'It did,' Malcolm responded, stacking his plate on the other man's and arranging their knives and forks in a neat row.

'More bourbon?' Mulligan asked.

'I don't know.' His eyes cut to the kitchen doorway and he pictured coffee granules, brown sugar and water boiling in a kettle. 'Perhaps a hot drink?'

Mulligan wrinkled his nose. 'Come on, one for the road. You've got a long drive ahead of you.'

'OK, but just a dash.'

After pouring out a couple more measures, the detective took their plates and carried them into the kitchen.

Tentatively, Malcolm picked up his drink and smelled it. But the thought of any more just made him feel dizzy. I'm drunk, he thought with disgust, hating the sensation of not being in control. The sound of a tap running was now coming from the kitchen and he toyed with the idea of asking for a glass of water. 'So,' he said, dismayed to hear a slight slur in his voice. 'Is there any hope at all of catching this man?'

'No,' Mulligan called back. 'I don't think we ever will.'

The detective's cell phone started ringing and Malcolm's

gaze swung round. He looked at it stupidly, aware his head was beginning to loll.

'That'll be work,' said Mulligan, making a strange swishing sound as he re-entered the room.

Malcolm tried to lift his eyes but they suddenly seemed so heavy. The detective moved back into his line of vision. He was now dressed in white, some kind of paper-like garment that even encompassed his shoes. The hand that picked up the phone was covered by a latex glove.

'Hello? You got my message from earlier? Yes, Mr Slater, that's right – he's here. Arrived about ninety minutes ago. Of course I can. The usual fee is fine. I'll have a full report for you by morning.'

Heart now hammering, Malcolm tried with all his strength to look up. The glass started sliding from his hand and he couldn't even clench his fingers.

'Whoops,' Mulligan said, plucking the drink from Malcolm's slack grip. 'You really should have passed on that bread and butter. I did.'

The detective moved back into the kitchen and Malcolm could now only listen to the sounds coming from the adjoining room. When Mulligan reappeared, he placed a tray on the low table. Malcolm swivelled his eyes. On it was a roll of bin liners, four lengths of nylon twine and a fish knife, its cruel blade tapering to an incredibly fine point.

Malcolm could feel drool coming from the corner of his mouth as his tongue stirred sluggishly. 'You . . . you're . . . it's you . . .'

Mulligan crouched down and secured the other man's wrists, then his ankles, to the chair. The detective straightened back up with a slight grunt. The sound of bin liners being unrolled started to fill the room. Malcolm watched helplessly as they were laid on the timber floor around his feet. Mulligan's voice floated down from above. 'That's right, Malcolm. I am. And you? You're not the one that got away.'

MARTIN EDWARDS –
THE OTHER LIFE

'I can't believe I'm actually doing this,' Jean Parkinson said, as she and Irina turned off the main street.

'You will enjoy.' Irina gave a wolfish smile. 'Good for you. Change.'

Jean grunted. It was all very well for the girl – all right, she was in her mid-twenties, but any female under forty was a girl as far as Jean was concerned – to say that. Already she wished she'd stayed at home, safe and secure at home. As for this fool's errand . . .

'Here is church.' Irina pointed to a small, single-storey building with a flat roof.

Jean stared. 'If that's a church, I'm a vestal virgin.'

'Church,' Irina repeated.

For all her pleasant manner, Jean thought, Irina was as stubborn as they come. Perhaps she'd needed that strength of character while making the long journey from Bosnia, wherever that was, to this quiet backwater in semi-rural Staffordshire. Certainly, it took something special to persuade a Parkinson to set foot inside a church. Arthur's funeral had taken place at a crematorium; forty-seven years ago, they'd married at a registry office. There hadn't been any children, but it wasn't much of a regret. Jean had never been the maternal type. Her satisfaction had come from helping Arthur in the business.

Jean halted, and leaned on her walking stick. 'Church? It's a glorified Portakabin!'

Irina shook her mane of blonde hair, dismissing any objection. She might be an immigrant, she might not have the right papers, Jean couldn't care less; she was a hard worker, and only charged half as much as those useless cleaning companies. She certainly knew her own mind. Jean could respect that, even if all this malarkey about the Other Life was a load of garbage.

Without more ado, Irina strode to the door of the building. Turning, she beckoned the older woman.

'Come.'

Grumbling, Jean followed her inside. In the cramped entrance hall, a table tottered under a pile of pamphlets and a vase of white roses. Two shelves on the wall were devoted to books about angels, meditation, dreams, and spirit guides. Above the shelves, a notice was pinned: *Feel Free to Borrow or Browse.* From the ceiling hung angel mobiles and dream-catchers.

A stout grey-haired woman greeted them with a broad smile. 'Welcome, welcome! First time here, is it? Come in, do.' She thrust pamphlets on them. 'Take a seat, and make yourselves comfortable. Would you like a raffle ticket? There's a draw after the service.'

Irina fumbled vaguely in her bag. Jean realized this was her cue to pay up. Dipping into her purse, she withdrew a twenty-pound note.

'Keep the change,' she told the woman. 'I expect to win, mind.'

Irina gave a giggle of apology, but the stout woman simply beamed. 'Very generous of you. The prize is a bottle of prosecco.'

Jean raised bushy eyebrows. As they moved into the main room, she muttered under her breath. 'Gambling and alcohol. Funny sort of church, if you ask me.'

At one end of the room, beyond a wide strip of crimson carpet, was a table covered with a white cloth. On it stood a crystal glass filled almost to the brim with red wine, and another vase of roses. Two chairs flanked the table, and to the left was a wooden lectern. On a shelf at the side was a CD player so ancient it was almost an antique. A thick red cord, suspended from two makeshift posts, separated the carpet and table from about twenty people seated on canvas chairs. All but two were female, and most looked Jean's age or older. Several of them broke off from their conversations to nod and smile as Irina and Jean made their way to seats at the back of the room.

Suddenly a hush fell as a tall, bespectacled woman came

into the room. She unhooked the cord and took up a position behind the lectern.

'Good evening, ladies and gentlemen. I'd like to bid you welcome, especially those of you who are new to our church. And without more ado, I'd like to introduce someone many of you will remember from her previous visits here – Emily.'

As she spoke, a door to the right of the lectern opened, to reveal a small, bird-like woman. Her appearance was greeted by an appreciative murmur from the congregation. She was dressed from head to toe in black, and Jean guessed she was seventy-five if she was a day.

'And now,' the tall woman said, 'would you please turn to hymn number two?'

Irina opened her pamphlet, and nudged Jean to do likewise. On the front cover was printed *HYMNS*. Turning over a page, Jean found hymn number two.

'Oh my God!' she murmured, even though she didn't believe in God. 'You couldn't make it up.'

Music burst from the CD player, a karaoke version of Abba's 'I Believe in Angels', and everyone got to their feet. After a moment's hesitation Jean also rose, stiffly and with the utmost reluctance. Irina and the rest of the congregation sang lustily, but Jean kept her mouth clamped shut. She'd never liked Abba. Arthur had once had a bit of a crush on the blonde one. He'd always had a roving eye. Come to think of it, he'd have taken a shine to Irina if he'd had the chance. Not that he'd have been much use to her after all that trouble with his prostate.

There weren't any rings on Irina's long, slim fingers, but the gold bracelet on her wrist looked, to Jean's practised eye, like the real thing rather than a fake. There must be a man in the background. Irina was pretty, for sure, and it would take a year's cleaning to pay for a bracelet like that.

Jean frowned. Was Irina as naive and innocent as she seemed? Jean had taken her on shortly after Arthur's death, when she was at her lowest ebb, and the osteoarthritis was taking hold. Of course, the girl was under strict instructions about where to clean, and where to keep out. Even so. Jean wasn't accustomed to letting other people into her life. She

and Arthur had been a tightly knit team, and before his retirement he'd done the necessary with people who worked in
the firm. Jean wasn't much of a mixer, and she wasn't soft,
either. If you'd told her, even twelve months ago, that she'd
wind up in a spiritualist church, surrounded by pensioners
singing a mindless pop song from the seventies, she'd have
said you were mad.

Not before time, the song came to an end, and people
resumed their seats. The stout woman asked Emily to lead the
prayers, and warm words were spoken about absent members
of the congregation who were suffering from illness. Hope
was expressed that there would be an end to wars and famine.
Jean let it all wash over her. You had to make your own luck
in this world, that was her belief. There wasn't anybody up
there looking after you.

As the room fell silent, Emily said, 'Can anyone take the
name Bill?'

A huge woman in a pink cardigan who seemed to be occupying two separate seats on the front row nodded. Her response
galvanized Emily into a flurry of hand-waving and pacing up
and down the red carpet. Speaking much more rapidly than
before, Emily announced that Bill was very happy, and no
longer in pain. He hoped that now he was gone, his beloved
wouldn't carry out her plan to have the back garden paved
over. Why not keep growing the hydrangeas, and celebrate the
wonders of Mother Nature?

The fat woman nodded soberly, and Irina leaned close to
Jean, to whisper in her ear.

'You see? She made a connection.'

Jean sniffed. It would take more than a bit of chit-chat about
hydrangeas to impress her.

Emily took a sip from the wine glass and, after closing her
eyes for a few seconds, asked, 'Will anyone take Brenda?'

A well-dressed bald man just in front of Jean raised his
hand. Emily had news from the departed Brenda, who wanted
her husband to keep his spirits up. If that meant making a new
lady friend, that was fine by her. She only wanted him to be
happy. A busty woman sitting next to Brenda's widower patted
his hand and gave him a smile of encouragement.

Emily turned to a woman at the far end of Jean's row. 'Will you take an elderly gentleman with lovely brown eyes, just like yours, who passed from a heart attack on Boxing Day?'

'His name isn't . . . Richard, is it?' The woman was almost stammering. 'Richard . . . Latham?'

Emily's eyes were shut again. Jean saw the woman's small hands clenching and unclenching as she waited.

'Richard Latham, yes. And are you his precious Hayley?'

'Oh, yes!'

The woman's eyes shone, and her lips parted in a joyful smile. How did they do it? Jean supposed that the stout woman knew her congregation well, and gave Emily plenty of tip-offs. Grief and wishful thinking did the rest.

Richard wanted his daughter to know that he thought about her constantly, and that he'd never meant to be so harsh and distant. Her husband was a good man, he understood that now. Would she forgive him for the pain he'd caused?

'Of course, Dad!'

Emily nodded, and murmured something Jean couldn't catch, as if in private conversation with someone nobody else could see. Jean thought she wouldn't fancy a conversation with her own father. He'd been a butcher, and as a kid she'd helped in his shop on the outskirts of Birmingham. Dad had trained her up in the hope she'd take over the shop one day, but then she'd met Arthur, and followed a different path.

'In the Other Life,' Emily told the daughter, 'people strive to redeem themselves. Make up for all the wrong turnings they took in this world.'

Irina was rapt. Jean wondered if a message might come from Bosnia. If so, would Emily transmit it into English, so that everyone could understand?

Emily took another sip of wine. 'Will anyone take Arthur?'

Nobody responded. Irina dug Jean in the ribs with a sharp elbow.

'Arthur!' she hissed. 'Your husband, no? Tell her!'

It wasn't an uncommon name, not in that generation, at any rate. But still nobody moved a muscle. Emily scanned the congregation.

'No?' She looked intently at Jean. 'Ah, is it you, dear? Come along, don't be shy. Will you take Arthur?'

Irina nudged Jean once again.

Slowly, Jean nodded.

Emily chirruped away, seemingly to herself, for sixty seconds, before clearing her throat, and addressing Jean.

'He was a home-loving man, was Arthur.'

Despite herself, Jean inclined her head.

'You were a homebody too, and he worked hard to give you a good life.'

Jean nodded again. It was undeniably true.

'He built things up nicely for you.'

Of course he did, Jean thought with a touch of impatience. The man owned a building company.

'Left you well provided for.'

Jean frowned: she didn't like talking about money. All this was bland and hopelessly vague, the sort of stuff anyone might say about anyone else. As a matter of fact, she'd played her part in making sure the business prospered.

'You're on your own now, but he's looking down on you. Keeping an eye out to make sure you're safe and sound.'

Oh yes, he'd always been good at that. Those occasional flings meant nothing, really, Jean had never bothered about them. Arthur pushed things to the limit. It was in his nature to go to extremes, but he never forgot which side his bread was buttered, all right.

Suddenly Emily chuckled, as if Arthur had told her a joke. He always had a wry sense of humour, Jean would say that for him.

'He's glad you have such good friends all around you. Giving you love and support.'

Irina squeezed Jean's hand. Jean felt a slight prickle of disappointment. For a few moments she *had* felt a strange connection with Arthur, but Emily was over-egging it. Arthur had been the one who went out and kept the business going. Jean took a quiet pleasure in doing her work well, but she'd never been sociable, never gone in for friends. She didn't find it easy to trust people.

Emily seemed disappointed not to have received yet

another nod of assent, and within a few moments, the connection faded. It was time to move on to someone else making contact from the Other Life.

Jean's canvas chair had become appallingly uncomfortable by the time the tall, bespectacled woman stood up, and said that unfortunately, the clock was against them. She gave profuse thanks to Emily, who smiled sweetly, sank down on to one of the chairs by the lectern, and treated herself to a gulp of wine.

'Hymn number four, please.'

Jean barely stifled a moan of dismay. John Lennon's 'Imagine'. Load of garbage. A world without possessions? You'd be back in the Stone Age. She stood up with the rest of the congregation, but didn't allow any of the ridiculous words to pass her lips.

When everyone was sitting down again, a collection was taken by the stout woman who had greeted them at the main door. The raffle was drawn, and the busty woman claimed the prosecco, giving Brenda's husband a triumphant wink as she returned to her place; Jean suspected that she was planning a connection of her own. Details of a forthcoming healing service and a meditation meeting were announced. Everyone was invited to mingle over tea and biscuits at the back of the room.

'Come,' Irina said, opening up her purse. 'Tea and . . .'

'Not for me, thanks,' Jean said.

'But you must! You made a connection with Arthur!'

Jean pursed her lips. 'Thanks for inviting me,' she said, 'but I really must get back. You know I don't like to be away from the house for long.'

'You must get out more!' Irina gestured to the people shuffling in the direction of the tea urn. 'These are good people. You make friends. Dear friends.'

Jean contemplated the busty woman, who had plunged into animated conversation with the well-dressed widower. 'Some other time.'

'I come back with you.'

'No need.' Jean realized she sounded ungracious, but that had never bothered her. 'It's only half a mile. I'm not a cripple.'

'It's dark outside.' Irina shivered. 'Bad things happen in the dark.'

Jean snorted. 'Not to me.'

Irina snatched at her sleeve as she turned to go. 'Please. Let me walk to your house.'

'You live in the opposite direction. Don't worry about me.'

Irina sighed. She seemed irresolute. 'I don't like.'

Good manners had never come easily to Jean, but she felt she should make a token effort. 'Mark my words, I'll be fine. Thanks for asking me along. It's been – interesting.'

Irina shrugged. 'OK, Mrs Parkinson. You win.'

Jean suppressed a chuckle. How often had she heard old Arthur say exactly the same thing?

She dropped the so-called hymn book on the table by the door as she made her way outside. One thing was for sure: Arthur would have been lost without her. It was good that he'd been the first to die. Even with some floosie at his beck and call, he'd never have managed on his own. He'd not been the same man after giving up the business, there was no denying it. They'd talked about moving abroad, maybe to the Algarve, but it had never come to anything. Once the doctor diagnosed cancer, things went slowly downhill.

Thankfully, the road home was well-lit, and there was a pavement all the way to the lane on which Jean lived. It wasn't yet nine o'clock, but there wasn't much traffic about. Her house was at the far end of the town, on the edge of the green belt. It was a huge converted barn, a ridiculous size for a couple on their own, let alone a single person, but she couldn't bring herself to leave. Arthur must have foreseen this, and that was why he'd taken so much trouble over the place. He used to boast that it was the best construction project he'd ever masterminded, and Jean didn't doubt it. For all his faults, he hadn't been *such* a bad man.

Her left knee was hurting tonight. The doctor reckoned she was pretty much ready for the operation, but she kept putting it off. She'd go private, but it wasn't meanness that held her back. Neither she nor Arthur had been afraid to spend when it made sense to do so. But she didn't fancy the prospect of an anaesthetic. Needles bothered her, she'd seen the damage they could do. In fact, she didn't mind admitting it, foolish as it seemed, she was a coward when it came to feeling pain.

As she limped along, she wondered about Irina. The girl reckoned she was a regular at the spiritualist church; maybe she'd tipped them off about Arthur, and the fact that he'd been a builder. Irina didn't know much about him, of course; she'd only arrived in this country around the time he died. That might explain why Emily hadn't been able to give much chapter and verse. Then again, it was as well.

Funny about that bracelet, though. Irina hadn't mentioned a man in her life. Presumably she wanted to guard her privacy. Fair enough, Jean and Arthur had always felt the same.

She turned off the main street, passing a van parked at the side of the lane. There were no streetlamps, but the house was only two hundred yards away, and from the moment darkness fell, it was always brightly lit. Arthur was a great believer in security. He was obsessive about it, right to the end of his days.

Caution, ingrained habit, call it what you will, prompted her to look back over her shoulder, and give the van a second glance. It didn't have any lights on, and there seemed to be nobody inside. Nothing odd about that, but there wasn't any reason for anyone to park there. The fields were fenced off, there were no shady paths down which courting couples might wander, and nothing on the main street worth stopping for; just a bus shelter and a convenience store that had inconveniently closed six months ago, driven out of existence by competition from an out-of-town retail park.

Jean was hobbling now. This knee really would have to be sorted out, there was no point in pretending any different. At least, Jean thought, she'd always been good at facing up to grim reality.

The front gate, seven feet high, was illuminated by a lamp on each brick post. She was about to tap in the number code (Arthur's birth year, no point in making things too complicated at her time of life) when her walking stick brushed against the iron rails of the gate. It moved silently but visibly under the lamplight.

Jean stiffened, and for once it was nothing to do with her creaking joints. Every six months, Paul Currie checked the security system. Paul was retired now, but he'd once worked for Arthur's old firm; he was a genius when it came to electronics. He'd assured her that everything was fine. Paul, like the rest of the old gang, was not quite the man he used to be, but when push came to shove, he never let her down.

Who had opened the gate and disabled the alarm system? And how had they managed it?

There was no sign of life in the house, but then you wouldn't expect burglars to advertise their presence. For a fleeting instant, Jean thought about calling the police. But it wasn't a good idea. Anyway, she'd never considered herself as helpless. Her toughness had been a source of pride to Arthur; he used to say it was why he'd married her. Even now, at seventy-one, she wasn't entirely incapable of looking after herself.

No, there was nothing for it but to walk up the front path and let herself in. She squared her shoulders. If there was anyone inside, she'd give them what-for.

The front door had both mortise and Yale locks; she let herself in, and switched on the lights. For a few moments, she listened intently, but couldn't hear anything. Mind you, her hearing wasn't what it once was; trouble was, the hearing test people only wanted to sell you fancy hearing aids, and she hated being conned out of the money Arthur and she had worked so hard to earn.

She walked across the hallway, and opened the door to the dining room. So far as she could see, nothing had been disturbed, but that didn't mean much. In the adjoining room, she kept the family silver in a couple of display cabinets. The connecting door was ajar. She could have sworn she'd closed it before leaving for her spiritual experience earlier that evening.

Jean hesitated, something she didn't often do. No sense in trying to make a dash for it. Given the state of her knees, they'd catch up with her before she got out into the open air. They, yes, she was sure there would be more than one of them.

She made up her mind. At her age, there was no point in being frightened by anything. She'd suffered from high blood pressure for years, and her father had died at forty-five following a stroke. Anyway, you could take all the care in the world, and still die in your sleep.

She opened the door, and pressed the light switch. The living room was T-shaped and a vast open space. To her left gleamed a beautifully equipped kitchen. To her right, framed by an archway, was a large sitting area, minimally furnished, with leather chairs and reclaimed pine flooring. Beyond a further archway was a huge conservatory.

Two men slouched in their chairs, looking at her as a cat might regard a mouse with nowhere to hide. The men were unshaven and one of them held a knife in his right hand. He was pointing it straight at her heart, and she realized they had been sitting patiently in the dark, waiting for her to return home. They hadn't found everything they wanted; the silver obviously wasn't enough. The fellow with the knife looked to be in his mid-twenties, his colleague was perhaps ten years older. Not opportunistic teenagers, these men, but professional criminals; she could sum them up in a single glance.

'Where's the money?' the man with the knife hissed.

He spoke good English, but with a strong accent. It reminded her of Irina's. Now she was certain that her cleaner had betrayed her. Irina had not only copied her keys but somehow made sense of the security system, and told her confederates how to fix it. Then she'd lured Jean out to the spiritualist church to allow them a free run. Jean swallowed hard. She was getting old. Past it. This simply wasn't like her – to be taken in so easily, fooled like a child.

These men wouldn't settle for easy pickings. They were hard men, unsentimental. Jean knew the type. They'd learned that there was a great deal of cash in the house, and they were determined to lay their hands on it. So they'd resolved to wait for the old lady to come back home, and force out of her the information they wanted. The whereabouts of the safe that Arthur had installed, and the combination to unlock it.

'The money?'

'Don't mess us around.' The older man seemed calmer than his colleague and twice as menacing. 'We know you've a lot more than a few bits of silver. There must be jewellery. You're not wearing any bling, so you must have hidden it away somewhere. What is there? Diamonds, rubies?'

Jean wondered how far the men were prepared to go to get what they wanted. Something in the younger man's eyes made her think he might enjoy hurting someone old and helpless. Someone who possessed what he did not. Her wealth was reason enough for him to want to cause her pain.

'There's . . . there's a safe.' Stammering slightly, she lifted her walking stick, and the younger man sprang to his feet, waving the knife.

'Put that down!'

She dropped the stick on to the carpet and the young man applauded sarcastically.

'Where's the safe?' the older man demanded.

A large watercolour of the estuary at Barmouth hung on the far wall. She gestured towards it.

'Right behind you. It's covered by the painting. If you stand up, you can see.'

As the men got to their feet, she reached behind her, and pressed a concealed button beside the dimmer switch twice. At once, the lights went out, and steel grilles slid noiselessly down from concealed cavities in both archways. Jean couldn't see or hear anything, but she knew that, behind the curtains, grilles for the windows were gliding into place. Paul had designed the electrics so that they were separate from the main system. This was her last line of defence.

One of the men shouted something. It sounded like a curse, but it wasn't in English, and Jean couldn't care less. All that mattered was that, within moments, the men were trapped.

'Open this!' the older man bellowed.

Jean pressed the button four times, and the two halves of the cage's wooden floor began to slide back into their recesses. She heard a scream of rage, along with the crash of falling furniture. Pity about those lovely chairs, but as Arthur used to say, you can't make an omelette without breaking eggs. The basement below the living space was fifteen feet deep, but when the flooring above it shifted back into position, you'd never guess it existed. Paul Currie called it a sort of panic room, one in which you were *meant* to panic. The men didn't have a hope in hell of getting out, even if the fall didn't break their spines. As they groped in the dark, they'd find something on the wall that seemed to be a light switch. Anyone who touched it would be electrocuted. Their hell, in fact, was that there wasn't any hope at all.

She stepped into the kitchen, and put on the lights. The safe was actually concealed within the central island. Arthur maintained that nobody would ever guess, and he'd been proved right.

What would her late husband have made of tonight? He'd predicted that the threat would come from some of the gangsters who had envied his success. Younger men who wanted a slice of the fortune he'd made without going to the lengths that had made his firm so feared.

He'd dreamed of leaving England and heading for the sun, but Jean had put her foot down. Why should they run away, just because they'd retired, and the old firm had broken up? In the end, she'd had her way, as she usually did. He'd insisted on ensuring that their new home was a fortress, equipped to resist an onslaught from half a dozen men armed with machine guns. She'd told him it was a stupid waste of money, but he'd insisted on going ahead and she didn't have the heart to stop him. It had been a labour of love, a last outlet for the darker side of his nature. All the planning had taken his mind off his deteriorating health, given him an interest.

And what had happened? Nothing, sod all. People, she supposed, were still afraid of them, long after they'd grown too old and weary to want to keep working. In the end, kidney cancer had killed Arthur, not a knife in the guts or a bullet in the brain. Funny the way things turned out.

To think that the home invasion, when it finally came, was so amateurish. Two blokes from somewhere she'd barely heard of, helped by a woman who had the gift of the gab. Honestly, it was a joke.

Jean sighed. She must be losing her grip if a kid like Irina could pull the wool over her eyes. It depressed her to think how much clearing up the mess would cost, but it served her right for being so gullible. A woman of her reputation, too. It was embarrassing. She daren't think what Paul Currie would say.

Irina would start to fret before long. Eventually desperation would lead her back here, as she tried to find out what was going on.

She'd deal with Irina at her leisure. Now, there was work to be done. Really, she ought to wait, but she wanted to attend to the two thugs in the basement. It would do her more good than all the pills in the world. Hobbling over to the kitchen island, she opened the bottom drawer, where she kept her old knives. One of them in particular had sentimental associations. It had belonged to her father. He'd been a good butcher, almost as good as her.

She paused for a moment, casting her mind back to the old days, and the way she'd helped Arthur when people stepped out of line.

Jean ran her finger along the blade. It was still as sharp as anything, and it drew a little blood. She felt a tingle of excitement, so unfamiliar these days that she couldn't help smiling. *That* was the connection she'd felt with Arthur, when she'd been surrounded by the spiritualists. *That*, for her, was the Other Life.

ANN CLEEVES – A WINTER'S TALE

In the hills there had been snow for five days, the first real snow of the winter. In town it had turned to rain, bitter and unrelenting, and in Otterbridge it had seemed dark all day. As Ramsay drove out of the coastal plain and began the climb towards Cheviot, the clouds broke and there was a shaft of sunshine which reflected blindingly on the snow. For days he had been depressed by the weather and the gaudy festivities of the season, but as the cloud lifted, he felt suddenly more optimistic.

Hunter, sitting hunched beside him, remained gloomy. It was the Saturday before Christmas and he had better things to do. He always left his shopping until the last minute; he enjoyed being part of the crowds in Newcastle. Christmas meant getting pissed in the heaving pubs on the Bigg Market, sharing drinks with tipsy secretaries who seemed to spend the last week of work in a continuous office party. It meant wandering up Northumberland Street where children queued to peer in at the magic of Fenwick's window, and listening to the Sally Army band playing carols at the entrance to Eldon Square. It had nothing to do with all this space and the bloody cold. Like a Roman stationed on Hadrian's Wall, Hunter thought the wilderness was barbaric.

Ramsay said nothing. The road had been cleared of snow but it was slippery and driving took concentration. Hunter was itching to get at the wheel. He had been invited to a party in a club in Blyth and it took him as long as a teenage girl to get ready for a special evening out.

Ramsay turned carefully off the road, across a cattle grid and on to a track.

'Bloody hell!' Hunter said. 'Are we going to get up here?'

'The farmer said it was passable. He's been down with a tractor.'

'I'd better get the map.' Hunter was miserable. 'I suppose we've got a grid reference. I don't fancy getting lost out there.'

'I don't think that'll be necessary,' Ramsay said. 'I've been to the house before.'

Hunter didn't ask about Ramsay's previous visit to Blackstoneburn. The inspector rarely volunteered information about his social life or friends. And apart from an occasional salacious curiosity about Ramsay's troubled marriage and divorce, Hunter didn't care. Nothing about the inspector would have surprised him.

The track no longer climbed but crossed a high and empty moor. The horizon was broken by a dry-stone wall and a derelict barn, but otherwise there was no sign of habitation. Hunter felt increasingly uneasy. Six geese flew from a small reservoir, circled overhead and settled back once the car had passed.

'Greylags,' Ramsay said. 'Wouldn't you say?'

'I don't bloody know.' Hunter hadn't been able to identify them even as geese. *And I don't bloody care.*

He wouldn't give the boss the satisfaction of asking for information. The information came anyway. Hunter thought Ramsay could have been one of those guides in bobble hats and walking boots who worked at weekends for the national park. He pointed to a black rock, which seemed to grow out of the land.

'It's part of a circle of prehistoric stones,' the inspector said. 'Even if there weren't any snow you wouldn't see the others at this distance. The bracken's grown over them.' He seemed lost for a moment in memory. 'The house was named after the stone, of course. There's been a dwelling on this site since the fourteenth century.'

'A bloody daft place to put a house,' Hunter muttered, 'if you ask me.'

They looked out on to an L-shaped house, built around a flagged yard, surrounded by windblown trees and shrubs.

'According to the farmer,' Ramsay said, 'the dead woman wasn't one of the owner's family.'

'So, what the hell was she doing here?' The emptiness was making Hunter belligerent. 'It's not the sort of place you'd stumble on by chance.'

'It's a holiday cottage,' Ramsay said. 'Of sorts. Owned by a family from Otterbridge called Shaftoe. They don't let it out commercially, but friends know that they can stay here. The strange thing is that the farmer said that there was no car.'

The track continued up the hill and had, Hunter supposed, some obscure agricultural use. Ramsay turned off it down a pot-holed drive and stopped in the yard, which because of the way the wind was blowing, was almost clear of snow. A dirty green Land Rover was already parked there and, as they approached, a tall, bearded man got out and stood impassively, waiting for them to emerge from the warmth of their car. The sun had disappeared and the air was icy.

'Mr Helms.' The inspector held out his hand. 'I'm Ramsay. Northumbria Police.'

'Aye,' the man said. 'Well, I'd not have expected it to be anyone else.'

'Can we go in?' Hunter demanded. 'It's freezing out here.'

Without a word, the farmer led them to the front of the house. The wall was half-covered with ivy and already the leaves were beginning to be tinged with frost. The front door led directly into a living room. In a grate the remains of a fire smouldered but there was little warmth. The three men stood awkwardly just inside the room.

'Where is she?' Hunter asked.

'In the kitchen,' the farmer said. 'Out the back.'

Hunter stamped his feet impatiently, expecting Ramsay to lead the way. He knew the house. But Ramsay stood, looking around him.

'Had Mr Shaftoe asked you to keep an eye on the place? Or did something attract your attention?'

'There was someone here last night,' Helms said. 'I saw a light from the back.'

'Was there a car then?'

'Don't know. Didn't notice.'

'By man, you're a lot of help.' Hunter was muttering again. Helms pretended not to hear.

'But you might have noticed fresh tyre tracks on the drive,' Ramsay persisted.

'Look. Shaftoe lets me use one of his barns. I'm up and down every day. If someone had driven down using my tracks, how would I know?'

'Were you surprised to see a light?'

'Not really,' Helms said. 'They don't have to tell me when they're coming up.'

'Could they have made it up the track from the road?'

'Shaftoe could. He's got one of those posh Japanese four-wheel-drive jobs.'

'Is it usual for him to come up in the winter?'

'Aye.' Helms was faintly contemptuous. 'They have a big do on Christmas Eve. I'd thought maybe they'd come up to air the house for that. No one's been in the place for months.'

'You didn't hear a vehicle go back down the track last night?'

'No, but I wouldn't have done. The father-in-law's stopping with us and he's deaf as a post. He has the telly so loud that you can't hear a thing.'

'What time did you see the light?'

Helms shrugged. 'Seven o'clock maybe. I didn't go out after that.'

'But you didn't expect them to be staying?'

'No. Like I said, I expected them to light a fire, check the Calor gas, clean up a bit and then go back.'

'So, what caught your attention this morning?'

'The gas light was still on,' Helms said.

'In the same room?'

Helms nodded. 'The kitchen. It was early, still pretty dark outside and I thought they must have stayed and were getting their breakfasts. It was only later, when the kids got me to bring them over, that I thought it was strange.'

'I don't understand.' Ramsay frowned. 'Why would your children want to come?'

'Because they're sharp little buggers. It's just before Christmas. They thought Shaftoe would have a present for them. He usually brings something for them, Christmas or not.'

'So, you drove them down in the Land Rover? What time was that?'

'Just before dinner. Twelvish. They'd been out sledging and Chrissie, my wife, said there was more snow on her kitchen floor than out on the fell. I thought I'd earn a few brownie points by getting them out of her hair.' He paused, and for the first time he smiled. 'I thought I'd get a drink for my trouble. Shaftoe always kept a supply of malt whisky in the place and he was never mean with it.'

'Did you park in the yard?'

'Aye, like I always do.'

'That was when you noticed the light was still on?'

Helms nodded.

'What did you do then?'

'Walked round here to the front.'

'Had it been snowing?' Ramsay asked.

'There were a couple of inches in the night but it had stopped by dawn.'

'What about footprints on the path? You would have noticed if the snow had been disturbed.'

'Aye,' Helms said. 'I might have done if I'd got the chance. But I let the dog and the bairns out of the Land Rover first and they chased round to the front before me.'

'But your children might have noticed?'

'Aye,' Helms said without much hope. 'They might.'

'Did they go into the house before you?'

'No. They were still on the front lawn chucking snowballs when I joined them. That was when I saw the door was open and started to think something was up. I told the kids to wait outside and came in on my own. I stood out here, feeling a bit daft, and shouted out the back to Shaftoe. When there was no reply, I went on through.'

'What state was the fire in?' Ramsay asked.

'Not much different from what it's like now. If you bank it up, it stays like that for hours.'

There was a pause. 'Come on then, 'Ramsay said. 'We'd best go through and look at her.'

The kitchen was lit by two gas lamps mounted on one wall. The room was small and functional. There was a small window covered on the outside by bacteria-shaped whirls of ice, a stainless-steel sink and a row of units. The woman, lying with one cheek against the red tiles, took up most of the available floor space. Ramsay, looking down, recognized her immediately.

'She's called Joyce,' he said. 'Rebecca Joyce.' He looked at Helms. 'You don't recognize her?'

The farmer shook his head.

Ramsay had met Rebecca Joyce at Blackstoneburn. Diana had invited him to the house when their marriage was in their final throes and he had gone out of desperation, thinking that on her own ground, surrounded by her family and friends, she might be calmer. Diana was related to the Shaftoes by marriage. Her younger sister, Isobel, had married one of the Shaftoe sons, and at that summer house-party they were all there: old man Shaftoe, who had made his money out of scrap metal, Isobel and her husband Stuart, a grey, thin-lipped man who had brought the family respectability by proposing to the daughter of one of the most established landowners in Northumberland.

Rebecca had been invited as a friend – solely, it seemed, to provide entertainment. She had been at school with Diana and Isobel and had been outrageous apparently even then. Looking down at the body on the cold kitchen floor, Ramsay thought that – despite the battered skull – he still saw a trace of the old spirit.

'I'll be off then.' Helms interrupted his daydream. 'If there's nothing else.'

'No,' Ramsay said. 'I'll know where to find you.'

'Aye, well.' The farmer sloped off, relieved. They heard the Land Rover drive away up the track and then it was very quiet.

'The murder weapon was a poker,' Hunter said. 'Hardly original.'

'Effective though.' It still lay on the kitchen floor, the ornate brass knob covered with blood.

'What now?' Hunter demanded. Time was moving on. It was already six o'clock. In another hour his friends would be gathering in the pubs of Blyth, preparing for the party.

'Nothing,' Ramsay said, 'until the pathologist and the scene-of-crime team arrive.' He knew that Hunter wanted to be away.

He could have sent him off in the car, arranged a lift for himself with the colleagues who would soon arrive, earned for a while some gratitude and peace, but a perverseness kept him quiet and they sat in the freezing living room, waiting. When Ramsay met Rebecca Joyce it had been hot, astoundingly hot for the Northumberland hills, and they had taken their drinks outside on to the lawn. Someone had slung a hammock between two Scots pines and Diana had lain there, moodily, not speaking, refusing to acknowledge his presence. They'd argued in the car on the way to Blackstoneburn, and he'd been forced to introduce *himself* to Tom Shaftoe, a small squat man with silver sideburns. Priggish Isobel and anonymous Stuart he had met before. The row had been his fault. Diana hadn't come home the night before, and he'd asked quietly, restraining his jealousy, where she had been. She had lashed out in a fury, condemning him for his Methodist morals, his dullness.

'You're just like your mother,' she'd said. The final insult. 'All hypocrisy and thrift.' Then she'd fallen stubbornly and guiltily silent and had said nothing more to him all evening.

Was it because of her taunts that he'd gone with Rebecca to look at the Black Stone? Rebecca wore a red Lycra tube which had left her shoulders bare and scarcely covered her buttocks. She had glossy red lipstick and black curls pinned back with combs. She'd been flirting shamelessly with Stuart all evening and then had turned to Ramsay:

'Have you ever seen the stone circle?'

He'd shaken his head, surprised, confused by her sudden interest.

'Come on then,' she'd said. 'I'll show you.'

In the freezing room at Blackstoneburn, Hunter looked at his boss and thought he was a mean bastard, a killjoy. There was no need for them both to be here. He nodded towards the kitchen door, bored by the silence, irritated because Ramsay wouldn't share information about the dead woman.

'What did she do then,' he asked, 'for a living?'

Ramsay took a long time to reply and Hunter wondered if he were ill; if he was losing his grip completely.

'She would say,' the inspector answered at last, 'that she lived off her wits.'

Ramsay had assumed that because Rebecca had been to
school with Diana and Isobel, that her family was wealthy,
but had discovered later that her father had been a hopeless
and irresponsible businessman. A wild scheme to develop a
Roman theme park close to Hadrian's Wall had led to bank-
ruptcy, and Rebecca had left school early because the fees
couldn't be paid. It was said that the teachers were glad of an
excuse to be rid of her.

'By man,' Hunter said. 'What does that mean?'

'She had a few jobs,' Ramsay said. 'She managed a small
hotel for a while, ran the office of the agricultural supply place
in Otterbridge. But she couldn't stick with any of them. I
suppose it means she lived off men.'

'She was a whore?'

'I suppose,' Ramsay said, 'it was something like that.'

'You seem to know a lot about her. Did you know her well,
like?'

The insolence was intended. Ramsay ignored it.

'No,' he said, 'I only met her once.'

But I was interested, he thought. Interested enough to find
out more about her, attracted not so much by the body in the
red Lycra dress, but by her kindness. It was the show, the deca-
dent image that put me off, and if I'd been braver, I would have
ignored that.

Her attempt to seduce him on that hot summer night had
been a kindness, an offer of comfort. Away from the house,
she had taken his hand and they had crossed the burn by stepping stones, like children. She'd shown him the ancient black
stones hidden by bracken, and then put his hand on her round,
Lycra-covered breast.

He'd hesitated, held back by his Methodist morals and the
thought of sad Diana lying in the hammock on the lawn.
Rebecca had been kind again, unoffended.

'Don't worry,' she'd said, laughing, kissing him lightly on
the cheek. 'Not now. If you need me, you'll be able to find
out where I am.'

Ramsay was so engrossed in the memory of his encounter
with Rebecca Joyce that he didn't hear the vehicles or the
sound of voices. He was jolted back to the present by Hunter's

shouting. 'Here they are. About bloody time too.' And then by the scene-of-crime team bending to pull on the paper suits, complaining cheerfully about the cold.

'Right then,' Hunter said. 'We can leave it to the reinforcements.' He looked at his watch. Seven o'clock. The timing would be tight but not impossible. He'd still be able to catch up with his mates. 'I suppose someone should see the Shaftoes tonight. They're the most likely suspects. I'd volunteer for the overtime myself but I'm all tied up this evening.'

'I'll talk to the Shaftoes.' Ramsay thought it was the least he could do.

Outside in the dark, it was colder than ever. Ramsay's car wouldn't start immediately and Hunter swore under his breath. At last it pulled away slowly, the heater began to work, and he started to relax.

'I want to call at the farm,' Ramsay said. 'Just to clear up a few things.'

'Bloody hell!' Hunter was convinced that Ramsay was prolonging the journey just to spite him. 'What's the matter now?'

'This is a murder inquiry,' Ramsay said sharply, 'not just an interruption to your social life.'

'You'll not get anything from that Helms bloke. What could he know, living up here? It's enough to drive anyone crazy.'

Ramsay said nothing. He thought that Helms was unhappy, not mad.

'Rebecca always goes for lonely men,' Diana had said, cruelly, on the drive back from Blackstoneburn that summer. 'It's the only way she can justify screwing around.'

What's your justification, he could have said, but Diana was unhappy too and there had seemed little point.

They parked in the farmyard. In a shed, cattle moved and made gentle noises. A small woman with fine, pale hair tied back in an untidy ponytail let them into the kitchen where Helms was sitting in a high-backed chair, his stockinged feet stretched ahead of him. He wasn't surprised to see them. The room was warm despite the flagstoned floor. A clothes horse, held together with binder twine, was propped in front of the range, and children's jeans and jumpers steamed gently. The uncurtained window was misted with condensation. Against one wall was a large square table covered by a patterned oil cloth, with a pile of drawing books and a scattering of felt-tip pens. From another room came the sound of a television and the occasional shriek of a small child.

Chrissie Helms sat by the table. She had big hands, red and chapped, which she clasped around her knees.

'I need to know,' Ramsay said, 'exactly what happened.'

Hunter looked at the fat clock ticking on the mantelpiece and thought his boss was mad.

Ramsay turned to the farmer. 'You were lying,' he said. 'It's so far-fetched, you see. Contrived. A strange and beautiful woman found miles from anywhere in the snow. Like a film. It must be simpler than that. You would have seen tracks when you took the tractor up to the road to clear a path for us. It's lonely out here. If you'd seen a light in Blackstoneburn last night, you'd have gone in. Glad of the company and old Shaftoe's whisky.'

Helms shook his head helplessly.

'Did he pay you to keep quiet?' Hunter demanded. Suddenly, with a reluctant witness to bully, he was in his element. 'Or did he threaten you?'

'No,' Helms said. 'It were nothing like that.'

'But she *was* there with some man?' Hunter was jubilant.

'Oh yes.' Helms's wife spoke quietly but the interruption shocked them. 'She was there with some man.'

Ramsay turned to the farmer. 'She was your mistress,' he said, and Hunter realized that he'd known all along.

Helms said nothing.

'Did you meet her first when she worked in the agricultural suppliers in Otterbridge? Perhaps when you went to pay your bill. She probably recognized you. After all, she often came to Blackstoneburn.'

'I recognized *her*,' Helms said.

'You'd hardly miss her,' the woman said, 'the way she flaunted herself.'

'No.' The farmer shook his head. 'No, it wasn't like that.' He paused.

'You felt sorry for her?'

'Aye!' Helms looked up, relieved to be understood at last.

'Why did you bring her here?' Ramsay asked.

'I didn't. Not here.'

'But to Blackstoneburn. You had a key? Or Rebecca did?' Helms nodded. 'She was lonely in town,' he said. 'Everyone thinking of Christmas. You know.'

'So, you brought her up to Blackstoneburn,' Hunter said unpleasantly. 'For a dirty weekend. Thinking you'd sneak over to spend some time with her. Thinking that your wife wouldn't notice.'

Helms said nothing.

'What went wrong?' Hunter said. 'Did she get greedy? Want more money? Blackmail? Is that why you killed her?'

'You fool!' It was almost a scream and, as she spoke, the woman stood up, her huge red hands laid flat on the table. 'He wouldn't have harmed her. He didn't kill her.'

There was a moment of complete silence.

'Of course he didn't.' Ramsay's voice was gentle. Another pause. 'That was you, Mrs Helms. You must tell me exactly what happened.'

She needed no prompting; she was desperate for their understanding. 'You don't know what it's like here,' she said. 'Especially in the winter. Dark all day. Every year it drives me mad . . .' She stopped, realizing that she was making little sense, and then continued more calmly. 'I knew he had a woman, guessed at least. Then I saw them together in town and I recognized her too. She was wearing black stockings and high heels, a dress that cost a fortune. How could I compete with that?' She looked down at her shapeless jersey and jumble-sale trousers. 'I thought he'd grow out of it, that if I ignored it, he'd stop or that she would get bored. I never thought he'd bring her here.'

'How did you find out?'

'Yesterday afternoon I went out for a walk. I left the boys with my dad. I'd been in the house all day and just needed to get away from them all. It was half past three, starting to get dark. I saw the light in Blackstoneburn and Joe's Land Rover parked outside. Like you said, we're desperate here for company so I went round to the front and knocked at the door. I thought Tom Shaftoe was giving him a drink.'

'There was no car,' Ramsay said.

'No. But Tom Shaftoe parks it sometimes in one of the sheds. I didn't suspect a thing.'

'Did you go in?'

'Not then.' She was quite calm. 'When there was no reply, I looked through the window. They were lying together in front of the fire. Then I went in.' She paused. 'When she saw me, she got up and straightened her clothes. She laughed. I suppose she was embarrassed. She said it was an awkward situation and why didn't we all discuss it over a cup of tea. Then she turned her back on me and walked through to the kitchen.' Chrissie Helms caught her breath in a sob. 'She shouldn't have turned her back. I deserved better than that.'

'So you hit her.'

'I lost control,' Chrissie said. 'I picked up the poker from the grate and I hit her.'

'Did you mean to kill her?'

'I wasn't thinking clearly enough to mean anything.'

'But you didn't stop. You didn't see if you could help her?'

'No.' Her voice was flat. 'I came home. I left it to Joe to sort out. He owed me that. He did his best but I knew we'd not be able to carry it through.' She looked at her husband. 'I'll miss you and the boys, but I'll not miss this place. Prison won't be very different from this.'

Hunter walked to the window, rubbed a clear place in the condensation and saw that it was snowing again, heavily. He thought that he agreed with her.

MARGARET MURPHY – STILL LIFE

M y physiotherapist's name is Angela; inappropriate for one who inflicts such hellish tortures on me. I endure it, partly because I have no immediate way to communicate my distress, but also to avoid the terrible muscle spasms and distortion of the spine that will result from atrophy.

As a distraction, I look around at the others. It's hard not to envy their mobility, their potency. I would like to join in their laughter, the camaraderie that exists always where conquering pain and accomplishing goals are common aims. If I happen to meet another's eye, he – they are mostly male – will quickly look away and stare with a look of pensive abstraction out of the window. Embarrassment makes dreamers of these solid lads.

One alone is able to hold my gaze. She is the only girl I have seen here. She speaks loudly; perhaps she thinks I do not hear or cannot understand. Or perhaps she raises her voice to ensure that I *do* hear.

'God, it's disgusting!'

Her physiotherapist remonstrates with her, but she quivers with indignation.

'Well, they shouldn't inflict the veg-heads on us. Why can't you bring these sodding monsters some other time?'

She's right, I *am* monstrous: I caught my reflection once in the gilt-framed mirrors of the great hall. My head lolls, and my bad eye is sewn up; the other stares wildly. Fierce and fearful is what I saw before recognition made me lose the perspective of objective analysis. She has a right, I suppose, to object. At least she will look at me, unlike the others, who deny my existence by focusing on the distance and breathing softly, like one who tries to fend off a bout of nausea.

Anyway, it does me good to look at her. She is one of the

cripples: I use such terms freely now, within the confines of
my own head. If I am a veg-head, then she most certainly is
a cripple – her legs smashed in some accident. She is learning
to walk without limping.

'He's staring at me. I'll *scream* if he keeps his mad eye
on me!'

She is angry, but I think also afraid that, although she is
still in her teens, life has already passed her by, that there
is no hope – only boredom and frantic struggle in unpredictable measure.

Yes, looking at her does me good, because it is liberating
to feel sorry for someone other than myself. Ah, but now I
have disconcerted her with my scrutiny.

'I'm getting out of this fucking *freak* show!'

She has gone. Who, I wonder, does she consider to be the
freak in this show?

Locked-in syndrome, they call it. They say he hears like a
normal person. That he can think. But I've watched him. He
sits for hours. Just looking. His face doesn't change, he doesn't
do anything. They feed him through a tube and clean him up
like a baby. Yeah, really normal. If I was like that, I wouldn't
let them feed me. I'd make them let me die.

He gets letters. And people coming to see him. Sometimes
they read to him from books. I've heard them through the
door. Sometimes they take him for walks. All that effort, and
for what? *Locked in* – he should be locked away – out of
SIGHT!

At physio, I can see that she is repelled by my physical appearance. As I drool on my tweed jacket, I see her lips draw back
from her teeth in a sneer of disgust. Yet she is there every day,
although she, unlike me, can decide when she comes down
for her sessions. A month or two and she will be ready to
leave, her bones mended, nothing to show but a little scar
tissue. As for the rest . . .

Look at him! Won't wear the hospital-issue tracksuit like the
rest of us. Not good enough for the likes of him. Christ! All

that money and he can't stop himself slobbering down his good tweed jacket. I HATE him.

She watches me compulsively now. I have seen her standing at my door when the nurses forget to close it. I cannot bear the noise in the corridor. It swells and distorts like echoes in a drainpipe – my condition creates a paradox of deafness and hypersensitivity. The sound of footsteps batters my one functioning eardrum like a demented timpanist, and yet I never hear *her* come. She is silent, despite her damaged limbs; not entirely corporeal, she drifts soundlessly, watches me for a time, and leaves without a word. It is difficult to say how long she loiters, for time seems to run on two separate levels in this place: each second, minute, hour, day, week is unconscionably long, and yet months seem to streak by, overtaking the days, losing the hours entirely in their hectic pace.

She was already here when I was admitted. A veteran of convalescence. An impatient patient.

What's it like to be locked inside yourself like that? Does he get mad about things? Maybe he wants to do stuff, like – I don't know, anything. You don't have to even tell your body to do things – you just want it and it happens, but not him. He's not just locked in, he's locked up. God, sometimes when I think about it, I can't breathe! If he could talk, what would he say? If it was me, I'd scream – Get me out of here! Let me fucking *die*! Why does he go on? Why doesn't he just stop breathing?

Paula, my speech therapist, says I should teach my visitor the code – my new method of communication. It's achingly slow, yet transfiguringly beautiful, for it returns to me the power of communication, it conveys the thoughts that clamour for expression. I had never thought of communication as a power until I was deprived of the means of it.

I must be selective; my affliction teaches me brevity and clarity. What I want to say must be thought out, planned, deliberated over and memorized before I attempt to relay it. A blink of an eye becomes a letter, as my visitors reel off the

alphabet with such casual facility, and I, with my eye, signal
when to stop. Each letter is set carefully, one upon another,
building syllables. Syllables are built into words, and words
into sentences. Paragraphs are generally beyond me; repartee
is not worth the effort: before half the joke is completed, it
has gone cold. Misunderstandings are more often the cause of
humour: I tried to explain who Paula was to a friend who had
come to visit. I wanted him to understand her importance to
me. He wrote out each letter conscientiously, sat back and
puzzled over the two words he had written.

'I don't understand,' he said, blushing. 'You're saying Paula
is *the rapist*?'

Would my angry waif have the patience to learn the tech-
nique? Skim through the alphabet and watch for the drop of
a wink, note down the letters, construct the words? Even if
she did, would the trust that is implicit in the one-sidedness
of our relationship be shattered by the possibility of my making
a reply?

A woman comes, sometimes. His wife. Children. Two of them.
They skip along beside his wheelchair. Talk, talk, talk. What
do they find to say to him? The boy dabs at the dribbles on
his chin with a Kleenex. I'd throw up if I had to do that.

I have a look around his room when they go off for their
walkies. Pictures everywhere – and cards, letters, books. After,
when they've gone back to their nice life, he sits and stares
at the door like – I dunno – does he want to go with them?
They wouldn't *want* him – I mean, what would they *do* with
him? Park him in a corner, face to the wall, so they didn't
have to look at his ugly mush? He should be dead, but he
isn't. Isn't alive, neither. Not really.

I suppose he can't tell them to make him die. Too much
guilt for his perfect little wife to drag around after he's gone.
And then there's the police. But I bet if he could, he'd finish
it. Slip under the bath water, no fuss, not even a splash. Just
a few bubbles, and then it's over and he's gone. For good.

She comes to my room, now, every night after lights-out. I
wait for her shadow to flit across the doorway, ghosting ahead

of her, like the wraith she is. At first, she stood in the doorway, as before, simply watching. Then, she came inside, touching things, examining pictures and books. Now she sits by my bed, her head bowed like a penitent. The sibilance of whispered confessions insinuates into every corner of the room, until the air vibrates with it, yet her sins remain a secret to me, because she speaks so softly and – perversely – although my hearing is hypersensitive to trivial sounds in the corridor, I cannot distinguish the confidences imparted in the quiet of my room.

Since I do not know her sins, I cannot give her absolution, and yet I know she has suffered – still suffers. She wants to die, this girl, this *child* who hasn't yet lived, and it snatches at the heart of me to watch her and yet to be unable to comfort her. We are here as convalescents, both of us, but I feel the cruelty of the term used to describe me: I will never recover, neither gradually, nor all at once. I suppose it is heartless to predict a recovery for her, too, since she is so inwardly tormented. We're both locked-in cases, in our way.

I feel a kind of regret that I repel her. It isn't vanity – but I do not want her to find me repugnant. You see how my ambitions are circumscribed? There was a time when I might have contrived to make her fall in love with me, just to see if I could.

I tell him things about me, about what happened to me. About what I did – what I tried to do – to myself. Sometimes when I look at him, I see a look in his one mad eye – like he's willing me to – like he *wants* it. Who could blame him?

I think about it. A fall, maybe. Tipped out of his wheelchair. There's enough cracked flagstones and stone steps to end a hundred sad cases in this dump.

My two children do not come often to visit me, but when they do, it is as if they have brought a little corner of my old life with them. They smell of London, of our riverside flat, pockets of clean air and diesel fumes, the oily exhaust of the tugboats and barges. My children smell of soap and fresh laundry. I want to ask Clarissa to bring me some clothing – their clothing – so that I can imagine myself at home, make believe that a part of them is with me always, but I'm afraid she will think me morbid.

I see the girl watching them – I cannot call her the cripple any longer, it seems unkind, and anyway, she's stopped calling me veg-head. She is watching for my reaction. What she expects to see, I cannot think. If the strength of my love for those two little ones could be translated into a physical sign, I would leap from my bed and dance with them to the shoreline, turn cartwheels with little Cloë on the sands, and hug my son to me, rejoicing in the bony awkwardness of his ten-year-old's body. Instead, I sit, as always, mute, silent, expressionless but for a tear that oozes from my eye. James dabs at it with the same tissue he uses on my drooling chin. He comments that Daddy's eye is watering in the wind.

You see, I have learned to weep discreetly.

Perhaps I am more like her than I realize; a ghost, a fearful apparition, only half-seen, and yet I am able to see and hear and take a sad delight in the living world, while doomed to be apart from it. A sudden notion makes me smile. Smiling is no longer a physical thing for me, but I remember the feeling, and it warms me like a glow of evening light. I shall teach my little spectre to commune with me, through the medium of my Ouija board – my alphabet.

When the children leave, it is getting late and Cloë is cranky and tired: too much sun. I forget to ask for the curtains to be drawn and now the sun falls full on my pillow and I feel the right side of my face drying to parchment in the glare.

A shadow, a fleeting coolness, and I know it is her. She closes the curtains, looks at me and leaves. I think, this time, for the first time, she has seen me – not my hideous exterior, but the person inside. I feel acknowledged, and the affirmation gives me a soaring sense of worth.

They left him frying like a lobster. His face was all red. I was going to sponge some water on it. But I just couldn't. I should've taken a pillow, pressed it hard against his face. It's not like he could fight; I'd be doing him a favour – doing all of us a favour. 'Cos it's us who have to watch him all day, shut up inside himself, not his wife, with her Saturday visits.

She hardly looks at him even when she *is* here. I watch him every day, her big, drooling baby-man. I should've done it; it would be the kind thing to do.

I have dictated a note to Paula; I wanted to thank the girl for her kindness. When my visitor glides past my door this morning, Paula will hand her my note. Oh, but she is here!

She takes the scrap of paper cautiously, eyeing Paula with suspicion, and begins to read. Her eyes grow wide and round. I know that look: pure rage. She stares at me with such furious hatred I want to shy away, but I'm stuck fast like a fly in amber.

'All this time and you let me think—' She stops and tears up the slip of paper on which is written a greeting, my name, a request for hers. 'Fuck you!' she is screaming. 'FUCK YOU! You let me say those things—'

A little gobbet of spittle has formed at the corner of her mouth and now I understand my son's urge to dab at my chin when I drool: it's demeaning, this loss of control. She runs from the room and I am left gasping, coughing, and Paula tries to calm me, to help the spasm abate.

Night. A shadow, the merest rustle of denim seam on denim seam. She is on me! I think at first it is a night terror – for me, sleep paralysis has become my reality. Then she drags me into my wheelchair and I know this is no dream. She is surprisingly strong, and I, in my sickness, have wasted to a scrawny seven stone. I try to gasp a protest, but even in my extreme terror I am unable to make a sound. We fly down the corridors, along the terrace, down the lane to the beach.

She heads straight for the water. She plans to drown me, and I am powerless to stop her! She halts at the edge of the foam, watching the steady rise and fall of the waves, and I hold my breath. Presently I hear her weeping.

'I trusted you,' she says.

I understand. She told me her secrets because she thought I was incapable of giving them away. She thought they were locked within me. Now she knows that I am able to communicate, I am a threat. So, it wasn't trust at all: she shared her

confidences in the same way you would with a dog, or a
stuffed toy. She thought me inanimate, insensate.

It is still and warm. The waves shush and heave on the
shingle and the moon smiles palely down, one half of its
face gone, as is mine, so that its smile, like mine, is a
malformed grimace. After a while – I can't say how long
– she takes me back, and I feel a tremor of relief; I will not
die tonight.

For three nights following, she comes to my room and we
take the twists and turns of the hospital's deserted corridors at
frenetic speed. Fate decides our destination. Tonight, we tear
out through the French windows of the dining hall on to the
south terrace. She pushes me to the top of the steps that tumble
precipitously down to the lawns, and I am sure that this is
the night she will finish it.

The harbour is visible through a bank of trees at the garden's
boundary, and to our left, above the patch of rocky shoreline,
the lighthouse beams at us. It's so bright that I can almost feel
its heat. Imperturbable, silent, watchful, it performs its stately
pirouette, holding none in favour, giving its light generously
to all, a simultaneous warning and beacon of safety.

It seems to affect her as deeply as it affects me, this
ungrudging gift of light, for she stops her furious pursuit – it
does feel like we are chasing something in these frantic
midnight races. She stops and she looks with me. The hypnotic
sweep of the beam seems to soothe her, and after a time she
wheels me back to my room. I have never before seen the
lighthouse at night, and I would like to thank her.

Today, I am afraid of her again. She is here, as if some pre-
arranged signal has brought her: my visitors all gone, physio
and my dear speech therapist (the rapist) Paula. She looks at
me and I brace, readying myself for the rough handling, the
unceremonious dumping of my body into the wheelchair,
headlong flights down corridors, across courtyards, and into
the night.

But she remains by the door. Although the light is poor, I
can see that she is crying. She edges into the room as if she
knows she has no business here, and my breath catches. Then

she stretches out a hand, flattens it against Cloë's painting of her pony – her latest gift to me – and claws it from the wall. Cards, letters, drawings, postcards, poems; all are torn or knocked from their places, trodden on, ripped, destroyed.

When she comes to me and thrusts her face, more monstrous in its rage than mine has ever been in its ruinous state, she draws back as though I have spat at her. But I am only crying, softly, discreetly.

I wanted to kill him. Hell knows I tried – but I couldn't do it. So I took all his things – everything he had. But when he cried, it was for me.

I haven't seen her for days. I had thought she'd left, gone home – or to whatever place equates to home for her. But here she is, loitering in the doorway, like a mugger waiting her chance. Paula looks around at her and smiles – I've told everyone that I was asleep when the damage was done, that I didn't see the destruction. My wife wants me to move somewhere safer, but I've refused: in the months since I met this strange, angry girl, life has been so exciting, so precarious.

'Here's your friend,' Paula says. I signal my need to say something.

'No,' the girl says. 'You've got something to say, you say it to me.' She turns to Paula. 'Show me.' Every bit as imperious as I was in my directorial days.

She has a facility for the code, having spoken in fragments and hinted at hidden meaning all her life. She adapts to its quirks and anticipates with quick, intelligent joy, delighting in a sentence correctly completed, as if she has uncovered the secret meaning of a lost tongue. Which, I suppose, she has.

'Beginning,' she says, 'or end?' I am given the opportunity to blink. A blink on the word 'beginning' gives me the earlier letters in my alphabet code; end gives me the second half. It's faster than the method everyone else uses, and she's good at guessing my meaning. Perhaps it's all that time spent watching me.

I tell her my hopes: to be able to breathe without a respirator, perhaps even to make sounds eventually – not words, I am not unrealistic – but sounds, so that the letters of my alphabet may be made from my own larynx.

'Big ambition,' she says, dismissing me in two words.

Her sarcasm hurts. But she is also capable of kindness and sensitivity. She is watchful for signs of discomfort, and although my face is incapable of expression beyond that of a solemn wink, she is able to interpret my moods, and she notices when I am uncomfortable. Also, she is aware of the keen pleasure I take in our wheelchair adventures, and she is always willing to indulge me.

She stops, frequently, by the canteen and tells me what is on the menu for the day. The chef is good – I can tell by the smells that stimulate my palate and cause me to salivate (one reflex that remains intact, though it can be an embarrassment) – and I tell her of another ambition, to taste real food again.

'Sundays,' I say to him. 'A whole day when nobody comes. Not your friends, or your family. No one to talk to. No physio, no speech therapy. How come you don't go nuts?'

I tell her that my imagination is like a butterfly: it is free to roam where it will. On lonely Sundays I am a novelist, a film director, hero, politician. I have flown, swallow swift to my wife, Clarissa, I have caressed her skin, kissed the nape of her neck, slept beside her, serene, content.

'I wish I had your words.'

'I wish I had your future.'

She guesses the word two letters in. 'My future,' she says. 'D'you know what my future is?'

I don't want to hear her say it. I don't want her to confirm my fears. Sensitive, as always, she is halted by my frantic blinking. I tell her, 'Your future is what you make it. Your past is finished. You are not.'

I want to tell him he's talking shit. He had everything. A good start, a good life. But something stops me. Instead, I say, 'You've got friends.'

'So have you.' I could swear he smiled. 'Paula likes you.'

'Oh,' I say. '*Paula.*'

'And *I* love you.'

I can't talk to him for a bit. Then I say, 'What do you want most right now?'

I'll give him anything for what he's just said.

'It's not in your giving.'

In your giving. The way he says things . . . It's not just words. He says things and they mean more than the letters and sounds that make them. There's thought and feeling in them. And kindness.

I tried letting my thoughts float like a butterfly, today. It felt more like a moth buzzing around a light bulb. Just when I thought I'd got away, airborne, soaring, I batted my wings against the lamp.

'That's good!' he says.

'Good? I'm screwed if the furthest I can fly is the bedside cabinet of this mouldy old pit!'

He breathes in . . . out-out-out-out. He's laughing.

'The simile,' he says, 'is good.'

He had to explain that one.

'You're bound to find it hard at first. Don't give up.'

'What about the lamp?' I say.

'Switch—'

'It off. Very funny.' I did, though. Maybe it was a joke and he was winding me up, but I did flick the switch, and sit in the dark.

I didn't go far next time, but I saw the curve of the bay, like a big horseshoe, and the sky was blue. The water was right up on the shore and the sun bounced off it till I was almost blinded, and when I looked away, along the sands, I could still see millions of little candles of light on the back of my eyes.

He makes me tell him what I see. Tells me I've got to learn the gift of speech.

She takes me to such places! Today, she has wheeled my chair *right into* the dining hall. Someone complains they couldn't enjoy their food with me staring at him.

'Yeah?' she says. 'Well, he hasn't touched a mouthful since he saw your ugly mush.'

She is ready to fight, but the neurologist comes over. 'What are you thinking of, Felicity, tormenting him like this?' It's the first time I've heard her name.

'Shows what you know.' She turns to me. 'Am I tormenting you?'

Two blinks: No.

'D'you want to leave?'

Two blinks.

The fact is, these visits to the dining hall enhance my culinary fantasies; one might even say *feeds* them. I can discern the herbs that have gone into making the sauce, how much pepper, whether full-fat cream was used. I can almost feel the meat melting on my tongue, taste the juices stimulating my salivary glands. Almost. But this final, glorious sensation eludes me.

I am ill. A respiratory infection, despite all the pummelling and expectorating the physio inflicts on me daily. Clarissa tries not to look relieved. I cannot blame her. I have seen her age in the months since I came here. I see it's slowly killing her.

Felicity looks worried. I tell her it's futile.

Today, I told her what her name means. 'Delight,' I told her. 'A blessing, a happiness of expression.'

She did not know; no one had ever told her.

He's getting worse. His breathing rattles in his chest, gurgles like water down a plughole. I can't help it; once you get into this habit of describing things, you can't switch it off, it's not like a bedside lamp.

I brought him a surprise. He's too ill to go on our mystery tours now.

She comes to me, shyly, blushing. It fills my heart with such tender joy to see her so softened, so willing to show her true self, in such contrast with that first, hostile meeting. In these few months, she is altered, as I am altered: beyond all recognition, for the better.

'Lamb,' she says, closing her eyes to memorize the ingredients she has demanded from the chef, 'garnished with fresh rosemary and roasted, served with apple and cranberry sauce, roast potatoes, baby carrots and broccoli.' She leans forward and kisses me gently on the lips, and my taste buds are flooded with the flavours. She stands back, anxious for my reaction, fretting that I will be offended. She smiles.

'And now . . .' She disappears for a moment and I hear a clanking in the corridor which hurts my ears. The sound distortion is worse of late. When she returns she has a bowl full of strawberries and cream in one hand and a bag of sugar in the other.

'Had to steal this,' she says. 'They won't put it out on the tables – think it's bad for us.' She dips a strawberry in the sugar, then in the cream and puts it whole in my mouth.

Felicity: my happiness. My delight.

He taught me that words aren't like money. You don't have to store them up so they don't run out just when you need them. I had kept a store of words like stones, ready to use.

The first talk I remember was between my gran and my mother. We didn't have conversations in our house. A lot of talk, but not what you'd call a conversation.

Gran was talking to Mum. They were sitting at the kitchen table, sipping tea. Gran's talk was like hailstones, hard and sharp; well-aimed, too. She rattled them off, spraying insults like she sprayed biscuit crumbs from her hardened gums.

Mum sat, miserable, trapped by the barrage of sound, trying to please, putting a word in here and there to prove she was listening.

I learned early not to listen.

Mum died before Gran – left her with only Granddad to blame. They fired off words at each other, stockpiling, building a funeral pyre to her and to themselves. I was alone by the age of seventeen.

'You have to use words,' he would say. 'Using words doesn't wear them out, it will improve your skill in using them.'

He had a word for it. *Articulate:* being able to express yourself clearly. But it had other meanings – sometimes he'd use it to tell you what to do:

'Articulate! Say what you feel! Don't worry about getting the words right – they'll come as you grow accustomed to speaking. You've locked yourself up inside yourself.'

He should talk.

He had these words, sentences, sometimes paragraphs ready for me when I came to visit. Like he'd stayed awake all night, just to get them right.

He's gone.

He left me a little money, a lot of good advice. He'd been writing every day, getting his physio to write things down. For me.

I'm reading from one of his letters. They're dated, one for each day, to be opened only on that date. I think he was afraid I'd try it again, skydiving without a parachute. Oh, I wanted to, when I first came here. But that was before he loaned me his butterfly wings. Today's letter, like all of them, makes me cry. His kindness is almost more than I can bear.

'*I once told myself that we were both locked-in cases, you and I. But I was wrong. I am locked in, but you were locked out. And that is far worse. That is the real tragedy.*'

I wish he had said this to me, so that I could thank him for giving me words. For giving me the wings to fly.

ABOUT THE AUTHORS

John Baker was born in Hull, the setting for several of his novels. His principal characters are Sam Turner and the ex-con Stone Lewis. His most recent novel, *Winged with Death*, is partly set in Montevideo in the seventies in the midst of civil war. Another arm of the novel is set in the present day in the North of England. *Winged with Death* is about time and tango and revolution, abduction and denial.

Chaz Brenchley has been making a living as a writer since the age of eighteen. He is the author of nine thrillers, two fantasy series, two novels about a haunted house and two collections, most recently the Lambda Award-winning *Bitter Waters*. He has also published fantasy as Daniel Fox, and urban fantasy as Ben Macallan. He lost count of his short stories long ago; a 'best of' collection will be published in 2021. His work has won multiple awards; it has been translated into languages from Chinese to Estonian. In his fifties he married and moved from Newcastle to California, with two squabbling cats and a famous teddy bear.

Ann Cleeves' awards include the CWA Diamond Dagger, the highest honour in British crime writing, in recognition of the sustained excellence of her work. She has written five distinct crime series as well as stand-alone novels, and is especially well-known for her Shetland and Vera Stanhope series of police procedural novels. She began her writing career whilst she was resident on the minuscule tidal nature reserve of Hilbre. Her first two sleuths were amateur naturalist George Palmer-Jones and Inspector Ramsay, and in 1999 *The Crow Trap* introduced that redoubtable detective Vera Stanhope. A television spin-off series starred Brenda Blethyn. *Raven Black*, the first in a series of police procedurals set on the Shetland Islands, won the CWA Gold Dagger; this series also proved hugely popular and received an acclaimed television adaptation. September 2019 saw the publication of the first in the Two Rivers crime series, *The Long Call*, which is again to be televised.

Website: anncleeves.com

Twitter @AnnCleeves

Martin Edwards received the CWA Diamond Dagger in 2020, and is the author of twenty novels, including *Mortmain Hall* and *Gallows Court*. He also conceived and edited *Howdunit*, a masterclass in crime writing by members of the Detection Club which has been nominated for six awards in 2021. He has received the Edgar, Agatha, H.R.F. Keating and Poirot awards, two Macavity awards, the CWA Margery Allingham Short Story Prize, the CWA Short Story Dagger, and the CWA Dagger in the Library. He has been nominated for CWA Gold Daggers three times and once for the Historical Dagger; he has also been shortlisted for the Theakston's Prize for best crime novel of the year for *The Coffin Trail*. He is consultant to the British Library's Crime Classics series and a former chair of the Crime Writers' Association. Since 2015, he has been President of the Detection Club. His novels include the Harry Devlin series and the Lake District Mysteries; in addition to publishing nine non-fiction books and seventy short stories, he has also edited more than forty anthologies of crime writing.

Website: www.martinedwardsbooks.com

Twitter: @medwardsbooks

Blog: www.doyouwriteunderyourownname.blogspot.com

Facebook: @MartinEdwardsBooks

Kate Ellis has sold over a million books worldwide. Liverpool-born, she now lives in North Cheshire. She has written more than twenty books in the Wesley Peterson series, blending mystery and history, and set in a fictional version of Dartmouth; the most recent title in the series is *The Stone Chamber*. In addition, she has published five books in a series set in the ancient city of Eborby in North Yorkshire and featuring DI Joe Plantagenet. Kate has also completed a trilogy set in the

aftermath of the First World War and featuring Albert Lincoln. She is the author of a historical mystery, *The Devil's Priest*, and many short stories. In 2019 she was awarded the CWA Dagger in the Library.
Website: www.kateellis.co.uk
Twitter: @KateEllisAuthor

Margaret Murphy's novels include psychological suspense written under her own name; a trilogy of forensic thrillers penned as A.D. Garrett; and two serial killer thrillers, written under the pseudonym Ashley Dyer, with advice from policing and forensics expert, Helen Pepper. Margaret is the founder of Murder Squad and co-founder of Perfect Crime writing festival. A former RLF Writing Fellow and past Chair of the Crime Writers' Association, she has been shortlisted for both the 'First Blood' critics award and the CWA Dagger in the Library. She is a recipient of the Leo Harris award, and won the CWA Short Story Dagger jointly with Cath Staincliffe. Joffe Books have recently relaunched her backlist of psychological novels, and the recent publication of *Don't Scream* completed a trilogy in the DCI Jeff Rickman series. She has also embarked upon a new psychoanalyst/detective series, set in her home town of Liverpool, with *Before He Kills Again*.
Website: margaret-murphy.co.uk
Facebook: @MargaretMurphyNovels
Twitter: @murphy_dyer
Instagram: @murphy_dyer

Stuart Pawson (1940–2016) was the creator of the Detective Inspector Charlie Priest series set in the fictional Yorkshire town of Heckley (not far from where Stuart lived with his wife Doreen and their four tortoises). Stuart's trademark as a writer was the dry humour with which Charlie Priest lightened the squalor of his daily work. Charlie's beloved moors, in all their moods, provide a fitting backdrop to the stories. Stuart's career as an engineer in the mining industry came to an end with the demise of coalmining and he went on to work for the probation service for five years, where he began writing his first book. There are thirteen titles in the Charlie Priest series and art school graduate turned detective Charlie shares Stuart's own hobbies of oil painting and fell walking.

Chris Simms has worked in airports, nightclubs, post offices and telesales centres. He now lives in Marple, Greater Manchester, with his wife, four children and a scruffy little lurcher. Along with nominations for the Theakston's Crime Novel of the Year award and Crime Writers' Association Dagger awards (for his novels and short stories), Chris was selected by Waterstones as one of their '25 Authors For The Future'. To date, he has examined a wide variety of issues in his books, including cosmetic surgery, factory farming and the so-called war on terror. More recently, he took time out from his DI Spicer series to write two contemporary, novel-length ghost stories. Alongside writing novels, Chris edits *Case Files*, an online magazine that profiles forthcoming work from members of the Crime Writers' Association.
Website: www.chrissimms.info
Facebook: @AuthorChrisSimms

Cath Staincliffe lives in Manchester. She is the author of the Sal Kilkenny private eye stories and creator and scriptwriter of *Blue Murder*, ITV's hit detective drama starring Caroline Quentin. Cath writes the Scott & Bailey books, based on the popular police show. Her latest series centres on two lippy, northern detectives – Donna Bell and Jade Bradshaw. Cath's stand-alone psychological fiction explores the lives of ordinary people caught up in extraordinary events. Her radio work includes *Legacy*, investigative mysteries featuring brother and sister heir-hunters, and she writes for Danny Brocklehurst's detective drama *Stone*, winning the WGGB Best Radio Drama Award in 2019. *Trio*, a stand-alone novel, moved away from crime to explore adoption in the 1960s. Cath's own story, of being reunited with her Irish birth family and her seven brothers and sisters, was the subject of the television documentary *Finding Cath* from RTE. In addition to the New Blood Dagger, Cath has been shortlisted twice for the CWA Dagger in the

Library, and twice for the CWA Short Story Dagger, sharing the prize with Margaret Murphy in 2012.
Website: www.cathstaincliffe.co.uk
Twitter: @CathStaincliffe